The First Time

Nicole Baker

Contents

Chapter One

Layla

"I already told you that we have this under control. Please, please stop following me around," Zane, my assistant manager, snaps at me while I continue trailing behind him.

I don't care what he says. I'm going to stick on his ass like panties stick to towels in the dryer. For as long as it takes for me to feel comfortable leaving this place for a week, I will be on his ass.

"I trust you. I do. Really," I reply, not even convincing myself.

I'm awful at this. Why can't I just go on vacation like a normal person and trust her staff to take care of things?

He stops dead in his tracks and then turns around slowly. For a second, I think he's going to scream at me in front of my entire staff.

"You trust me? That is the biggest load of garbage that I've heard all day. Bigger than the dumpster behind our building."

My jaw goes slack. "It is not. I *do* trust you. I just want to make sure I have everything in order, so I set you up for success. I don't want to leave behind a big mess."

He still seems skeptical of my motives, but I think he eases up a bit as the muscles in his face start to relax. I know I'm being a pest, but this is the first vacation that I've taken since I bought this restaurant three years ago. My friend Charlotte has basically forced me to go on a trip with her. She says I will run myself into an early grave if I don't learn to trust others and step away once in a while.

Judging by the annoyed look on all my managers' faces throughout the day, I think she may be right. I may have control issues.

But this place is my baby. It's everything to me. It's years of blood, sweat, and tears. All the nights that I sat in front of my computer trying to learn how to run a business instead of going out and enjoying my twenties like most of my friends.

"I'll pretend like I believe you," he tells me with a look of sympathy. "Only because I actually love you and want you to try your best to enjoy this break. You need it."

"He's not lying. You need it," Madeline, my head chef, inserts as she walks past us in the kitchen.

Zane crosses his arms across his chest like he was just proven right. He looks at me expectantly, like he's waiting for me to argue against needing this trip.

"No one asked you," I shout to Madeline.

She waves her hand in the air like she could care less about what I say, then proceeds to help her staff plate the delicate desserts in front of them. Zane clears his throat waiting for me to respond.

"Okay, fine!" I throw my hands up in the air. "I may need this trip."

He smiles. "Yes, you do. Maybe try to get laid while you're at it. I haven't seen a member of the opposite sex near you since we first opened this place. I'm beginning to wonder if actual cobwebs are growing down there."

I gasp at him. "How dare you!"

He laughs, and then we walk back to our offices at the far end of the restaurant. As we turn the corner and walk down the quiet hallway, his words still poke at me.

"I'll have you know; I *have* slept with someone since I opened this restaurant."

I follow him into his office, which is directly across from mine. He takes a seat in his chair behind his desk and then smiles up at me.

"Ok. So, you've slept with one person. How long ago was it that you slept with this person?"

"I..." I stumble as I try to remember. Shit, come to think of it, did I even sleep with him, or did we just fool around?

"Exactly." Zane leans forward on his desk, his face turning more serious. "Look, I really do have all of this under control. I promise. I know it's your baby, but you have to trust me."

My shoulders slump when I see the hint of pain he's wearing with his words. It hurts him that this is such a struggle for me to let go of and give to him. It hurts me that I'm the reason for his look of pain.

"I'm sorry, Zane." I sink down into the seat opposite him. "I think part of me is terrified to leave and not be needed here."

His face turns to the side. "What do you mean?"

I've never admitted this to anyone, barely myself. But leaving this place behind for a week is making me face some harsh realities in my life.

"It's just…I'm the owner. Most owners step back and let their team take the reins once everything is running smoothly. But—I guess I'm afraid that once I step away and you guys prove you don't need me, I'll have no reason to be here all the time. I love being here with you."

"Layla Williams. You will always be needed here. You are the energy of this team. Just because we can handle a week without you doesn't mean we don't need you. I'd lose my mind if I didn't have our Sunday night bitchfest together after we close."

I chuckle as I think about our Sunday routine. At the close of the weekend, our busiest time, Zane and I get caught up on all the managerial tasks needed for the following week. It's our time together to be alone in the restaurant and vent about all the shenanigans that took place over the weekend. This is the restaurant business. Shit happens all the time that requires some major venting.

"There are many different types of owners in a restaurant. You know this. You're not in it to make a buck; you're in it because you love it. But maybe—just maybe, you can stop working so much and learn to enjoy your life too. It'll do you good," he says with concern in his eyes.

I try to hold back the tears that threaten to spill.

"I don't think I know how to be anything but the owner of this place anymore," I say as my voice cracks.

"Well, this trip is your chance to figure it out. I am putting a no-contact rule on you. I will call you if I have any questions, but you are in no way allowed to contact me unless it's an emergency or you need advice on how to give the best blowjob."

I cover my hands over my face. "Zane! You are so crass!"

He shrugs. "Nothing you didn't already know about me, darling."

"Ok. I will do my best to avoid all forms of communication with you. I'm sure Charlotte is planning on confiscating my phone anyway."

"Good. She knows how much you need this."

I don't know what I would do without Charlotte. She used to spend her summers here growing up. After her parents divorced when she was seventeen, they stopped coming, and their beautiful home remained vacant for a decade.

We lost touch after that. It wasn't until she showed up a decade later when her father had passed and left her the house.

She wasn't planning on staying here, but I guess I have my brother to thank for that. I don't know what she sees in him sometimes, but they are so happy together. And I have my best friend back!

"Well, I need to get home and pack, I guess." I stand up out of the seat.

"Girl! You leave for Italy in the morning, and you haven't started packing?" Zane says with a gasp.

"Stop judging! Baby steps here, remember?"

"You stress me out," he says as he stands and opens his arms. "Come here, give me a hug."

I step into his arms. "Thanks for doing this."

"It's my job," he chuckles.

"I know. Still. Thanks for putting up with me."

"Get out of here. I can't wait to see pictures when you get back."

I walk into my office to grab my bags and then lock the door behind me.

Once I make it home, I go straight to my closet and pull out my large suitcase. I don't know why packing for a week in Italy feels so daunting.

Charlotte decided for us to spend an entire week in Lake Como. We're going to eat and drink our way throughout the region, maybe even take the trains to see Milan and Tuscany.

I have to admit that being a foodie, I'm super excited about this trip. I just don't know what to wear.

July in Lake Como, which is at the northern tip of Italy, will be warm enough to swim in the water. I have a couple of bikini options on my bed. I think I'll be most comfortable in sundresses, flowy clothes, and cute sandals. I can add some jewelry to fancy it up at night.

I'm terrified that I'll forget something important. I have my ID, passport, and credit card safely tucked into my purse, as well as a European outlet adapter for my cell phone charger and my curling iron.

I've actually been practicing some Italian words to use. Mainly anything that has to do with eating since that's when most of my interactions will occur.

It's almost midnight by the time I'm showered and in bed. I'm glad I didn't decide to close down the restaurant tonight. I'm already going to be a drag on the plane tomorrow.

Our plane doesn't take off until noon, but I need to be at the airport by ten, which means I need to leave here by nine. I set my alarm for seven-thirty so I can eat breakfast and make sure I have everything without being rushed.

Part of me is itching to stop at the restaurant on my way to the airport, but I know Zane will literally lose his mind.

I close my eyes and picture the mountains of Como as I start to fall into a deep sleep. This trip is going to be exactly what I need. Nothing is going to get in the way of me finding myself.

Chapter Two

Josh

"You going to take your shot or just stand there and ogle those girls over there?" I shout at Liam as he not-so-subtly glances at some blonde in the corner of the bar.

"Fuck off, I was just trying to line up my shot," he lies as he moves his pool stick back while he leans over the table.

Eric, his brother, leans into me at our round, high-top table in the corner. "He's a shit liar, isn't he?"

"I heard that," Liam shouts after he takes his shot, which hits his solid ball but bounces off the corner pocket. "Dammit!"

"If Asher were here, we'd be kicking both your asses in this game," Liam growls before he takes a swig of his beer.

Eric and I both roll our eyes. "Yeah, well, looks like your brother has just proven that he's the real talent in this game," I reply.

Liam, Asher, and Eric are all brothers. I went to college with Asher years ago. They also have a little sister named Layla, but I try not to think about her. Actually, I try to avoid her at all costs. We have a history, and it's complicated.

"Can you believe that he bailed on us again tonight?" Liam says begrudgingly.

"He's got a lot going on," Eric points out, being the older, wiser brother and all. "With just moving into the new house with a three-year-old and now living with Charlotte."

"It's your shot," Eric nudges me. "Let's end this game between you two now so Liam can go work his magic on his little crush over there."

I chuckle as I grab my stick and move along the table, trying to find the perfect angle to sink the last ball. I'm down to just needing to sink the eight ball to win.

"Left corner pocket," I point with my stick, then line up behind the ball. The eight ball sinks into the intended pocket, and I hear Liam curse under his breath.

I stand up tall and smile widely at him. "Nice game, man. Better luck next time."

"Whatever, I'm outta here," he growls, then makes a beeline straight for the blonde. She smiles effortlessly up at him.

Yeah, he'll be going home with her tonight. If Layla were here, I'm sure she'd have some snarky comment about how she's surprised I'm not the one taking a woman home. She always seems to imply that I'm some massive man whore.

Now, I'm not saying that I'm a prude, but she acts like I'm out here taking women home left and right. Truth be told, it's been a while for me. I just haven't been feeling it lately. I don't know what it is that's making me feel this way.

"Well, I think I'm gonna head out," Eric says while clapping me on the shoulder. "I've got a big meeting tomorrow with an investor."

"Nice. Good luck. I hope it goes well."

He blows out a breath. "We'll see. Later."

I look around the bar, wondering if tonight should be the night I get back on the horse and try to pick up a girl. Liam is laughing it up with the blonde, who has a beautiful brunette sitting next to her. But once again, I'm in no mood to take someone home.

I nod at Liam to let him know I'm heading out. He gives me a confused look, probably expecting me to hit on the hot friend, but I just shrug my shoulders and walk out the door.

On my drive home, I start to think about what's been bugging me lately. Not that I want to admit it, but I think I know what it is, or who it is.

Layla.

Ever since my best friend, Asher, has been dating her best friend, Charlotte, we've seen a lot more of each other. It was easier to ignore our past when we didn't see each other all that much. But now, every weekend, I'm coming face to face with her. She ignores me, rolls her eyes at me, says sarcastic shit to me, and I should just ignore it like I used to. I just don't understand after ten years, why these feelings are resurfacing like this.

Just as I walk into my house, my phone lights up with an incoming call from Asher. What could he be calling for this late at night?

"Everything okay?" I ask as soon as I answer.

"Yeah. Why?" he replies, sounding confused.

"I don't know. You never call me at this hour on a weeknight."

I throw my keys on the entryway table.

"Well, I mean, nothing's wrong, but I do have a favor to ask."

"Oh, okay. What do you need?" I would do anything for him. He's like my brother.

I walk down the hall to my bedroom and plop down on my bed as I wait for him to reply.

He sighs into the phone, and I hear a muffled Charlotte in the background. I hear her say, "Just ask him."

"Dude, what's going on? What do you need to ask me?"

"It's not really a small favor," he starts. "So, you know how Charlotte and Layla are supposed to go to Italy tomorrow?"

"Yessss," I draw out, wondering where he's going with this.

Of course, I know that. It's all they talk about when everyone is together. Layla won't shut up about the Italian men she's going to flirt with, which is annoying as fuck.

"So," he stalls again, "Charlotte isn't feeling well."

"Oh, shit. And they're leaving tomorrow?" I ask, wondering if she could maybe just push through and sleep on the plane.

"Yeah. She's been getting sick a lot."

That doesn't sound good. Hopefully, it isn't the flu.

"Damn. Do you think it's just a bug? Maybe she'll feel better in the morning."

"That's the thing. She's actually pregnant. It's not something we've shared with people yet. We were waiting until she's further along."

"She's pregnant? Shit. Congratulations! I'm really happy for you guys."

I am. Asher has been through hell and back, and it has been such a relief to see him happy again.

"Thanks, man. We can't wait to share the news with everyone. But that's not why I called. She figured she could still go on the trip and just not drink. Her only symptom was being really fatigued. We didn't expect nausea to start so late, but she can't keep anything down and is sick around the clock."

"Damn. That's not good." I can't imagine having to go through that. I'm a wuss when it comes to getting sick.

"No. It sucks. I feel awful watching her and not being able to do anything about it."

"I can imagine."

"So, that brings me to my favor," he says matter-of-factly. "I was wondering...if maybe you could go with Layla."

My entire body freezes and my breath catches in my lungs. I can't really be hearing him correctly because I think he just asked me to go to Italy with his sister for an entire week—just the two of us.

I don't even know how to process his words.

"I'm sorry. What did you just say?" I ask in a suffocated whisper.

"Look, I know you two have had your differences," he starts, and I laugh bitterly, knowing he doesn't know the half of it, "but she really needs this break. She's gonna be devastated if it gets canceled."

I try to disguise my annoyance. I don't like being put in this situation when he knows Layla and I together is bad news. We can't get along for more than a second before one of us offers a snarky comment.

Why in the hell does he think that us spending a week alone together would bode well? Not to mention the weird feelings I'm having around her again.

"Why me? Why can't you ask Avery or someone else like your mom?"

He sighs, the worry evident in his voice. "Avery can't get off work for the week on this short of a notice, and my mom isn't fond of that kind of travel. Plus, a week of just my mother is not a relaxing trip for Layla."

Shit, he's right. Her mom would drive her crazy. Still, I don't see how I'm any better.

"Look, I appreciate that you trust me enough to ask, but I don't think it's a good idea. Have you even cleared it with Layla? There's no way she would agree to this."

He clears his throat. "We haven't even told Layla that Charlotte can't make it. We're in panic mode. Charlotte wants to have a solution before she breaks the news to Layla."

"Trust me, man. Layla would never get on that plane with me. I can promise you that."

Charlotte whispers something that I can't quite make out.

"Charlotte says she'll take care of Layla. She promises she'll be on board, even if she's hesitant at first. That's how much this trip means to Layla. Please, man."

"What about work?" I ask, knowing what he'll say next.

I work for Asher at his construction company. He likes to say we're partners in the business, but it's still his company. He makes the final decisions, even if he trusts most of my decisions.

"It's covered. I've got you. Ian can take over for the week."

There it is. Asher has everything figured out. I appreciate what he's doing for his sister, but he doesn't realize what our history is. He just thinks we annoy each other, that our personalities clash at times. No one knows our history.

I'm just about to tell him it's a firm no when he throws a wrench in everything.

"If you don't go, I'm going to have to resort to asking David. I know he's our buddy, but I just think Layla would be more comfortable with you there. I don't know why, but I do. Charlotte does, too."

David. Alone with Layla in Italy for an entire week.

Fuck. That.

"David is not going. Absolutely not," I growl into the phone a bit too forcefully.

I think I hear Charlotte chuckle in the background.

"Well, if you don't go then..."

"I'll go," I cut him off, sounding a bit too intense.

"Really?" he asks hopefully. "You'll do it?"

This is so fucking stupid. I know I shouldn't agree to this, but the idea of Layla alone with David is too much for me to bear. How could I let her be alone with one of my best friends in one of the most romantic countries in the world? Over my dead body.

"Yeah, whatever. I'll do it."

"He'll do it," I hear Asher whisper to Charlotte.

"Oh my god! Thank you so much, Josh!" Charlotte shouts in the background.

'Yeah, yeah, yeah. Just give me the details."

As they spout off a bunch of details I won't remember until they write them down or text them to me, a warning voice whispers in my head, telling me this is a bad idea.

I should heed the warning. I swallow hard as I try to hide the anger building in me for being put in this situation.

But there's also a faint bit of excitement in the pit of my stomach. As much as I want to deny it, a week alone annoying the hell out of Layla sounds kind of fun.

It isn't until we get off the phone and I'm lying in my bed that I start to regret my decision. Something is telling me this is going to blow up in my face, but for some reason, I'm not picking up the phone to back out of it.

Chapter Three

Layla

Layla, it's Italy. Get over yourself. Just because your best friend can't make it anymore doesn't mean the trip is ruined.

Charlotte said she and Asher spent all night figuring out who her backup should be. And really, how could I be mad when my best friend is having a baby with my brother? I'm going to be an auntie again! I feel like Monica in *Friends* when Rachel and Ross announced they were having a baby. Actually, I'm probably a lot like Monica in real life. I'm a chef, she was a chef. I'm a bit neurotic, so was she.

I just hate that Charlotte is feeling so sick. She seems optimistic about it all despite not being able to keep a single thing down at the moment. She looked like a ghost when she video-called me last night. I was slightly alarmed for her health. I spent the next hour googling symptoms to make sure she wouldn't die from this. See...neurotic.

I wonder who they found to come to Italy with me on such short notice. My hope is that Avery will show up here at the gate. She would be a great companion to eat and drink our way through Italy.

Although, she does have a pretty shitty manager. I would be really shocked if she agreed to a week in Italy without knowing if her boss would be okay with it.

I glance at the clock by the gate number. We start boarding in fifteen minutes. Whoever the hell is coming better get a move on.

And I swear, if my mother is the best that they could do, I will walk out of this airport and slap Asher across the face. There is no way I could do a week alone in Italy with her. She would drive me insane. I'm sure she would go on another tangent about how wonderful William is and how I should give him another chance.

William is my ex-boyfriend—from high school. I mean, seriously, she needs to give it up. I'm twenty-seven years old now. But William is a family friend and our parents have been friends for years. He comes to a ton of our family parties—always there to make me feel like I'm the crazy one for not giving him another chance. He always says that if I were with him, I wouldn't have to work another day in my life.

He never considers the possibility that I might want to work. It shows how well he knows me. My job is the very thing that breathes life into me. No, to him, he wants the nineteen-fifties wife who will be there to smile on his arm at parties and be waiting at home for him with an apron on and a home-cooked meal. As Taylor Swift would say, "No deal. The nineteen-fifties shit they want from me."

Just as I'm about to pick up my phone to call Charlotte to let her know I'm out if it's my mother, I hear someone behind me clear their throat.

When I turn around, my heart flutters for a second before my stomach sours. I hate that he can still cause even the slightest bit of butterflies in me, even after all of these years.

He smirks at me, like he can tell my body is recoiling at the sight of him. "Hey, Freckles. Surprised to see me?"

There's no way he's here for me. Asher and Charlotte aren't that stupid. Surely, they would know that I would rather stick a pen in my eye than spend a week alone with this man.

"Please, tell me you're here to get on another flight. Did you just happen to see me and decide you wanted to ruin my morning?"

He chuckles, clearly enjoying my discomfort. "Guess again."

"Cut the shit, Josh. There's no way you're Charlotte's replacement, right?"

"I believe I am. Surprised?"

He lifts his bag off his shoulder and places it on the ground at our feet.

"You are going to Italy—with me?" I ask, barely able to get the words out. "There's no way they would do this to me."

"Hey," he says, shrugging his shoulders, "I told them it was a stupid idea. But somehow, they thought I was a better choice than your mother."

I stop to think about that. Is he a better choice than my mom? I mean, he won't pester me about working less or finding someone to marry, and it's not like I have to spend every second with him.

Ugh, but this man in Italy is going to be annoying as hell. I'll bet he flirts with every woman in his line of sight.

But do I have a choice? Would I ruin my trip just because of him? That would be ridiculous. Zane would literally throw the biggest tantrum. He'd accuse me of finding any reason not to trust him and leave the restaurant to him for a week.

"If I let you come, are you going to spend the entire time flirting it up with the woman, or will you appreciate the culture and food like you're supposed to?"

I feel like I almost see a crack in his armor, showing a hint of pain at my insult, but then his eyes turn dark. "Will I flirt with all the women there? I don't know, you're enough of a mood killer to set the tone for a week of romancing all the women."

I gasp in surprise at his response. "That's it. There's no way in hell I'm going with you."

I grab my things and stomp away from him.

Okay, so I only make it like ten feet, but that's beside the point. I'm just trying to make a point that I don't want to be anywhere near him right now while I consider my options.

I grab my phone out of my back pocket and dial Charlotte.

"Hi," she says hesitantly. "I was waiting for your call."

"I thought you were my friend," I bark as my anger becomes a scolding fury. "How could you do this? And to not even warn me?"

"I know you're mad, but just give me a second to explain my-self."

"Well, you have all the time in the world. Our plane is boarding in two minutes, but seeing as how I'm not going, you have all damn day."

I feel his presence behind me, but don't have it in me to turn around and face him. Figures he can't even let me have this conversation alone.

"I knew if I told you last night, it would be impossible to get you to the airport," she starts.

"Yeah, exactly. You were correct. So, why the deceit?"

"Because Avery couldn't go! I mean, obviously, Asher was staying here with me, and your other brothers were busy working. It was nearly impossible to find someone who could just jet off the next morning without letting anyone at work know. But Josh works with Asher. Plus, I figured anyone was better than your mother," she says, her voice smooth but insistent.

"Yeah, but Josh?" I whisper into the phone. "You know how I feel about him. He'll make my trip miserable."

"No, he won't. He's been sworn to be on his best behavior. He knows how much you need this. Plus, we didn't get insurance on the trip. Are you telling me you're going to let all of this money go to waste just because of Josh?"

Dammit, she has me there. There's no way I can do that.

"See, you know I'm right," she continues. "Just get on the plane. And if he starts to act up, you give me or Asher a call and we'll have a word with him. And..." she stops talking abruptly.

"Charlotte? Are you okay?" I ask, wondering if I lost connection.

"I'm gonna be sick," she says in a faint whisper. "Gotta go."

"Shit," I mutter to myself as the line goes dead.

"We will now be boarding Group C for the flight from Savannah to New York," a male voice echoes on the intercom.

I glance down at the ticket in my hand, reminding me that I'm Group C.

"Shall we?" Josh grabs my bag from the ground and slings it over his shoulder.

I think this is happening. My brain is screaming at me to come up with a good excuse to get out of this as he walks towards the gate without a care in the world. Instead, I go through the motions of scanning my ticket and walking through the boarding bridge. Then as we walk on the plane, I realize this is it. There is no backing out now.

We take our seats in business class, which was one of my splurges for the trip. I push my purse under the seat in front of me, then let my head fall back on the headrest and close my eyes.

"Aw, come on. Cheer up. I'm not that bad, am I?" his voice washes over me.

I keep my eyes closed, not wanting to see the smug face he must be wearing. I can tell how much he is loving this. His favorite hobby is pissing me off.

"This is supposed to be a break for me. I'm supposed to be working on finding myself outside of my work," I whisper, more to myself than to him.

I expect him to say some smartass response, but when nothing comes, I open my eyes.

"What makes you think I will get in the way of that?" he asks with no hint of sarcasm.

"Are you serious? You seem to do everything in your power to annoy me. You know you get some kind of sick pleasure out of it."

His eyes are flat and unreadable. Instead of responding, he pulls out his headphones and places them over his ears. I guess that's my cue to leave him alone.

Fine by me.

I reach into my purse and pull out my earbuds, then find a movie on my phone. The short flight to New York is over quickly. I'm too focused on getting to our connecting flight to bother talking to Josh. He's been oddly silent since our flight took off. It's almost as if my comment hurt his feelings.

But it's not like I'm wrong. I've said that to him before. I don't know why he's acting like I haven't or like it's not true. He *does* like to annoy me.

Once we're settled on our connecting flight, the silence has gotten under my skin. Plus, we have an eight-hour flight ahead of us.

"Did I say something wrong before? Like... did I, uh... hurt your feelings?" I stumble awkwardly through my words. I'm not used to asking about his feelings, but if I'm forced to be alone with him for a week, I'm not going to be able to handle the cold shoulder. It'll grate on me.

He hesitates, taking his time to lower his headphones. "I'm not trying to ruin this trip for you. Did you ever think I'm doing this *for* you? I have a lot going on at work, but I packed up everything on a whim so you could have this time away from work."

I never thought of it like that. I guess he did put all his life on hold to come here with me. And here I thought it was just so he could torture me—like that's the only possibility there could be.

Before I can speak again, he continues, "And I know we don't always get along, but that's not all on me. Despite what you want to believe, you play a role in that, too."

Well, I don't know if I'd go as far as to say I play a role in it. I mean, I may give him shit, but it's only because he deserves it.

It has nothing to do with a broken heart or anything. I'm over what he did to me all those years ago.

Whatever the reason for our disdain for one another, it would be nice to try and put that aside for the trip. He's clearly trying to do that.

"I'm sorry," I whisper. "I guess I didn't think about you having to drop everything. Thanks, I guess, for doing that."

He chuckles to himself. "I'll take that half-assed apology."

Then he puts on his headphones and ends our conversation abruptly again.

Ugh, this man is so infuriating. I throw my head back against my seat and do my best to suppress my groan so I don't freak out the other person sitting next to me.

How hard is it to just accept my apology? I mean, it wasn't the best, but I tried.

This is going to be the trip from hell. Not only is my best friend not here, but the man who broke my heart and left me to pick up the pieces is accompanying me instead.

Chapter Four

Josh

As the plane comes to a screeching halt on the runway, I pack up my headphones and place everything in my backpack.

The plane ride was long. Eight hours of Layla ignoring me or giving me one-word answers.

I know she gave me an apology, and I should have just accepted nicely, but it seemed so forced. I'm giving up my time and money to fly halfway across the world for her, and all she could muster was a half-assed apology.

And now, here we are in *Italy*. I should be excited, but I'm dreading it.

How are we going to fill the silence of this trip if she isn't willing to talk to me? We have to spend an entire week together, and the plane ride alone has been miserable.

When we get to the train station, I find out I now have to endure a thirty-minute train ride to Como next to this ice queen. We're both clearly exhausted after the day of traveling, and our heads hang low as we try to fight off sleep.

Once we're in the cab and headed to our hotel, I let my head fall back against the seat and close my eyes. I was already struggling to get to bed last night knowing what I agreed to. I'm hanging on by a thread here, trying to stay awake.

I hear a gasp fall from Layla's mouth at the same time the warmth of her hand hits my thigh. My eyes fly open.

"Look," she whispers as she leans further over me, looking out my window.

The vast mountains surround the lake, and the crystal-clear water makes it look like a painting. As we weave through the roads, I can see large villas tucked away on the edge of the mountains.

"Wow," I gasp as we both stare out in awe of the beauty.

She leans even further over me, her mouth a mere couple of inches from mine. Her hand moves higher on my thigh as she looks for more leverage to hold herself up. My body is all too aware that it's Layla's hand on my thigh, her lips close to mine, and a growing problem is now arising in my pants.

I close my eyes and try to think of something else, anything else, but the placement of her hand. All that does is heighten my sense of smell, and I recognize her fruity, floral scent. It only makes my situation worse.

I need her to move.

"Umm," I cough as I squirm in my seat. "Yeah, it's beautiful."

She looks over at me with a smile on her face. I can see the moment she recognizes how uncomfortable I am, and her smile instantly fades. She moves back to her side of the seat. Guilt begins to gnaw at me. I hate that I'm the reason she lost that beautiful smile on her face. If only she knew why I had to put an end to the moment.

The cab driver stops in front of our hotel.

"Here we are," he says in his thick Italian accent.

We get our bags out of the trunk, and I look up at our hotel. It looks like a large palace on the side of a mountain. It's made out of some kind of white limestone with large Roman columns in the front.

Rolling into the front lobby is much of the same. I follow the red carpet up to the front desk.

"Hi, we're here to check in," I tell the woman standing behind the counter.

She looks young, maybe in her early twenties. Her name tag says Milana.

"Ciao. Benvenuti. Welcome," she smiles brightly. "Are you checking in?"

I turn to Layla. "Is it under your name?"

"Layla Williams," she ignores me, speaking directly to Milana.

"Ah, I see. Right here. A suite with a terrace and hot tub. King bed. A lovely view for your two," Milana says.

I look over at Layla, her eyes are wide. "Um, there was a last-minute change of plans. I was supposed to be here with my best friend. Is there any chance we could change to a new room that has two beds? Or maybe even two separate rooms?"

"Yes," I interject emphatically. "Two rooms would be best."

Milana looks between the two of us with concern. "I'm sorry, I'm not sure we have an extra room available for the length of your stay. Let me check."

The silence is deafening as she types away on her computer. I don't even risk another glance at Layla. I'm still trying to come down from the incident in the cab. If that's all it takes to get me going, there's no way I could survive sleeping in the same bed with her for an entire week.

I wonder if she sleeps naked or maybe she just wears a tank top and her underwear. Fuck, I love it when girls do that.

Please, tell me there's two rooms. I don't know if I could even survive two beds, knowing she's in the bed next to me.

"We do have an extra room," she says.

Thank God! I take the much-needed breath that I was holding.

"The cost is one thousand nine hundred euros a night for six nights. Would you like me to book it?"

What the hell? What kind of hotel are we staying at? That number is outrageous. There's no way I can afford it. That's like sixteen thousand dollars. The all too familiar shameful feeling washes over me as I realize I could never give this woman next to me the life she deserves.

I'm sure her douchebag ex-boyfriend William would be able to spend that kind of money in a heartbeat. Her mom would probably love it if Layla were here with William. Just goes to show he was right all those years ago.

I have to speak up and admit the sad fact that I just can't swing that kind of money on a room.

"Are you kidding me?" Layla gasps before I can admit defeat. "That is outrageous. I knew I shouldn't have trusted Charlotte with the rooms. I know Asher told me he would handle it, but I just didn't think they would spend so much."

"Does that mean…" I start to speak but have trouble saying the words out loud.

"That we're shacking up together in one bed?" she finishes for me. "Are you willing to pay that kind of money just to avoid being in the same room as me?"

I feel like that's a trick question. If I had the money to spend carelessly, fuck yes. But I can't tell her that I don't trust myself around her. She still thinks I can't stand her, that I feel nothing towards her, and that is how it needs to stay.

"You know I can't afford that," I grind out, a blanket of disgrace washes over me.

"Well," she turns to Milana, "it looks like we are keeping our original room."

Milana nods, looking uncomfortable at our exchange. She must feel the tension between Layla and me. She makes quick work of getting us checked in.

I stand behind Layla as she holds the keycard in front of our door. As soon as we walk into the room, my breath catches in my throat.

There is no way this is our room. To say it is big is an understatement. The large king-sized bed looks luxurious with its white comforter and large pillows. The room has polished hardwood flooring, which extends to the sitting area with deep blue couches next to the windows.

Speaking of windows, they are floor-to-ceiling windows with French doors that open up to a white limestone terrace overlooking the lake and mountains.

"Holy shit," Layla whispers.

She drops her luggage on the floor by the bed and then walks straight to the doors. When they open, the wind blows around her as she walks out to the terrace. I follow her out. We both lean against the white stone railing.

"It's beautiful," she says as she looks out at the view.

"It is," I agree. "I've never seen anything like it."

"The water," we both say together.

She smiles, and I can't help but do the same. "It's so clear," I add, struck by the sight.

"Josh, look!"

I turn around and she's standing next to a hot tub. Layla next to a hot tub, the two of us alone. My brain is conjuring up a bunch of inappropriate images that I try to push aside so I don't spoil the mood.

"Shit, I think we're getting in there all week. I can't believe we have our own private terrace with a hot tub. This is insane."

"This place is like a dream," she says with a bright smile.

Relief floods me as I watch the joy radiating from her. Thank God I was able to make this trip, so she didn't have to cancel. I've watched her work her ass off for years. She deserves this vacation. She needs this vacation.

"What do you want to do first?" I ask as I glance down at my watch. "It's a little passed five right now."

I rub the back of my neck, trying to ignore the tension there. I'm still exhausted from the travel.

"What time is it back home?" she asks.

"Lunch time."

Her eyes bug out. "That's it? Why am I so tired?"

"We just traveled for like fifteen hours. I don't know about you, but I didn't get good sleep last night, nor do I sleep well on planes."

"Ugh, same. What do you think about ordering room service and getting a good night's sleep?"

"I think that's the best idea I've ever heard. We could eat out here on the terrace."

We find a menu on the table near the couches. I make a call to the front desk and order us our food and a bottle of wine while Layla gets in the shower.

I'm sitting on my cell phone, trying to connect to the hotel Wi-Fi, when I hear the bathroom door open.

I look up, and every muscle in my body tightens.

"What are you wearing?" I growl, trying to compose myself.

She glances down at herself and then shrugs. "I know. I thought it was just me and Charlotte. Or that I was at least going to have the potential to bring back some hot Italian guy. These pajamas are all I have, and after the long day of travel, I just want to be comfy."

I grind my teeth as my eyes home in on her breasts. Her nipples are hard, and I can see every detail of them through her silk tank top. Her matching shorts are not any better, showcasing her toned legs.

"Can you at least put on a bra?"

She glances down and then places her hands on her hips. "What? Are my nipples that repulsive to you? I'm sure you can handle a little outline of a nipple at your old age."

She is so infuriating. I stand up and stomp over to the bathroom, grabbing a pair of boxers on the way. If she wants to play that game, I can play.

The bathroom is fucking insane. All white marble with a huge walk-in shower. Gold features throughout, giving it an upscale look. I turn on the shower until it's steaming hot. The water calms my muscles, which are still tense with anger.

Layla is so stubborn.

It drives me insane and turns me on all at the same time. My dick is aching as I close my eyes and picture her perfect tits again. That silk left little to the imagination.

I've been in Italy for all of an hour, and I'm already sporting a raging hard-on for her. I'm not gonna last.

But I refuse to touch myself with thoughts of her dancing around my head. That's dangerous territory. Instead, I bite my lip while I drive the shower handle all the way to the left until freezing-cold water comes out.

Shit, that's cold. But at least my dick is already shrinking up at the torturous temperature.

Once I'm done and dry off, I pull on my black boxer briefs. If she's just gonna strut around the hotel in next to nothing, I'll do the same. See how she likes it.

I open the door and walk back into the room. I spot her leaning against the railing outside, still in her silk pajamas.

My heart does a weird flutter in my chest as the beauty of the view and the woman compete for my attention.

Like she senses my presence, she turns around and looks at me. I walk further into the room until I'm at the doorway to the terrace.

"Enjoying the view?" I ask as her eyes look me up and down. The look of hunger in her eyes is obvious. It makes my dick stiffen slightly. Suddenly, I'm starting to wonder if this plan is about to backfire on me. Because Layla eyeing my bulging cock is starting to feel like I've taken this game in the wrong direction.

"What are you doing?" she grinds out, then looks away hastily, like she can't bear the sight of me for another second.

I shrug my shoulders and walk further onto the terrace, forcing her to look back at me.

"I'm just trying to understand the dress code here. It seems as if we're walking around in next to nothing."

I stop in front of her, maybe a foot away. Her breathing is labored as she looks her fill. I know when a woman likes what she sees.

"I told you," she says with a tremor in her voice. "I didn't pack anything else."

I cross my arms across my chest. "Well, it appears we are in a bit of a pickle here. If you're walking around with your tits on display, I'm walking around like this."

Her eyes turn smoldering. "What exactly would you like me to do? I'm not going to put on a dress or fancy top to soothe your growing erection. I know you're a man whore, but can't you keep it down for this trip? At least around me."

I laugh bitterly. "There you go again, throwing man whore out at me. If that's the reason for all this animosity, I think it's a little old. You might need to find a new reason to despise me so much."

"I have plenty of reasons not to like you," she folds her arms across her tits, matching my stance.

It pushes her breasts up so high out of her top that I see a bit of her nipple popping out. I advance on her losing all reason and control.

Chapter Five

Layla

His body almost collides with mine until I'm pushed completely against the stone railing. He cages me in with one hand on each side of me.

It's not just his presence that makes my entire body ignite, it's the compelling look in his eyes.

"I don't think you do," his deep voice answers indulgently. "I think you have plenty of reasons to *pretend* not to like me."

I gasp. His words cut right through my heart with their accuracy. I avert my gaze away as if they are the key to my soul, and without them, he can't stab me with any more words that cut.

But it only lasts a second because his scent is so intoxicating, and his body is so damn perfect. His muscles are big and defined from all the hours of manual labor his job entails.

Then I remember what it felt like that night so many years ago. After he kissed me, and we poured our hearts out to each other only days before. I walked into the party and his eyes met mine. I thought he was going to call me over. Instead, he wrapped an arm around another woman's waist and turned away.

I shove his chest, so he falls backwards, just barely catching himself on a chair behind him.

"No, you're wrong. I have reasons to not only not like you, but to hate you."

Without giving him time to respond, I stomp back inside. A knock at the door comes at the perfect time. We need a reset on this moment so I don't slap him, or worse, give into my stupid body's desires.

"I'll get it," he grumbles as he walks to the door.

The plates and a bottle of red wine, perfectly chilled at fifty-eight degrees, are placed on our table outside. I take a seat on the side of the table that faces the water so I can look out at the view. Hopefully, the view will keep me from peeking down at Josh and his stupid sculpted body. Oh, who am I kidding? His body beats the view by a mile. There's no hope for me keeping my eyes off of him.

"Can you please put some clothes on while we eat?" I bark at him just as he's about to take a seat.

He lifts an eyebrow. "You're still half naked. Why do I have to put more clothes on?"

"I told you; I don't have anything else comfy to wear."

What is so hard for him to understand? He's really pissing me off with this. Besides, him in just his tight-ass underwear is not the same as my pajamas.

He groans then pushes his chair back out. He comes back in grey sweatpants and a black t-shirt. I'm not sure that's much better. He somehow still looks just as good. Can I ask him to put something less sexy on? No, I think he'd kill me.

"Here." He extends his hand out. "Put these on."

He's holding another pair of similar pants and a shirt. As much as I want to defy anything he says, it would be nice to feel a bit more covered up around him. I grab the clothes and make a big production about giving in, like I'm only doing this for him.

In the bathroom, I strip off my silk pajamas and step into his clothes. I'm swimming in them, and they smell like him. It feels insanely intimate to be wrapped up in his clothing. I don't see any of this going well.

I walk back outside and take a seat at the table. The food smells heavenly, and I'm starving. I pull the silver dome off my plate. The scallops are sitting over a bed of noodles in a white wine sauce.

"Wow," I sigh with contentment. "This looks incredible. I can't wait to dive in."

I look up at Josh. He's looking at me with a strange, dark look in his eyes. He scans my body, but I can't quite figure out what is making him look at me like that. Then I remember I'm in his clothes.

Does he...like seeing me in his clothes? Of course, he does. He's a guy. I'm sure he likes seeing any chick in his stuff. It's some weird possession thing. It has nothing to do with me.

As if he was in a trance, he shakes his head and clears his throat.

"Yeah, lucky for us, the restaurant here comes highly recommended. I looked it up while you were in the shower."

He picks up his glass of wine and raises it. "To a truce, so we can enjoy the food and view in peace."

My mouth curves into an unconscious smile. He always has known how to make me hate him one minute and laugh the next. "To one of many truces throughout our trip."

I raise my glass as his head falls back with laughter. We clink them together. I sip the wine, enjoying the delicious flavors swarming around my palate.

We both moan in response. It's a local wine. The grapes were grown right here in the mountains.

"It's so fresh. I swear I can taste the breeze of the mountain air in this wine," I tell him.

He smiles at me. "I was gonna say it's really good. I wish I'd known I was gonna be here so I could've studied up on sophisticated phrases to say when drinking wine."

I giggle, picturing him saying something completely out of character. "Well, it *is* really good. No need to fancy up your words on my account."

"Let's dig in. I need to eat and then sleep."

The food is just as good as the wine. We manage to eat in peace without any further bickering. When it comes time to sleep, we are in bed by eight. I put up a wall of pillows in between us, but I think we're both too tired to even be aware of the other's presence. I think I passed out seconds after hitting the pillow.

Chapter Six

Josh

I turn my head to the side, feeling the soft pillowcases against my skin. It's my first reminder that I'm not in my own bed. Luckily, sleeping next to Layla wasn't so bad. I think she even passed out before I did. The Great Wall of China she constructed with pillows made it feel like I was alone most of the night.

I peek to my right and notice her side of the bed is empty. There's no sign of her on the couch or at the table.

The clock lets me know it's seven in the morning. I think I slept for almost twelve hours. Shit, I hope that at least means I slept through any possible jet lag.

I should get up to see where Layla is. I don't know what the plans are, but I think I'm supposed to spend the day with her. Why else would I have come? At least, I don't think she's planning on going off on her own.

The warm summer breeze comes through the door leading to the terrace. I spot her outside, sitting on a comfy chair, coffee in hand.

Damn. I forgot she was in my clothes. Seeing her in them last night was a sucker punch to the gut. A chance to see what she would look like if she were mine. If I were good enough for her and made enough money for her to bring me home to her parents.

Not that I don't know her parents, but I don't think I'm what they had envisioned for their little girl.

"Mornin'," my sleepy morning voice rasps.

She turns around quickly with a bright smile. A strange sensation takes over in my chest, familiar to the one I had yesterday. I don't know what she is doing to me.

I'm used to putting her in a certain category at home while having to be on my best behavior because her brother is around. I think this one-on-one time is getting to me, making me feel things I shouldn't be feeling. Things that are easier to ignore in a group of loud, obnoxious friends.

"Good morning. There's a nice single-serve coffee maker over there. Lots of options."

"Nice. I'll grab some. Be right back."

After I make my coffee, I grab the seat next to her. The first sip hits the spot. It's different from the kind we have at home. Stronger.

"Ever have a view like this with your morning coffee?" I ask.

She smiles behind her cup. "Not even close."

"I still can't believe we're in Italy. Never thought I'd be here."

Her eyebrows raise. "Is that a good or a bad thing?"

I smile. "It's a good thing. So, uh, what's on your agenda for the day?"

Her head tilts to the side as she looks at me uncertainly. "My agenda?"

I shrug my shoulder. "I didn't want to just assume you wanted me with you."

"Oh, you don't have to spend the day with me if you don't want to. I can just..."

I stop her before she even finishes. "I never said that. Layla, I'm here to spend the time with you."

She bites her bottom lip, drawing my attention to her mouth. I've only felt those lips on mine once, but I could never forget the feeling. Soft and full, perfectly kissable lips.

"Okay," she gives me a small, tentative smile. "Well, I wanted to start with taking a water taxi to Como to do some sightseeing. Just kind of stroll around, then get some lunch there."

"Sounds cool with me. Do we want to grab some breakfast first?"

"I might grab a bar or something to have on the way. But I know I'm about to eat my way through this place, so I'd rather save the calories for lunch and dinner."

"You got it. No breakfast. Shoving our faces for lunch and dinner. I'm down."

She shakes her head at me, but her smile tells me she might actually be lightening up around me.

After we get ready, we walk towards the water right outside of our hotel. She looks beautiful in a pair of light green shorts and a white top with brown sandals. Her hair is down, and she's wearing minimal makeup, which she pulls off easily because she's so damn beautiful.

We are led to the hotel's dock which, apparently, has a water taxi that stops by every thirty minutes. We don't talk much as we wait. We both continue to look around at everything around us. It's easy to just get lost in thought while you take in what surrounds you.

When the boat finally arrives, I motion for Layla to go ahead of me.

"Buongiorno bellezza," a young, attractive-looking male says to Layla as he holds his hand out for her to step onto the boat.

I make a mental note to look it up, but I think he called her beautiful.

"Grazie," she replies flirtatiously.

I follow her to the front of the water taxi, where she takes a seat next to the railing. The water around us is so clear you can see the rocks and fish everywhere. It looks like a swimming pool instead of a lake. You don't see water like this in America.

"I think he's checking me out," Layla whispers to me.

"Who?" I reply roughly as I scan the boat.

I'm ready to beat whoever is making her feel uncomfortable until I look up at her and see her smiling and fixing her hair. Is she fucking kidding me? I follow her line of sight and see the Italian guy who works on the boat ogling her.

He's not subtle, nor is she, and I'm not thrilled.

"You two on a romantic vacation?" he dares to speak to us in his thick accent.

I move to put my arm on the railing behind her, trying to signal to the man to back off.

Layla lets out a ridiculous giggle. "Oh, we aren't together. He's just a friend. If you could even call him that."

I swallow hard, trying not to reveal the anger that her words evoke in me. I didn't sign up to be some loser who follows her around while she flirts with every guy in sight.

"A woman like you shouldn't be out with a *friend* in beautiful Como. You should be treated to all the luxuries this place can offer by a man who knows what he has in front of him." He raises his eyebrows at me with a challenge, as if daring me to be man enough to be that guy.

And there Layla goes with another hideous giggle. This time, I can't hold in my groan.

"What's your problem?" she asks with a hint of annoyance.

"Nothing at all. Just enjoying the beautiful views around us," I say, then turn my head away from her.

Thankfully, Fabio gets pulled away to do some actual work on the boat. The rest of the ride I'm able to actually take in the scenery and slightly enjoy myself, even though his words echo in the back of my head.

Even if I was interested in exploring this with Layla, which I'm obviously not, I can't afford to spoil her with all the luxuries this place has to offer. I'm no fool. I know George Clooney doesn't have a place here for its affordability. I could never give Layla what he was referring to. I'm just your average man who works a blue-collar job and brings home enough to be comfortable.

And I'm okay with that. I'm happy with that, actually. It's not until I'm near Layla that I'm reminded of my lack of success in this world.

"What's first on the agenda?" I ask her as soon as we're off the boat.

She looks up at me through her sunglasses. "I wanted to stroll around first if that's all right with you."

I shrug my shoulders. "It's your trip. I'm just here to tag along."

Como looks exactly like any Italian city I picture when I close my eyes. It has cobblestone streets, old buildings made of stone or cement.

We stroll through the streets as crowds of people take up every inch of space. There are restaurants, stores, and bakeries every-where. It seems like every other yard someone is walking with their dog. Layla squats to greet all of them. I never knew she was such a dog lover.

"Oh, look at this restaurant," Layla wanders over to a corner restaurant with seating out front on the cobblestone. "Can we eat here?"

"You're the food expert. I trust your instincts."

Layla manages to charm her way to the last open table outside. The restaurant is on the outskirts of the town, so we also have views of the mountains and the lake.

"Should we order some wine?" she whispers like she's asking me to do something illegal.

I chuckle. "It's vacation. Don't you know you can drink alcohol morning, noon, or night on vacation without any guilt?"

"So, if I order a bottle, you'll drink it with me?"

"I think I'd be okay with that. As long as you pick out my lunch for me. This is mostly in Italian, and I don't know what I'm reading."

"Done."

She smiles, and I realize I like it when she forgets that she hates me. I wonder how long it will last.

After the waiter has poured our wine, Layla puts in our food order in Italian. I have no idea what I'm about to eat, but I kind of like the mystery of it all. I lean back in my chair and rest my hands behind my head. I must admit, it's nice being on a vacation. I've been working like crazy this past year. It's taken a toll on me.

"Have you thought about your restaurant at all since we've been here?" I ask Layla.

"Ugh, yes. I'm doing everything in my power to trust Zane and not check in on him."

I've met Zane a bunch of times. I'm pretty sure he's tried flirting with me in hopes of flipping me to the other team. He's a good guy, though. Works hard and is good to Layla.

"Zane can manage. You know he's more than capable."

"I know. It's just...that place is my baby."

"And you've done an incredible job with it. You have it running like a well-oiled machine." Her eyes open wide as her mouth falls slightly. "What? Why are you looking at me like that?"

"Nothing," she shakes her head. "I'm just surprised to hear you say that. I didn't think you cared much for my restaurant."

"Wait...what? Why would you think that?"

She turns her face away from me as she answers. "Just always seems like you do what you can to avoid going there or forcing Asher to pick somewhere else."

I stiffen in my seat, momentarily abashed. "Shit, I never knew you noticed that. I just got the impression that you didn't want me there. But you have to know," I lean forward and grab her hand, "I think your food is incredible."

A blush runs along her cheeks. "Thanks. That means a lot."

Just as I'm pulling my hand away from hers, our food comes out. The waiter places some kind of pasta in front of me. Whatever it is, it looks better than anything I'd eat in America. It's not pasta drowning in a sauce.

"Wow, look at this," I say as I get a glimpse of her plate. "I can't wait to dig in. What am I eating exactly?"

She looks amused as she scoops up some of her food. "You are eating tagliatelle in a wild boar sauce, and I have risotto with braised veal in a lemon sauce."

We both eagerly grab our forks and start to eat.

It ends up being a surprisingly peaceful lunch. Neither of us seem to annoy one another. Maybe that's what good food and wine do to people; makes them get along.

We take the water taxi back to our hotel and change into bathing suits to take a dip in the pool while we enjoy some drinks.

As soon as we get to our lounge chairs, I reach behind my back and take my shirt off. I don't miss the gleam of interest in her eyes as they roam my body.

I guess there's one benefit to working in construction. I may not bring in the kind of money that most women dream of, but the manual labor has blessed me with a body that tends to make women go crazy.

She bites her bottom lip, never tearing her eyes away. My dick grows hard watching her reaction. I try to hide my smirk, even though I want to gloat and point out how she's still attracted to me, even if she hates me.

Then karma slaps me across the face when she takes off her black coverup. Her white bikini doesn't cover much. Her large breasts are spilling out of each side of the triangles. I look over and see a group of men on the other side of the pool pouring all their attention on Layla.

I know it's not my damn place to say anything to her, but I don't relish the idea of other men seeing so much of her body.

Then she reaches down for some sunscreen, and I see half of her ass is hanging out as well. My head falls back as I use every ounce of willpower that I have to keep my mouth shut.

"What's wrong with you?" she asks nonchalantly.

"Nothing," I bark back through gritted teeth.

"Geez, what's with the sudden mood change? You suddenly realize you may have an STD from all your slumming around?"

I don't even give her comment any attention. It's bullshit, and she knows it. She's just trying to get a rise out of me. I swear, I think she gets off on it.

I grab my own sunscreen and work it onto my chest. I'm not sure what pisses me off more, the attention she's getting in her bikini, if you could even call it a bikini, or her insult about my sex life. I refuse to look up at her, knowing she is rubbing her lotion all over her body right now. I don't think my dick can handle it.

"Shit," she whispers, which finally draws my eyes back to her.

"What's wrong?"

Her hand is reaching behind her back while her face strains. "I can't reach. Can you put this on my back?"

The asshole in me wants to prove a point to the onlookers who are still watching her. One guy pushes the other, then points to Layla. Fuck it. I'll make sure they know she's off-limits.

"Sure. Lie down on your stomach."

When she's on the lounge chair, her fucking luscious ass in my face, I squirt some of the lotion on my hand and scoot to the edge of my chair. I start in the center of her upper back and begin to rub it in. Her skin is flawless and smooth.

Her head is turned towards me, but she has her eyes closed.

I squeeze more lotion on my hand and start to rub it along her lower back, just above the top of her bikini bottoms. I make sure to get her sides, then I move my hand up her side until it hits the side of her breast that's spilling out of her bikini.

Her eyes fly open, and I wait for her to yell at me, but she says nothing. Instead, she watches me as my hand rubs along her breast. What starts as something to show up the guys across the pool, turns directions quickly.

I move my hand down her side again, then dare to push it even further when I continue all the way down to her ass. Her eyes show no sign of surprise or apprehension, they just hold mine like this is exactly what she wants me to be doing.

I cup one cheek in my hand and resist the urge to spank it. Shit, she has some nice cheeks. They would look incredible taking her from behind. I move to the other cheek and give it the same treatment. At this point, there's no way in hell I can stand. My dick went from semi-hard to a full-fledged, raging hard-on.

Before I get to a point where I do something stupid like think she possibly wants me again, I pull my hand away.

Clearing my throat, I try to act indifferent. "There you go."

I lay back on my lounge chair and close my eyes, willing my body to calm down. I hear her whisper a thank you, but I need to focus right now.

I take a couple of deep breaths.

The entire thing has completely backfired. My body is all of a sudden acutely aware of the beauty next to me, and I'm afraid the desire it stoked can't be tamed.

Chapter Seven

Layla

Layla

Horny doesn't even begin to describe what I've been feeling since Josh rubbed suntan lotion all over me. What the hell was I doing just watching him intently as he felt me up? I was in a daze, watching his muscles bulge as he touched me in places I've only ever dared to let myself fantasize about at night when I'm alone with my thoughts.

Even then, I tell myself it's just because he's attractive, but that I still hate the guy.

I tried to find extra pillows last night to block myself from somehow ending up touching him in the middle of the night. I don't trust myself in the dead of night to make the wisest decisions. Not with him sleeping next to me in nothing but his sweatpants.

I don't understand what's going through his head. Sometimes, he'll look at me in a way that makes my heart skip a beat, not that I want him to look at me that way. But other times, he'll pretend like I'm not in the room while he laughs and flirts with another woman.

What am I supposed to make of that?

All I know is that I'm all kinds of confused. These days, I'm not the type of person to make super rash decisions, but I find myself thinking about what it would be like to just give in to my desires just once.

All these years, I've tried my best to hate the man, but I can't deny that my body feels another way.

I need a breath of fresh air before I do something stupid. I look over at him lying on the bed in his stupid grey sweats and no damn shirt on.

"I thought we agreed to wearing clothes," I grumble from the table across the room.

He looks over at me. "I got hot last night."

"Well, morning is here. You should be wearing a shirt."

He smirks at me. "Is it that distracting to see me without a shirt on?"

"Ugh, I'm going for a walk. I want to see if they have any granola bars or something downstairs."

I grab my purse and walk out the door without a second thought. I hate how he can be so damn cocky. But what I hate the most is how right he is. It *is* distracting to see him without a shirt on.

What time is it in Georgia? I think I need to talk to Charlotte. I reach for my phone, only to come up with an empty pocket. Shit. I left it in the room.

Luckily, my purse has my hotel key in it. I wouldn't put it passed Josh to refuse to let me back in without apologizing or something equally annoying.

I open the door and stroll back in, determined to keep my head down and retrieve my phone. But his sudden gasp of surprise forces my eyes in his direction.

"Oh my god!" I scream as I watch Josh gripping his dick.

"What the fuck! I thought you were going downstairs," he shouts.

"I forgot my phone."

His eyes bore into mine, but I can't hold them for long. I'm too busy looking at the most perfect dick I've ever seen in my entire life. I mean, like long, thick, and the sexiest vein running through it. His tip is swollen like his dick is just straining to get some attention.

"Geez, Layla," he screams in frustration.

"What are you doing jerking off the second I leave the room?"

"Because you piss me off!"

"What the hell does that have to do with anything? Wait a minute," I hesitate, "were you thinking about me?"

His head falls back on his pillow, but he doesn't answer. Holy. Shit. He was totally thinking about me.

"Well, don't stop on my account. You were thinking about me. Why not finish while looking at the real thing?" I say as I throw my hands up in the air.

I don't know what the hell I'm suggesting. I can't watch him do this. I'd literally never be able to look at him the same again.

My panties are already soaked from the excitement of the idea. I don't know if it's knowing he was thinking of me, even if it was in some kind of weird, angry way, or just the sight of his sexy abs as the backdrop of this perfect image. But all I know is my body is fully on board for this weird show I've just requested.

Hell, I said I needed to find myself on this trip. Before I owned the restaurant, I was bold and free. I did what I wanted. Maybe this can be my first experience back to that girl. Zane would totally be high-fiving me right now.

"I'm not gonna jack off in front of you, Layla," he bites out.

"Really? Cuz your dick is still in your hand, and it looks like it's even harder now. Do you like the idea of me watching?" I raise my eyebrow with a challenge.

I watch a little bit of precum drip out of his tip. It lands on his thumb, and I think I might pass out. I rub my legs together and feel the friction ease the ache that's building.

"Fuck, I'm going to hell for this," he says. "Alright, Freckles. You asked for it."

"Don't call me that," I bite back, but he just smiles.

I always hated his nickname for me. I have scattered freckles on my nose and cheeks, which I've always been self-conscious about. Sometimes, I try to cover them up with makeup. His nickname has always felt like an insult to me.

He ignores me. Instead, I watch him gather his cum on the tip of his dick and spread it all over himself. It's without a doubt the hottest thing I've ever seen.

I wish I could crawl onto the bed and lick it off, but I'm stuck standing at the foot of the bed by myself.

His hand wraps around his thick length, and now my eyes are fighting between watching the veins on his hand versus the one running along his dick. His eyes are hooded as he focuses on watching while his hand pumps up and down along his shaft.

"Is this what you wanted, Freckles? You wanted to be a perv and watch me touch myself? I can tell you, I'm not gonna last long with all those little moans and whimpers you're making over there."

My hand flies over my mouth. I had no idea I was making any noises. But hearing my nickname being used in such a dirty way is starting to make me feel like maybe I don't hate it after all.

"Fuck," he growls as he starts to stroke harder and faster. "I wish I could come all over your sexy ass instead of on myself. Did you like it when I touched you there yesterday?"

I can't answer. The truth isn't something I'm willing to speak out loud yet. But that doesn't mean I'm willing to tear my eyes away for a second. His eyes hold onto mine with such intensity that I feel like I'm somehow a part of this with him instead of just an onlooker.

His movements begin to get jerky as I watch his stomach muscles tense up. He's close. But I don't want this to end. I want to live in this moment forever.

"I'm coming. I want you to watch every drop of cum shoot out of me. Just know, you were the one who got me off, Freckles."

His head falls back deeper into the pillow in ecstasy as he moans through his release. Thick white ropes of cum rush out of him, landing all over his perfect set of abs. I find myself licking my lips, wishing I could run my tongue along his stomach.

When he's done, his entire body relaxes as his eyes open. The reality of what we just did together hits me like a ton of bricks. What the hell did I just do?

I'm supposed to hate this man, not give him any more ammunition to hit me with. I race back out of the room, phone forgotten, as I make quick work to get downstairs for some fresh air.

This is only day two of the trip, and I've already forgotten to keep my guard up. This is exactly why this was a bad idea. I should've never gotten on the plane. Now I'm stuck here with him in the same bed.

I pace back and forth outside until I feel like I've got my composure. On my way back to the room, I try to pump myself up so I have the confidence to walk in there and pretend like nothing ever happened.

Somehow, I feel like moving forward without discussing it is the safest plan of action. I don't trust myself to let my brain go back to the moment we shared together.

Chapter Eight

Josh

What the hell just happened? What was I thinking?

I wasn't thinking, that's the problem. I can't be expected to make any good decisions when I have my throbbing cock in my hand and my dream girl standing in front of me.

She just looked so sexy as the desire sparkled in her eyes. Then she took control, and I saw the Layla I knew years ago come to life. The one who didn't take shit from anybody, the one who knew what she wanted and went after it.

I was a goner after that.

What am I supposed to do now? I need to see where she stands. I know she enjoyed it, but I saw it in her eyes when it was all over, she panicked. She regretted it.

I fucking hate that. What went from the single hottest moment of my life turned into an awkward clean-up filled with uncertainty.

The door opens, and I feel my heartbeat accelerate. I turn around and watch Layla stroll in with some granola bars in her hand.

She looks at me hesitantly. "You want one?"

"Uh, sure. Thanks," I say as I grab one from her hand. "Look. About what happened."

"Can we just…not talk about it?" she asks quickly. "It was stupid. I don't think we need to make a big deal out of it."

Stupid? Don't make a big deal about it? I knew she wasn't going to react well, but hearing the words out of her mouth hurt.

"Yeah, sure. It was stupid. Got it. It's forgotten."

She straightens her back. "Thanks. Are you ready? We have to get going if want to make that cooking class."

"Yeah, sure." I grab my phone and wallet, then tuck them in my back pockets.

Thirty minutes later, we walk into the kitchen, where several stations are set up. People are laughing and talking all around us.

As I'm tying my apron on, I look over at Layla, who is ready with a big smile on her face.

"Tell me again why someone like you needs a cooking class?" I ask, struggling to get this damn thing tied behind me.

She watches me with fascination. "Turn around," she smirks then starts to tie my apron for me. "Because it's in Italy. It's also more of an advanced class about making pasta from scratch."

I turn around quickly, almost knocking over the stack of bowls in front of me.

"Advanced? Layla, I don't know the first thing about cooking."

She smiles. "That's why you have me as a partner."

When the class starts, Layla tells me she wants me to start, and she will assist. I personally think she just wants to watch me screw everything up.

I'm instructed to measure eight hundred grams of flour.

"What the hell are grams?" I whisper to Layla.

She points to a scale in front of her. "America is actually one of the few places that measure ingredients in cups."

Somehow, I magically make it through measuring the flour with Layla's assistance.

"Now go ahead and form your well in the center of your flour for your eggs," the instructor says as if I'm supposed to know what she's talking about.

I glance over at Layla, who is moving the eggs next to me, and at the station next to us to see what they're doing.

"Seems simple enough," I mutter to myself as I move some of the flour to the sides to create a hole in the middle.

I start cracking my eggs into the center, one by one, until I'm on my final egg. Just as I crack it, the entire contents of my eggs start to flow over my flour walls and onto the counter.

"Eggs overboard, Layla. Eggs overboard! What do I do?" I shout in a moment of panic.

Layla reaches over me and starts to push flour around the sides as she snorts. "You just need to close the gap that was allowing the eggs to escape."

She is clearly getting a kick out of this. We both work to move the flour around and clean up the mess that I created. Once the panic subsides, I realize our arms and hands are touching as we work. Her scent surrounds me, and our earlier escapade is all that I can think about now.

She must notice the change in the air because she looks up at me, and her smile fades. She bites her bottom lip, and I think I let out a low growl.

Dammit. It's been ten years since I've had those lips on mine. Three thousand, six hundred, and fifty days. That's far too long. It's eating away at me to keep my distance.

"Now, you need to...ummm," she looks around and clears her throat, "you need to start slowly mixing the flour into your eggs until it starts to form a dough."

"Got it," I reply hesitantly.

"It looks like I need to start on the lemon sauce," she says as she glances around the room. "Just let me know if you need anything. I'll be right here."

I don't even remember the teacher telling us to do anything else besides add the eggs. I've been far too caught up in noticing every little breath Layla takes and what her hands feel like against mine. I want to take that hand and run it along my dick.

How am I this turned on when I just jacked off an hour ago and am currently kneading pasta dough?

There is something seriously wrong with me that my dick is behaving like a teenager when he's around his crush. That's what it feels like with Layla. Every move she makes goes straight to my dick.

I watch her measure her lemon juice, her lips puckered to the side in concentration. She's so damn adorable and sexy at the same time.

"You gonna stop rolling and get out the pasta machine?"

I realize Layla is talking to me.

"Wait, what?" I ask, embarrassed that I was just so lost in watching her. "What pasta machine?"

She smiles at me. "That one, right there. Did you not hear anything she just said?"

"I was busy kneading this dough," I defend, hoping she doesn't call me out.

With the help of Layla, we manage to get our pasta run through the machine. It's actually really cool to see the final product and know it all started from eggs and flour.

"Damn, this is kinda fun," I admit as I add the pasta to the boiling water.

Layla looks at me skeptically. "Says the guy who's been whining almost the entire time."

"Hey, I don't want to screw this up. This is our lunch. I don't want you blaming me for a bad lunch because you brought the man who eats out all the time."

"Aw, you're worried about making me happy?" She puts her hand to her heart jokingly.

I drop the rest of the pasta in and turn to face her. "I always worry about your happiness, Layla. Maybe you don't see it, but I do."

Her smile falls from her face. I'm good at making that happen. She opens her mouth to say something but then shuts it. Looking around the room, she clears her throat.

"The pasta should only take about two minutes to cook. We need to keep an eye on it."

Right. Message received. Move on.

We both turn awkwardly to the pot as the moment passes us by. I let Layla take the lead and plate our food. She grates fresh pecorino cheese on top of our lemon sauce along with fresh chopped basil. Watching her work is like watching a painter making a masterpiece or a dancer in their element during their favorite number.

Every movement she makes is fluid. I can feel the love behind her work. She isn't just making food, she's creating something with her heart.

We are instructed to carry our plates outside, where a bottle of wine awaits our private table.

Our table is perched under a lemon tree with an impeccable view of the lake. It's wild how everything you see looks like a painting. There's so much beauty that your brain doesn't know how to process and take it all in.

Layla takes a seat across from me, and I realize nothing can compete with her. She's always stolen my focus wherever we go.

"What are you doing?" I ask after we get into our room after dinner. She's rummaging through her suitcase like she's looking desperately for something.

"I'm trying to find my sparkly top."

She pulls out some black glittery scrap of material.

"Why do you need that top?"

"Because...I thought I might go to a bar tonight. I kind of wanted to check out the nightlife here. Don't worry, you don't have to come."

I pop off the bed. "Like hell I'm letting you go out at night in that top in a foreign country."

"You can come. I just didn't want to pressure you. I'm gonna go put this top on."

She goes into the bathroom, and I open my bag to find a black shirt that fits my biceps a bit tighter than my other shirts. It has nothing to do with wanting to impress Layla. It's just a nice shirt, and I like to wear it. And while we're at it, the extra spray of cologne has nothing to do with her either.

She comes out in white shorts and her little top. Her hair seems fuller, and her eyes look darker. If she thinks she's picking up a random Italian man at this bar, she's delusional. I can't let her risk her life. For one thing, her brothers would kill me if I let that happen.

Plus, fuck that.

"You have a place in mind?" I ask as I open the door.

"There's a bar over in Como that is supposed to be where all the locals like to hang out. We need to take the water taxi to get there."

"You lead the way."

As soon as we step foot off the boat, I can hear live music. Layla leads me along the street until we turn the corner, and the bar appears before our eyes. It's actually kind of cool looking. The large openings in the brick walls allow you to sit at the tables outside on the cobblestone while still feeling like you're in the bar.

There are people dancing inside and all along the streets while lights hang above us.

"Oh my god! Isn't this the cutest?" she claps excitedly.

We walk up to the bar, and I motion to her that it's on me. "What do you want?"

"I'll take a glass of Chianti. Thanks."

All the wine has been incredible these past two days, but having a nice cold beer in this heat sounds pretty amazing, too.

I grab our drinks from the bartender and turn to Layla. "Where do you wanna sit?" I scream above the loud Italian music.

"Outside seems fun," she replies.

"Cheers," I say after I take a seat at the table she picked. "To learning how to make pasta. It will certainly come in handy on my next date night."

I wink at her, and she scoffs, which just makes me chuckle. I don't know why I like getting under her skin, but I do. If only she could admit that there is some kind of powerful attraction between the two of us.

I know I thought I regretted this morning, but come to find out, the only thing I regret is her reaction afterward.

"So, how is the finding yourself thing going?" I ask, wanting to understand more about the woman she has become.

I want to know everything there is to know about her. I want to be the one who knows her secrets, things she doesn't tell anybody.

"It's been…interesting. I definitely feel like I'm detaching from work."

"Interesting…that's a horrible answer. I'm completely failing you in helping you succeed. Tell me—what would the younger version of Layla be doing right now?"

She purses her lips as she considers my question. "I mean, I'm in Italy. I'm single. I would probably be taking some shots right now. Dancing with some handsome man who can't take his eyes off of me. I'd be wild and free."

Jealousy swarms in my gut at the thought of her dancing with another man. It makes me want to let her know that she doesn't need another man. I'm right here. "Does this morning not count as being wild and free?"

Her eyes go wide. "I can't believe you're bringing that up."

I smile over my beer. "What? I can't let you downplay that and act like it wasn't wild. Come to think of it, you were the one who initiated it, too."

She covers her face with her hands. "I don't know what I was thinking."

"Were you thinking? I think you were just going with your gut."

"It was hard to listen to my brain when your thing," she says as she waves her hand at me, "was in my face. How weren't you more embarrassed?"

I shrug. "I have a nice thing. Plus, I saw the look in your eyes when you saw it. You liked it. Admit it."

Chapter Nine

Layla

The nerve of this asshole. To claim that I liked his thing.

I did not. It wasn't anything special. I've seen better.

Ugh, okay, I'm full of shit. Even I can smell it. It was the nicest *thing* I've ever seen. I want to see it again. I want to suck on it like a damn popsicle.

But I won't. I will not fall for his charm again. I look over at him and I can just tell he knows what I'm doing. He knows I'm arguing with myself.

"Who won?" he asks with a raised eyebrow.

"What are you talking about?"

"Who won in the little argument in your head? The you that hates me or the one who wants me?"

"Didn't your parents ever teach you how to talk to a lady?" I fire back.

He looks away from me, the tension evident in his shoulders. "My parents didn't teach me shit," he says under his breath.

I know he grew up in Texas and his parents are still there, but I don't know much beyond that. Asher told me once that he doesn't go home very often. He's spent quite a few holidays with us since he met Asher in college.

"Are you not close with your parents?" I ask, suddenly curious to know more about his upbringing.

He scoffs. "That's an understatement."

"You never talk about them."

He tips back the last of his beer. "I don't like to," he says, then slams down his glass. "What do you say we loosen you up and make this night a little wild and crazy? We can bring back the old Layla. Although, I like the one right in front of me too."

His eyes roam up and down my body. He's not subtle with his appreciative gaze.

"How do you propose we make it a crazy night?"

He gives me his megawatt grin. "Shots."

He leaves our table and comes back with a tray of drinks. Thank goodness we ate a massive amount of carbs today. I'm hoping it helps absorb this alcohol.

"A secret for a shot?" he suggests with a knowing look on his face.

I cross my arms across my chest. "If you want to pretend that we're in high school. Fine. But you have to go first."

He rubs his hands together in anticipation. "Bring your best, Layla. Let's get personal."

I tap my finger to my chin as I ponder all the things I want to know about this man. Without any liquid courage yet, I think our first round of questions should be easier. We can get to the good stuff after I have some hard liquor in my system.

"Best sex you've ever had?" I challenge him.

Am I torturing myself with this question? Yes, I am. But I still want to know the answer.

He shakes his head as he grabs his shot glass. "You go straight for the tough questions."

He has no idea what's coming if he thinks this is a hard question.

His eyes trail down the length of my body again, making me break out in goosebumps. "I have a feeling I haven't had my best sex yet, but it'll happen soon."

I wiggle in my seat as my body scorches with desire. He throws his shot back. I should point out that he didn't answer the question, but I think he just insinuated sex with me would be the best he's ever had.

"Alright, Freckles. I believe it's my turn to pick a question." He slides a shot glass my way. "Are you ready?"

"Bring it on, Josh."

"What's the most important quality you're looking for in a man?"

I'm stunned. This is not the type of question I was expecting. "You're making my question look bad. I didn't realize we were asking serious questions, not dirty ones."

"Just answer the question, Freckles."

"Fine. That's easy. I want a man who will be supportive. I'm a career woman, and I don't want someone who expects me to play the stereotypical housewife."

I take the shot, the whiskey burning all the way down my throat. I cringe at the taste. It's been years since I've taken a shot.

Josh is rubbing the stubble on his chin when I look up at him.

"What?" I ask.

"Nothing. Just wasn't expecting an answer like that. I thought maybe you were interested in settling down and being taken care of eventually."

"Ugh, why do all men think women want that? It's like feminism never happened. There's still this assumption that women will quit their jobs when they get married. They will obviously not be a working mom because somehow that's neglecting their children if they continue work."

"I'm sorry. I know you're passionate about what you do, and you are amazingly talented. I would hate to ever see you give up your career. I guess I just thought it's what you wanted because he told me..." he leans back in his chair, "Never mind. It doesn't matter."

He's holding something back from me. Who told him something? And what did they tell him?

"Your turn," he breaks through my thoughts. "Make it a good one."

"What's your favorite sex scene from a movie?"

He throws his head back and laughs. I smile in return. I figured he'd like this question,

"That's such a random question, but I love it. Okay, let me see. I think the hottest one that comes to mind is the rollercoaster scene in Fear between Reese Witherspoon and Mark Wahlberg. I was just a teenager when I first saw the movie, and I got hard every time I watched it."

I can't help but laugh hard as I picture a teenage Josh popping boners from a movie scene.

"Don't laugh at me. That scene could probably still get me hard. It was freaking hot."

"You got a thing for public orgasms or something?" I ask.

"Not particularly," he winks at me. "Just thought the thrill of having an orgasm at the brink of falling down the hill of a coaster would be a huge rush." He takes his shot and winces. "Damn. Whose stupid idea was it to do this again?"

"I believe it was yours."

"Alright. I guess that makes it my turn. Nice question, by the way. Now, let's see. When did you have your first orgasm?"

Damn. I think I deserve my shot first for this question. Of course he would pick a question like this. I've definitely never told anyone this story.

"Seriously, Josh," I sigh.

"It's gonna be good, isn't it? Come on, fess up."

"I was in a hot tub once…" I start, and he instantly smirks. Fucking asshole will never let me live this down.

"How old were you?" he interrupts.

"What does it matter?"

"Trust me, Freckles. It matters."

"Sixteen if you must know. Anyway, I was in the hot tub with friends. It was at some party, and we were all hanging out in someone's backyard."

"What were you wearing? Was it a two-piece?"

"Control yourself, Josh. Let me finish answering the question. Are you going to have another uncontrollable boner like your teenager movie?"

"I just might, Layla. We're talking about you in a hot tub at sixteen years old, having your first orgasm. The only thing that will ruin it is when you bring the guy into this story."

He's going to blow a gasket when I finish this story. Lucky for him, there is no boy involved.

"So, I had a couple of beers that night. I was really loose and relaxed. Everybody went inside to get some food, and I didn't feel like it. I told them I'd wait until they came back. So, I leaned back and propped my feet out of the tub. I didn't realize it was going to line one of the jets right up against me. I'm guessing you can see where I'm going with this."

Josh's elbows are on the table, a hand covering his mouth while his eyes are practically bulging out of the sockets. He's silent as he just stares at me.

"Josh. Say something."

He takes a deep breath and lets his hand fall from his face. "So, your first orgasm was with the jet of a hot tub?"

I scoff. "Well, it wasn't on purpose! I was sixteen. Give me a break!"

"It wasn't on purpose?" he asks with an eyebrow raised. "You mean you didn't keep your pussy there in front of the jet because it felt good, and you wanted to see what happened? You wanted to chase that feeling until you came."

Why does it sound so damn dirty and yet, hot when he says it? I'm suddenly extremely aware of the temperature.

I reach for my shot to try to ease the ache between my legs. It's not fair that he got to release his pent-up sexual tension this morning, and I'm sitting here suffering in silence. Men can be more vocal about getting aroused, whereas women have to hide it, or they come off as wild or promiscuous.

"Ok, fine," I admit. "I could've pulled away. Now you know my first orgasm. Are you happy?"

"There are a lot of words to describe what I'm feeling right now."

I suddenly want to change the direction of this conversation. I don't know where this question comes from. It's probably the wine and shots going to my head.

"Moving on. I have my last question."

"Shoot."

"Do you regret kissing me?"

I hold my breath, terrified of finally learning what I've feared all along. His actions certainly indicated it was all a mistake, but hearing the words will solidify it for me. I don't know why I live to torture myself like this.

I can see it in the way he's looking at me. Pure shock and disbelief. He can't believe I'm rehashing this shit either.

Maybe I should take it back. Ask another question. I suddenly don't think I can stand to hear the words out loud anymore.

"Freckles," he whispers. "There are things I've done in my life that I regret, but kissing you is not one of them. Kissing you was one of the best decisions I've made in my life. It changed me forever."

Tears well up in my eyes. I do my best to blink them away, not wanting him to see the effects his words have on me. I watch on as people dance and laugh all around us, speaking in their beautiful language.

"Look at me, Freckles. Tell me you understand what I'm saying. There is nothing about our kiss, about that evening, that I regret. I'm sorry that I've made you think differently. It's...complicated."

I smile through my tears. I don't think I'm ready to dive into what happened all those years ago. Right now, I think I just want to stay in this moment where I know he doesn't regret that night.

"Take your shot," I say softly with a smile.

He takes it, then stands up and walks up to me, holding his hand out. I give him a questioning look in response.

"Let's dance," he says insistently. "Come on. Tonight was supposed to be fun. I believe I've watched you over the years in bars. I know you want to let loose over there."

After a deep breath, I place my hand in his. He gives a reassuring squeeze, and it goes straight to my chest. The electricity between us from a simple touch of the hand is startling.

He brings me over to the cobblestone street where others are dancing and twirls me around. A smile instantly spreads across my face. Then he surprises me by pulling me all the way against his hard body, wrapping his arm around my waist.

The alcohol is pumping through my veins, clouding my judgment, making it hard for me to remember why being with him is a bad idea.

We start to sway to the music, our breaths mixing together. The entire world around us fades away, and it's just me and him together in this moment.

His other hand lands on my hip, and I feel his fingers grip me as he tries to pull me closer.

I smile. "I don't think I can get any closer."

His eyes are dark as they study my face. "I want more. I need more."

I wrap my arms around his neck and press my entire body against him. His forehead falls to my shoulder, and I feel his shuddering breath against me.

"I don't know what the hell this song is talking about," he whispers.

I start to crack up. "Neither do I. It's kind of fun to just focus on the beat."

He pulls away for a second and kisses my forehead. Next thing I know, he's moving us around the street without a care in the world, leading me like an expert. He spins me around and dips me.

The songs switch between sweet and sultry, and so does his dancing. One second, we are laughing and moving along with the beat, the next, my body is flush against his, and his hands are roaming all over me like he can't get enough.

We laugh and talk all the way back to our hotel. He wraps his arms around me on the boat ride after I shiver from the cold air. It only made me shiver more, but for an entirely different reason.

As soon as we're back in the hotel, I turn to him.

"Hot tub time?" I say with a smile.

"Absolutely. I'll open a bottle of wine."

I grab my suit and am sinking into the tub when he comes in with two glasses.

"Thank you," I say as I take the glass. "This really is an incredible room. I can't believe Asher and Charlotte were willing to pay for it."

"You know how Asher is when it comes to Charlotte. He'll drop his life savings to make her happy."

"True," I laugh. "It's still ridiculous. Very out of character for Asher."

"I guess we get to reap the benefits of his poor financial decisions."

He holds his glass up, and we cheers to my brother's financial missteps. I'm definitely feeling the alcohol that I've consumed.

Another glass of wine might not be the wisest choice, but this night has been so much fun, I don't want it to end.

We spent the next hour drinking wine, laughing over untold stories about my brother, and reminiscing about family get-togethers at my parents' house.

"I didn't realize you were at so many of my family get-togethers. I feel like I don't have many more stories to tell that you don't know about or were there."

"I'm an honorary son to your parents. I guess whether they like it or not."

"Shut up. They love you," I tell him, though I feel like I see a hint of sadness on his face before it's gone. "Well, I think we should probably get in bed so we can get up in the morning."

He stands up out of the water before I have the chance to. For a moment, he's towering over me as water runs down every muscle in sight. Nothing but the lights of the hot tub shine around us, and I'm completely lost in my thoughts.

His bathing suit bottoms are molded to his skin because of the water, and I see the outline of his dick. A dick I have now seen but have not touched or tasted. I can't seem to tear my eyes away from it. It must be the alcohol because my brain is screaming that it's massively obvious that I'm staring, but my body isn't moving. My eyes won't look away.

Until I see it start to grow in his shorts, then my eyes go directly to his. I stand up in the hot tub until we are inches apart. I raise my hand until it cups over his hard length. We both groan at the same time, and his head falls back.

A small smirk plays at the corner of my lips as I feel him grow even harder in my hand. He curses to the sky then reaches down for my hand. He moves it off him and leans down to give it a soft kiss. I'm not sure what's going on.

"Freckles, you're drunk," he croaks out like he's in pain.

"So are you. What's the problem?"

He sighs then tucks a wet piece of hair behind my ear. "I don't want you regretting it in the morning. Come on, let's go to bed."

I'm left standing alone in the hot tub, humiliated and rejected.

Chapter Ten

Josh

"Are you excited to see Milan?" I ask as I drive our rental car along the Italian streets.

We decided to venture out the rest of the trip, starting with Milan since it's only an hour's drive from Como.

"Yep," she replies shortly.

"It's a beautiful day. I can't believe we lucked out on this weather so far."

"Uh huh."

"What's your problem this morning?" She's been short with me since the moment we woke up. We had an incredible time last night. Sure, we had too much to drink and are feeling it this morning, but I don't understand why she's acting like she's mad at me.

Maybe she just feels worse off than me from the alcohol. Perhaps the shots weren't such a good idea.

"I don't have a problem," she bites back, looking out the window.

"Is it the alcohol? Are you feeling sick? If you need me to pull over, just let me know."

A bitter laugh escapes her. "Of course, you don't even know why I'm mad. Typical Josh. Not a care in the world, oblivious to other people's feelings."

"What the hell is that supposed to mean? What did I do?"

She crosses her arms across her chest. "It doesn't matter."

"Layla, let's not act like teenagers. If I did something wrong, tell me."

"Fine! You humiliated me last night." Her head stays focused on the windshield, refusing to look in my direction.

"Wait a minute. Is this because I didn't take advantage of you when you were drunk?"

She doesn't reply.

Unbelievable! I can't believe it. I try to do the right thing. Stopping her so she didn't give me the same damn face she gave me after I came all over my stomach in front of her, and this is how she reacts. What the hell? It's like I can't win with her.

Damned if I do, damned if I don't.

"I wasn't that drunk. You could at least be honest and not use being an honorable man as the reason you rejected me."

My hands are gripping the steering wheel tightly, trying not to lose my shit on her. This entire trip is giving me whiplash.

"Think what you want, Layla. You always do."

She scoffs and then goes back to looking out the window.

After a long, painful car ride, we are now standing just outside the Duomo of Milan. It's the fifth largest cathedral in the world, but I can't imagine anything being more impressive than this structure. It's massive.

"Holy. Shit," Layla mutters as we both crane our necks to see the entirety of the cathedral.

"This is the most incredible thing I've ever seen. I don't even understand how they accomplished such a massive structure so long ago."

She looks over at me. "Are you in some kind of architecture heaven right now?"

"I am. I really am. Can we go to the top? I bet the view is stunning."

"Oh, um. Yeah, sure. I think we can purchase tickets over there."

I'm like a damn kid in a candy store as we wait in line for the tickets. I'm so excited to get inside. We walk into the line for the elevator, which we're told is an hour wait, or we can take the two hundred and fifty steps to the top, which has no line. I'm starting to feel antsy in this line.

"Ugh, do you want to take the stairs?" Layla grumbles behind me.

"Why do you say that?"

"Because you literally can't stand still and keep looking over at the stairs. Come on, let's go."

"It's only a couple hundred stairs," I tell her as I lead her to the stairs. "We're young. I'm sure it'll be fine. They said it'll only take five to ten minutes if we climbed the stairs. How bad can that be?"

I'm eating my words within a couple of minutes. It's definitely gotten me huffing and puffing as my thighs are screaming at me. But I'm used to my muscles screaming at me to stop but pushing through to get the work done.

Layla, however, is not.

"These mother fucking piece of shit stairs," she curses for the hundredth time behind me. "Why the fuck did you make me do this?"

"It was your idea," I say through breaths.

"I only did it for you," she huffs out.

"I didn't ask you to. I'm sure we're about halfway. It'll be over soon."

"Oh my god! Only halfway? I'm gonna die. There's literally no way I'll make it."

I chuckle to myself, careful to hide it from her so she doesn't kick my ass when we get to the top. She's being a bit dramatic.

By some miracle, we get to the top, following a whole lot of cussing behind me. I turn around to see Layla with her hands on her knees.

"Give me a second," she pants. "Okay," she breathes deeply. "Okay, I'm okay."

I smirk. "Let's go."

As soon as I step foot onto the roof, my entire body breaks out into goosebumps. The view is even better than I thought it would be. You can see all of Milan from up here. The Italian Alps are off in the distance, far beyond the city, but still visible from up here.

The entire cathedral is made from Italian marble. The pinnacles are intricate and appear to reach into the clouds, with large statues on top of them that seem to defy gravity.

I turn around and realize Layla has her head down.

"Don't you want to look at this? It's amazing, Freckles."

"Ummm, I might have forgotten to mention I'm afraid of heights."

"What?" I close the distance between us. "Why did you agree to this?"

She shrugs her shoulders, face still looking down. "You just seemed so excited. I figured you wouldn't do it if I didn't."

Her admission does something to me. I can't believe she did this for me. She's clearly petrified. I can see her legs shaking.

I reach my hand out for hers. She doesn't hesitate in latching onto it. Another sign that she's terrified.

"Like...do I think you're going to throw me over the edge? No."

I sigh. "I guess that's a good enough answer. You at least trust that I won't murder you. I'll take it."

With her hands in mine, I try to move forward, but she's frozen in place. Instead of leading in front of her, making her feel alone behind me, I position myself behind her and wrap an arm around her waist.

"First," I lean in and whisper in her ear, noticing her body shiver in response. "Look ahead. We don't have to move yet."

She follows my instructions. "Just look at the length of this church, Freckles. It's breathtaking. It's all made of marble. Can you imagine lugging this material on whatever boats they built six centuries ago?"

"Wow," she exhales. "It really is amazing."

"I heard someone downstairs say that they started building this in the thirteen hundreds. I wonder what their vision was back then or if they had any idea what it would become one day. It took six centuries just to finish it." I look down at her. "You think you can walk a little further? I'll hold onto you the entire time."

She nods. "Just don't leave me."

I give her body a squeeze to let her know that I've got her and I'm not going anywhere. We walk slowly until we are in the center of the entire cathedral. We both look around in silence as we take in the view. I start to turn us around so we can get the three-hundred-sixty-degree view. I'm honored that she's letting me do this, that she's trusting me with her fear.

"Those things remind me of these drip sand castles I used to make on the beach growing up. Minus the life-size statues on top of them," she says.

I chuckle. "The pinnacles. Yeah, I can see that. They're stunning, aren't they? I've never seen anything like it. The statues look like they're about to touch the sky."

My hand glides along her stomach as I try to secure her closer to me. I can hear her sharp intake of breath. Next thing I know, my hand is sliding under her shirt and caressing her stomach.

"Just so you know, last night was the hardest thing I've ever done. I was not rejecting you under the pretense of being honorable. I had to go into the bathroom after you fell asleep to take care of myself. You don't know what you mean to me, Freckles. I would do anything to protect you, to make sure you're treated the way you deserve. And you deserve more than our first time being a night of drunken sex. I wasn't willing to risk you not remembering our first night together."

She looks up at me, into my eyes. "I don't know what to do with that."

I smile at her and then kiss her forehead. "Just enjoy the view. You don't need to do anything."

I'm not sure how long I stand there holding her with the entire city of Milan on our horizon. It's a moment I know will live with me forever. I like being able to have her in my arms under the pretense of her fear.

Last night, it was the alcohol; today, it's helping her face her fears. Maybe one of these days, she'll be in my arms because she's mine, and that's where she chooses to be all on her own.

After a long day spent walking around the city, we almost fall into our seats at dinner.

"I need wine and sparkling water," she demands as soon as we sit.

"I second that. I need alcohol to forget about the pain in my feet and water because I think I'm dehydrated."

"And I need a huge bowl of pasta because I burned enough calories to not give a fuck what I eat," she adds.

"We'll get you all the carbs you want."

"Ah, good evening," our waiter says as he lays out a plate of bread for us. "Our homemade bread with olive oil using our locally grown olives. Can I start you off with something to drink?"

"Yes, we would like a bottle of your finest red wine and some sparkling water," I tell him.

"Treating your beautiful woman tonight, I see."

I know I should correct him, tell him she's not mine, but I like how it sounds. And I like that she hasn't corrected him either. She's been so quick to make the correction since we've gotten here.

After our wine arrives, we order our pasta and sit back, enjoying our drinks as we watch the sunset over the city. From here, I can see the cathedral lit up.

"So, tell me, what else did you dream of doing on your trip to Italy?" I ask her as we begin to eat our food.

"Oh gosh. I know I need to come back, there's too much. There is one stupid thing I kept picturing, but it's stupid."

I lean forward. "Now you have to tell me."

"You'll make fun of me," she says as she rolls her eyes and takes a sip of wine.

"Probably. You still have to tell me."

She glares at me. "Whatever. I don't even care anymore. I kept picturing having a picnic on a hill in Tuscany overlooking a vineyard with the rolling hills ahead of me. I would have local cheeses and wine. I would be with some sexy Italian guy who would feed me the cheese."

I bite my lip, trying not to laugh. "I see."

"Ugh, I can tell you're trying not to laugh at me. I told you it was stupid."

I chuckle. "I mean, it's an interesting thing. I get the picnic in Tuscany. The Italian man feeding you cheese is a little... cliche."

"That's me, one big cliche. I also want to visit Venice. I'm not sure if we will have enough time to drive over there. It's only a couple of hours away from here."

"I don't see why we can't make it there."

Our car ride back is pretty silent, as we are exhausted from the day. Layla starts to nod off, and I get to spend some time watching her, thinking about our past. I wonder what would have happened between the two of us if I hadn't let her ex get in my head.

Was he right? Is he still right? Or did I let my insecurities get the best of me all these years?

Our connection just feels too big to be wrong. I know I don't make much money, not compared to what her father has provided for her all her life, but I could love her more than any bank account could.

I just want her to be happy. That's all I've ever wanted. And I'm starting to wonder if I could make her happier than anyone. But I could never give her these lavish trips.

Fuck, I don't know anymore. What I do know is that I want to make this trip everything she's dreamed it to be. I look over at her, confident she is passed out now.

I pull my phone out and make a phone call to the front desk of our hotel. Thank goodness they speak fluent English; I can clearly tell them what I want to do, and Enzo confirms he can get it done.

As soon as we get back to the hotel, I nudge Layla awake. She is still half asleep as we make our way into our room, where she falls face-first onto the bed. I chuckle as I strip off my clothes and get under the sheets in my boxer briefs.

She's clearly too exhausted to build her wall of pillows. Sleep doesn't come quickly as I think about the surprise I have in store for her tomorrow.

Chapter Eleven

Layla

I've never felt so comfortable in my life. I wiggle around in the bed, enjoying the warmth the covers provide. I love mornings like this when you just wake up feeling cozy.

I hear a groan in my ear, and my muscles go rigid. I realize my entire body is warm because of the man I have climbed like a damn tree in the middle of the night.

My head is in the crook of his neck, his arms wrapped around me while our legs are tangled together like pretzels. Sometime in the middle of the night, I stripped down to my thong and tank top.

My right hand is on his chest. His naked chest. The man is only wearing boxers, and my thigh is basically resting over his slightly hard dick. Seriously, why have I seen his dick hard more times this week than I've seen of any man in the last three years? And it's not like it's led to me getting anything out of it. I'm still horny and unsatisfied.

Without permission from my brain, my hand runs across his chest, mixing with his chest hair. His arms squeeze me tighter as I hear him stir around. Crap. Why did you have to do that, you stupid hand?

I'm ready for him to jump off the bed and ask what the hell I'm doing.

"Morning," he croaks out in a fog instead.

"Morning," I whisper as I try to pull away, but he doesn't let me.

"How did you sleep?" he asks, like it is completely normal to wake up like this.

"Umm, good. I mean, I'm sorry about this. I have no idea how we ended up like this."

He chuckles, and I feel it vibrate through his chest. "Well, you hit the bed face first last night. You were too tired to build your pillow wall. And it looks like somewhere in the middle of the night, you lost your clothes."

"I was exhausted last night."

"It was a long day," he says. "Are you feeling recovered enough for a surprise this morning?"

I lift my head off his shoulder, careful not to open my mouth too much and scare him away with my morning breath. "What do you mean a surprise?"

"Like, you want me to explain the definition of surprise, or you want me to repeat that I have a surprise for you?"

I glare at him. It's too early for his sarcasm. "Don't be a dick."

He smiles. "Sorry. It just comes naturally. Come on, we need to get ready."

He kisses my forehead and then gets out of bed. I don't understand this new thing where he kisses my forehead like I'm his girlfriend. Mostly, I want to scream WHAT THE HELL DOES ALL OF THIS MEAN?

"How am I supposed to dress for this surprise?" I ask as he digs through his suitcase.

"There's not a lot of walking involved. You can get away with anything, really."

"And when do I get to find out what the surprise is?" I ask as I get out of bed.

"When we get there, Freckles."

Whatever. I'm too tired to try to analyze what's happening. Josh is in and out of the shower so fast I barely have any time to think.

"I'm gonna be downstairs. Take your time, it's no rush," he yells out before he walks out of the hotel room.

"Pfft, take my time," I mutter to myself.

I'm in Italy, and the man I've pined over for years wakes up to tell me he has a surprise for me. And he thinks I'm gonna just mosey around while getting ready.

Not a chance in hell. I practically sprint to the bathroom and then jump into the shower. I opted for a black and white sundress with my brown sandals.

After spraying my perfume, an absolute must for me at all times, I grab my purse. On the way down to the main lobby, I take a deep breath. Why am I nervous? It's not like this is a date.

When I get downstairs, Josh is talking to a man at the front desk and then breaks out into a laugh. He looks so good: a white button-down shirt with the sleeves rolled up and blue shorts.

"Ready?" he says with a big smile on his face when I approach.

"I'm ready."

"Alright. I'll catch you later, Enzo. Thanks for all your help. Come on, Freckles."

As soon as we get in the car, he grabs two cups of coffee out of the holders. "One for you," he says, handing a cup over.

"Wow," I reply. "You really thought of everything. Thank you."

"Let's get this show on the road," he says as he starts to back out of the parking space.

The navigation system on his phone begins directing him through the winding roads along the mountains. It looks like our trip is over two hours, but I don't recognize the address of our end location, and the city isn't showing.

It's not until I start seeing signs and recognizing the trees that I begin to sit up straighter in my seat. "Are we in Tuscany?" I ask.

He smiles. "I figured I wasn't gonna fool you for too long. But we are only thirty minutes away, so I made it most of the trip."

"Oh my god, Josh! I'm so excited! Where are we going?"

"It's a vineyard in the Chianti region. Some family-owned vine-yard that generally only sells its wines here in Europe."

"How did you get it booked so last minute?"

He shrugs. "I had the help of Enzo at the hotel. I called him last night when you were sleeping in the car."

"That was really sweet of you." I try to blink away the tears that are threatening to spill over.

He reaches for my thigh and squeezes. "I'm just trying to make this trip what you pictured it to be."

This trip is nothing like I pictured it to be with this man sitting next to me, but I'm beginning to think it's better than I could have imagined.

When we get to the vineyard, Josh and I are taken on this incredible tour that starts with the vineyard itself. We walk along some of the vines while this adorable old man, Lorenzo, tells us all about their growth and the kinds of wines they make.

Josh gets really into, asking all kinds of interesting questions that spark a lot of laughs with Lorenzo. It's just so easy to be around him. He doesn't take life too seriously. There's nothing stuffy or pretentious about him. I may have blocked all those qualities out for years, but they are there.

"Alright, let's go down to the cellar. I'll give you a special tour. It's not part of the package, but I like you two," Lorenzo says as we walk back to the main building.

Josh makes a funny face at me, and I try to hide my laugh. He knows he won this guy over and is definitely gloating, but I'm happy to reap the benefits.

An hour later, I'm tipsy from the wine as we leave the building.

"That was so much fun," I say, then somehow manage to trip on a rock in front of me. "I'm not that drunk, I swear. The rock came out of nowhere."

He chuckles. With his hands in his front pockets, he turns towards me as he walks backward. "I wonder how many people leave this building claiming they're not *that* drunk."

I scoff. "How are you not feeling it?"

"Who says I'm not? But I am like twice your size, so I can handle a lot more than you. Come on, let's get some food in you."

He walks along the grass like he knows where he's going. I look around us and only see trees and vines, besides the building behind us that is getting smaller in the distance.

"Um, Josh. I don't think there's any places to eat around here."

"I think you might be wrong about that. What about right here behind this tree?"

I think he's losing his mind until we reach the tree, and I see it. A picnic. There's a blanket with an entire charcuterie board of meats, cheeses, crackers, and a bottle of wine and glasses set up.

It's exactly like I had described. The warmth of his actions spreads through my body. It's overwhelming what I'm feeling.

"Josh," I whisper, then look over at him.

His hands are still in his pockets as he rocks back and forth like he's a bit nervous.

"Do you like it?"

"I love it," I tell him. I don't even know how to respond to adequately show my appreciation. This is the sweetest thing anyone has ever done for me.

"Well, let's take a seat. I think we should start with getting some food in you before you go for any more wine."

"Yeah," I laugh as we take a seat. "I was eyeing this food either way. It looks incredible. And this view," I continue as I look out at the rolling hills of Tuscany. "It's exactly what I had envisioned."

He leans back on his arm, letting his legs extend out, oblivious to how good he looks.

"Oh, and just so you know, I'm twenty-five percent Italian," he says with a wink.

Oh, boy. My heart is beating erratically in my chest, but I try to play it cool like he has little effect on me.

I smile at him, then take a piece of cheese. "I guess you'll do."

He laughs loudly. "Thanks, Freckles."

I clench my teeth. "Must you call me by that nickname? You haven't used it in years. Why are you saying it again all of a sudden?"

"What's wrong with my nickname for you?"

"Freckles? It always felt like you were making fun of my freckles. I used to get picked on for them, so it just felt like another person teasing me."

I can't even look at him when I say it. It's embarrassing to admit, but I'm just over hearing that name on our trip. But after the silence drags on too long, I look over at him. His eyes are brimmed with tenderness as they hold onto mine.

"I love your freckles. They're the first thing I noticed about you when we met. I instantly fell in love with them."

I suck in a quick breath of astonishment. With hesitation, I grab a grape and bring it to my mouth, biding my time to respond. Because how do I respond?

I swallow hard. "Umm, thanks."

"Anytime, Freckles."

We continue to eat our food, but every time his gaze meets mine, my heart turns over.

It's the perfect afternoon. I'm trying like hell not to analyze what all of this means.

After we finish our food, we both lay back on the blanket and look up at the sky. I turn to my side to face him.

"Thanks for coming," I tell him.

His hands are behind his head, his biceps on full display. He doesn't look over at me, but I see a flash of humor across his face.

"That's not the reaction I received at the airport."

"Well, you're different in Italy."

"How so?" he asks as he faces me, matching my position.

His thigh brushes against mine. I swallow hard. "I don't know exactly. For one thing, you aren't mean."

"Freckles, when am I mean to you?"

I huff. "Come on. Please don't act innocent in all of this."

A muscle flicks angrily in his jaw. "I'm serious. I may have teased you, enjoying the reaction it gets out of you. But maybe it's because if I didn't do that, I was invisible to you."

"You have never been invisible to me," I reply softly.

"Maybe not, but that's how I felt. You were either ready to hate me or ignore me. I guess I would rather have you hate me than nothing at all."

I'm not sure what to say back to him. After what he did to me, am I supposed to feel bad for him?

I roll over to my back and sigh. It's always been so complicated between us. The most frustrating thing is that I don't even understand why he did what he did to me. But I just can't bring myself to rehash it on this trip.

"We should get going. It's a long drive back, and I'm not sure we want to be driving around in Italy in the dark for too long."

After we pack everything up and bring it back to Lorenzo, thanking him profusely for all his kindness and generosity, we get into our car to start the long drive back to Como.

Josh pops the address into his phone before we hit the road. He follows the directions while I lie my head back and think back to our conversation.

All these years, Josh thought the only way he could get my attention was by making me angry. Is that true? Probably.

I put a wall up after he hurt me. There was likely nothing he could say or do to make me like him again. The man I thought I knew, the man I'm with on this trip, doesn't seem like the kind of person who would hurt me the way he did. It doesn't add up.

"You wanna look up places to eat on your phone?" he asks as the sun begins to set. "It looks like we're about an hour away."

"Yeah. Good idea." I grab my phone out of the cup holder. "Shoot. No service."

"Dammit. I guess we can just wing it when we get back. It might be a bit of a late dinner."

"That's fine. I think we…" I stop talking when the navigation system starts to tell Josh something, but then it cuts out, and his phone goes black.

We look at each other and then back at his phone. "What the hell," he growls as he taps at his phone. "Shit."

He begins to slow down as he continues cussing to himself.

"What's going on?" I ask. "Did your phone just die?"

He sighs. "Yes. I don't have a charger. We will need to use your phone. Can you type in the address?"

"Sure." I open my app and type in the name of the hotel, but nothing happens. "Shit."

"What?" he asks.

"No service."

"You're serious right now?" he bites back at me.

I shoot him a penetrating look. "Yes, Josh. I'm freaking serious. I have no service. What do we do now?"

He glares at me. "I don't know, Layla. Let me think for a second."

He runs his hands through his hair and then grips the steering wheel. "Can you check the glove compartment? Maybe there's a map in there."

"A map? What are we—explorers?"

He seems to be growing impatient. "Just open it, Freckles. I don't have time for this."

"Whatever," I reply as I open the glove compartment. Sure enough, there's a map sitting on top. "Here you go, Galileo."

He opens the map and begins to study it like he actually knows where the hell we are on that ginormous thing.

"Ok. We're right here," he says, shocking me. "It looks like we could take this road for another fifty miles or so; maybe by then, we will hit an area with service to get us all the way back. Here, you look at the map; just get me to that highway."

He shifts the car into drive and begins to drive along the road with far too much trust in my mapping abilities. I start to turn the map in circles, trying to understand if we need to take a right or left at the next road.

"What the hell are you doing with that map? Just keep it still."

"Just let me read the damn map the way it makes sense to me," I bite back at him. "Ok. It looks like you are going to go right up here at this stop sign."

We somehow manage to get through a couple of turns, but I'm all lost in this damn map again as I get our direction mixed up in my head.

"What the hell, Josh. How could you let your phone die! This is insane. I can't believe I'm reading a map in the middle of Italy with no backup if this goes south."

He rips out his words impatiently, "I need you to please watch your next words. I'm trying like hell to behave here, to get us through this, but you're not making it easy on me."

I glower at him over my map. Instead of responding, I try to figure out our next turn. "Up here, you make a left."

He begins to turn then I realize I had it mixed up. "Shit, no, a right. Make a right! A right!" I shout.

I fly forward as he slams on his brakes.

"Dammit, Freckles!"

"Ouch! Did you have to break that hard?" I ask, rubbing my chest where the seatbelt bit into my skin.

"That's it," he pulls to the side of the road and cuts the engine.

He gets out of the car and I watch him walk to the grass on the side of the road as he paces back and forth. What the hell is he thinking? We don't have time to waste out here with him having a pity party. It's getting dark, and I'm starting to freak out.

I push the door open and stomp over to him.

"What the hell are you doing? Get back in that car! We need to turn around and get back on the road."

He ignores me as he continues pacing back and forth.

"Josh! Did you hear me?" I shout even though I'm standing right in front of him. "Josh!"

He stops in his tracks. "Don't push me, Freckles. I'm doing my best not to lose my shit on you right now."

"On me? What the hell did I do wrong? You're the one who let his phone die while we're in the middle of a foreign country with no cell service. I can't believe you're putting this on me...it's so typical, just like," I say but am cut off when his hand grips the back of my neck.

"I warned you not to push me, Freckles," he says before he pulls me into him by my neck.

Before I know it, his lips are on mine. It's not soft or slow. It's all-consuming. The way they dance over mine, it's like each movement is a testament to the depth of our longing.

His tongue mixes with mine in the most satisfying way. It doesn't feel like it could get any better until he fists my hair and growls into my mouth like he's hanging on by a thread. We are kissing like he's going off to war, and we may never see one another again.

Our first kiss ten years ago was sweet and gentle. It was passionate in a different way than it is now. Right now, it's smoldering and desperate. A decade's worth of mixed emotions culminated in this kiss.

He bites my lower lip. "You piss me off," he growls before his lips are back on mine.

I should protest. I should tell him the feeling is mutual, but I'm too lost in the moment. In the way his lips feel while they stake their claim over mine.

My hands clutch his t-shirt as I tug him closer. His hands reach around my waist and grab my ass as he pulls me against him. His hard length presses against me. My body is on edge, begging for a release.

I feel the cool air against my body as he slowly pulls away, breaking our kiss. We are both panting as we stand here looking at each other.

"Shit," he says as he looks around. "We really should get back on the road. It's getting dark."

I nod my head, not sure how to transition from our kiss to thinking about the placement of the sun. But he takes off towards the car, so I follow.

Once we're back on the road, the mood has shifted. It's awkward, neither one of us acknowledging the kiss because we have to focus on finding our way back to the highway. I feel the tension as he takes his turns. He's nervous about getting back safe.

"Okay, here's the highway," I say as we both seem to breathe a sigh of relief.

The signs are already more familiar once we get back on the main road. I know I've seen some of these on our way here. And just like that, I look down at my phone and have service.

"I have service again. I'll type in the hotel."

"Thank God," he replies as his shoulders visibly relax. "We should be there in thirty minutes now."

The last of the car ride, now that we know we aren't lost in the middle of nowhere, is spent with my brain replaying our kiss. Once we get back, we decide to eat at the restaurant next to our hotel since it's already late. Although, eating late to Americans still seems to be early to Europeans.

The restaurant is fancy, so I throw on a simple black dress. Josh has on a black button shirt with grey slacks, and my body is literally melting at the sight. Why must he be so good-looking?

And why are we not acknowledging the kiss?

Josh opens the door for me and guides me out with his hand on the small of my back. He leaves it there until we're outside, where he silently grabs my hand. I swallow down the words that are threatening to spill over.

The ones that want to ask him what we're doing right now. Instead, we enjoy a nice evening together over a candlelit dinner, where he insists on paying once again.

The entire evening he finds reasons to touch me. Whether reaching for my hand under the table, running his hand along the back of my neck aimlessly while we wait for our food, or keeping it placed on my back while we walk.

It's sweet but driving me crazy. I've been shivering all night from the feel of his hands on me. I need more.

When we get back to the hotel, I take off my makeup and put on his t-shirt and sweatpants for bed. He's already under the covers by the time I get out of the bathroom.

Between being exhausted, angry, or drunk...I've yet to spend a night with him where I've been quite so aware of who's in the bed next to me.

I pull back my side of the covers and crawl into bed as my heart beats out of my chest. I can't find it in me to put any pillows between us. I don't want to. I want to feel him against me. I want to hear his breathing. I want him to touch me, dammit.

He faces me on his side, just watching me with a curious look. I roll over until we're only inches apart.

"What's happening between us?" I finally whisper into the darkness.

His hand comes up and tucks my hair behind my ear. "We're finally being honest with how we feel."

"I need you," I admit, as my body craves him.

His lips curve up in his sexy smirk. "I'll tell you what, Freckles. I'll give you what you need tonight, but not everything. If you wake up tomorrow and don't regret what we did, like you seem to every other time, then you're mine."

A ripple of excitement passes through me. He moves until he's hovering over me then his lips brush gently over mine.

"Is this pussy wet for me already?" he whispers into my mouth.

I'm gonna die. I'm not going to make it through this night if my reaction to this one line is any indication. Am I wet for him? I've been in constant need of changing my underwear this entire trip. But that doesn't sound sexy, so I keep that bit of information to myself. Plus, I'm pretty sure he wasn't expecting a response.

I'm sure he knows exactly what he does to me.

He pulls my sweatpants down a bit until I'm exposed to him but doesn't take them all the way off. His hand gently caresses my skin along my stomach, then down one thigh. He continues this pattern as he seems to stare at me in awe.

"I've never in my life been affected by anyone the way you affect me, Freckles. I'm going crazy here trying to hold myself back."

"Don't. Just don't hold back."

His lips come down on mine with more force this time as his tongue slides over mine.

"I'm not rushing this. I'm not rushing anything this time." He adjusts my leg so it's bent, allowing him to see all of me. Then his fingers slide along my slit. "I knew it. I knew you'd be fucking dripping wet for me."

His eyes hold mine as he slides his fingers inside of me. I whimper as I feel them stretch me. It's everything, and not enough.

"Memorize this feeling of my fingers fucking you," he growls as he moves them inside of me. "If you're a good girl, it could be my dick tomorrow."

Oh, god, it's like being touched by his words. The pleasure they evoke is incredible. It's been ten years of this back and forth. Of hating him and yet responding physically to him. A decade of foreplay.

He pulls his fingers out and rubs them over my clit, getting it wet, then pushes his fingers back inside of me. Now, his fingers work me from the inside while his thumb rubs my clit at the same time.

His lips are back on mine. I can barely match his kisses. I'm too focused on what his fingers are doing to me.

"Are you gonna come all over my fingers, Freckles?" he says between kisses. "I wanna feel your pussy squeeze them. I want them to be soaking wet by the time I'm done with you."

"Oh, gosh. Josh. Please," I whisper in response.

I'm so close. His thumb is working magic on my clit, bringing me closer and closer to the release I need so desperately.

"That's right. Beg me, baby. Beg me to let you come."

"Please! Please, Josh!"

He hisses as he pulls his lips away from me and watches his own hand in awe. I didn't think he could do any better, but then he pushes them in harder and, instead of releasing them quickly, shakes them inside of me. It hits my g-spot perfectly.

"Come me for, Freckles. Now!" he demands.

And I listen. I come all over him while he violently shakes his fingers inside of me.

"Fuck, yes. I knew you'd come all over me. My entire hand is soaking wet."

I can barely register what's happening until he pulls his own sweatpants down then grips his cock and starts pumping himself while he hovers over me. He's using the hand soaked with my release to spread it all over his dick. It's the hottest thing I've ever seen.

"Please," I whisper as I reach for him. "Let me finish you off."

He lets go of himself and props himself up with both his hands right above me. I reach for his length, and he hisses the second I wrap my hand around him.

"Freckles, I'm going to embarrass myself here. It's not going to take very long."

I smile and lean into him for a soft kiss. "I'll take that as a compliment."

Then I glide my hand back and forth over his thick cock. It's hard as a rock, and I can feel the thick vein that runs along it on my thumb. After only a couple of pumps, he's panting and breathing heavily.

"I'm coming," he growls as thick spurts of his cum coat my stomach.

We both try to catch our breath as we watch the last of his cum hit me. He leans down and kisses my forehead gently.

"Let's get you cleaned up," he whispers.

He climbs out of bed first, then takes my hand and leads me to the bathroom. We jump into the shower and rinse off quickly. He takes his time drying me with a towel and then helps me back into my pajamas.

As soon as we're back in bed, he reaches for me and pulls me into his chest.

"Goodnight, Freckles," he whispers.

"Goodnight." I lie awake on his chest for a while, afraid to wake up and realize that all of this was just a dream.

Chapter Twelve

Josh

I'm in the bathroom, brushing my teeth in nothing but my grey sweatpants in an effort to stall from going back out into the room. Layla is still asleep, and I'm terrified to wake her up. What if she regrets last night? Is she going to wake up and remember how much she hates me?

After last night, I can't go back to being friends—or enemies—or whatever the hell we were.

When I woke up with her in my arms, I felt relieved that it wasn't a dream, until I realized that if she does regret this, our relationship would be ruined forever.

Since I can't hide in the bathroom forever like a creeper, I check myself in the mirror, then open the door and walk back out into the room. She rolls over when I walk out, then yawns as she rubs her eyes.

"Morning," she says as she stretches her arms above her head.

Images flash in my brain of what it felt like to touch her last night, and my dick starts to twitch in my pants.

"Mornin'" I reply, as I walk over to the coffee maker. "Did you sleep okay?"

I lean against the counter, not wanting to turn my back to her just yet. I'm desperate and will overanalyze every single movement she makes.

"I slept great," she says as she throws the covers off her. "I'll be right back. I'm gonna use the bathroom."

I nod my head. Great. She's been up for thirty seconds and is already trying to avoid me. I start to make myself a cup of coffee as I feel a heaviness in my chest.

I'm not sure why I thought it would be any different. I watch the coffee pour in a steady stream into my cup as a dark cloud hangs over me. I must not have realized she was back in the room because I feel her fingers glide over my shoulder.

I turn around and she's standing in front of me with a smile. I hold my breath, waiting for a rejection. But instead, she gets on her tippy toes and throws her arms around my neck. Her lips are on mine in a searing kiss that I feel all over my body.

She kisses me with a hunger that I match in an instant. I wrap my arms around her and pull her against my body. The kiss is a mix between slow and fast. I grip her ponytail as our tongues work together, exploring each other's mouths lazily like we have all the time in the world.

When she pulls away, she looks at me with a bit of humor in her eyes.

"Are you done freaking out?" she asks coyly.

"What are you talking about? I wasn't freaking out," I lie.

"Really? So, the look of complete devastation when I said I had to use the restroom was all in my head? I just wanted to brush my teeth before I threw myself at you."

I smile, keeping her in my arms, refusing to let her go. I tickle her side, then slap her ass as her head falls back with laughter. "You just love torturing me, don't you?"

She shrugs as she bites her lip. "You seem to like doing the same thing to me."

I'm not about to get into that argument with her right now. Instead, I pull her in for another kiss.

"I have another idea for today," I tell her. "How about we go to Venice?"

"Venice?" her voice raises an octave. "You want to go today?"

"Why not? You want to go. We only have three days left. Let's do it. It's only a three-hour train ride from here. We can leave now and get there before lunch. Go on, get ready. I'm gonna look into a few more things on my phone."

While she is getting ready in the bathroom, I get on my phone and find a hotel that has an availably for tonight. If we're going to Venice, it's not gonna be for a couple of hours just to turn back. These websites that have all the hotels with their availability make it simple to find something within minutes.

I'm not picky. All I need is a place to sleep, and this one looks nice enough. It's right on the main canal too, with really good reviews. I grab my backpack and start throwing a change of clothes into it, making sure to leave enough room for her things as well. I don't want her trying to carry her own bag through the streets of Venice.

"Just booked a hotel for the night. Pack whatever you want in my backpack," I tell her the second she walks out of the bathroom.

"You're serious right now?" she says with a smile.

I laugh to myself as I hand her the bag. "Why is this so hard for you to believe?"

She seems to ponder my words. "I don't know. I've never been with anyone who's willing to be so spontaneous."

I'm not sure what to do with that. Who would be with a woman as incredible as her and not strive to make every single day special for her? It irks me that she's been with such selfish assholes.

She packs her things in my backpack while I purchase our train tickets. By the time she's done, I have a car waiting downstairs for us. I don't know how people traveled in foreign countries before everything was available in the blink of an eye on your phone.

We grab a breakfast bar and a to-go cup of coffee, then hop in the car.

On the train ride, she scoots closer to me and leans her head on my shoulder. I wrap my arm around her, and we both sit there in silence while I hold her like she's mine. It's a bit surreal that I get to do this.

The moment we walk out of the train station, it's like we're magically transported into another world. We're immediately in front of the water of one of the canals. There is a row of public water buses and private water taxis docked directly in front of us.

Without the hassle of lugging two large suitcases around, we don't really have to worry about hopping on a bus or taxi.

I grab her hand and lace our fingers together. "Where to first, Freckles?"

"Food?" she asks with excitement. "Somewhere on the water."

I smile. "I don't think we'll have a hard time finding that here."

We stroll across so many bridges that I lose count, walking along the water until we find this great place right on the main canal that has outdoor seating. Of course, we order a bottle of wine because it's Italy, and why not?

I struggle with the menu as usual since it's all in Italian. "What's this?" I ask Layla as I point to the menu.

"Oh, Spaghetti al Nero Di Seppia. It's spaghetti cooked in black squid ink. It's a Venetian specialty. You should try it."

"Cooked in squid ink? Interesting. I guess I'll give it a try. When in Rome," I say with a wink.

She chuckles. "Haha...you're hilarious."

We drink our wine and admire the view of boats and gondolas going by. Once our food is out, I look down at my pasta, wondering what the hell I got myself into. It's completely black. I've never even heard of putting squid ink on something; the color in itself is intimidating.

"I promise if you like seafood, you'll like this," she tells me, clearly picking up on my hesitation. "Ooh, they even put some scallops on top for you."

I'm not so sure, but I spin the spaghetti on my fork and give it a try. Layla watches me intently, trying to gauge my reaction.

I nod my head as I chew. It's actually delicious. The pasta is cooked perfectly, while the lemon and garlic sauce seem to have a saltier taste to it. I wonder if it's the ink.

I smile up at her. "It's incredible."

Layla's eyes open wide. Her head falls back as she begins laughing. "Oh my god!"

"What?" I ask, looking behind me.

She claps her hands together as tears begin to roll down her cheeks. She grabs her phone on the table. "Please, please, smile for me again."

"Smile for you? Why?"

"The ink," she continues through her laughs. "Your teeth are black."

I try to picture what the hell I must look like, grinning like a fool with black teeth, but the thought of it makes me laugh myself. I'm sure I'm giving Layla more lovely views of my teeth because she just laughs harder and then holds her camera up and takes a picture.

I grab a glass of water and try to swirl it around my teeth.

"Better?" I ask with a smile.

"Better." She takes a bite of her own pasta. "I think that's going to be my screensaver from now on."

I shrug. "If it makes you smile every day, I'm okay with it."

After lunch, we walk over to the famous St. Mark's Square to get some gelato and see St. Marks Basilica. We stroll around through the streets, hand in hand, as we walk into shops and buy some souvenirs.

It's a slow day where we wander around seeing nothing and yet everything. It seems like every turn you make, there's another bridge, another small canal, an alleyway. Gondolas float by, and I hear the gondolier serenading his passengers.

We get dinner after we check into our hotel, the place recommended by our hotel concierge.

Venice, as the sun is starting to set, is truly something else. We happen to walk by a canal with several gondoliers standing next to their gondolas.

"You wanna be cheesy and take a ride?" I ask Layla.

"You'd take a ride with me? I'd love to do that!" she bounces on her toes with excitement.

I walk up to one of the gondoliers to see if he's available. He looks over at Layla behind me and winks. "I was done for the day, but I can make an exception."

I thank him profusely and pay him the obscenely expensive amount for a ride and a bottle of champagne to accompany it. We sit down on the red, velvety seats as our gondolier hops on the back and begins to paddle away from the dock.

"Ah, Venice. The city of love," he says as we move along the water. "Perfect for a couple like you."

Neither of us correct him. This time, being called a couple seems fitting. I hand her a champagne flute and wrap my arm around her. The lights are beginning to shine brighter, reflecting off the water as the sun goes further down.

She leans her entire body into mine and we sit in silence as we drink and watch the scenery pass us by.

"I'll never forget this trip," she whispers to me as her hand rests on my thigh. "Thank you for making it so perfect."

I smile down at her. "Even with all the fighting?"

Her hand starts to run up and down my leg. "It's kind of been like a little bit of foreplay. Don't you think?"

She leans up and kisses me softly on the lips.

"Fuck, Freckles. You're creating a bit of a situation for me in my pants."

Her hand lifts a bit higher until it grazes my dick. My jaw falls as I suppress the groan I want to release.

"Over here. Bridge of Sighs," our gondolier shouts. "Legend has it that if you kiss while passing underneath, you will enjoy eternal love."

He turns down the canal for us and starts singing some song in Italian while we approach the bridge. Layla seems a bit uncomfortable.

"You don't have to kiss me," she fidgets in the seat. "Eternity is a long time."

I raise my eyebrow. "You don't want to spend eternity with me? Am I that annoying?"

She loosens up and laughs lightly. "No. I just wouldn't think you would want to spend eternity with me. You know, it's me. Just your best friend's little sister."

Everything gets darker as we head further into the small canal. The bridge is approaching, and I don't know what makes me do it, but I lean in and kiss her while we glide under the bridge.

My hand reaches for her cheek and tilts her head so I have the perfect angle to open my mouth and deepen the kiss. Her tongue against mine sends shivers of desire racing through me.

I pull away slowly. "You're more than just my best friend's little sister, Freckles."

Her voice cracks as she starts to reply, but I crush my lips back onto hers. We lean back in the seat and enjoy the slow, drugging kisses. I don't even know how long we make out in the gondola, but all of a sudden, we are out at the main canal as our gondolier drops us off.

My dick is stiff as hell in my pants as I reach down and help her out of the gondola. There is eagerness in her eyes when she looks down at my dick while we're walking hand in hand back to the hotel. The prolonged anticipation is almost unbearable. I can't take another second.

We cross over a small bridge, and there's a dark alley between two buildings. I pull her into the alley and press her up against the wall, and then my mouth covers hers hungrily. There's urgency in my kiss as I chase some sort of relief.

I grab her hands and place them above her head on the brick wall. "Do you feel what you do to me, Freckles?"

I push my dick against her hip so she knows what these kisses are doing to me.

"I could fuck you right here," I growl. "Pull those damn shorts down and fill you with my cock."

I kiss down her neck as our hands clutch each other's above her head.

"We should go," she exhales, "to our hotel room."

I kiss up her neck and behind her ear, then take her face in my hands and kiss her swollen lips again. "Baby, I'm trying to figure out how to keep my hands and mouth off you long enough to get from here to the hotel."

She giggles through my kiss. "Who said you need to keep your hands off me? Come on," she grabs my hand and pulls me. "The hotel is like two minutes away."

I don't know how I manage it, but we make it to the hotel without me taking her right in front of everyone. I've wanted this woman for a decade, craved her every night. I've compared every woman who came into my life to her, and they all failed miserably because there is no comparison.

As soon as we get to our room, she turns around and smiles brightly at me. She walks backwards towards the window and pulls her shirt over her head.

"Is this what you want?" she teases me.

I grab my straining dick in my shorts and rub it just to ease the pain. "Fuck yes," I say as I slowly follow her.

"Do I get your cock now that I've proven I don't regret last night?" Her shorts fall to the floor. She's standing in front of me in a red lace matching set of underwear. I don't know when she managed to sneak those on without me noticing, but I'm thankful I had no idea. If I knew that was underneath, I wouldn't have made it through the day without having her.

Her eyebrows raise suggestively. "Are you going to take your clothes off?"

I reach behind my head and pull my shirt off. She bites her lip as her eyes ogle my chest. She watches as my hand unbuttons and unzips my shorts. Then I pull them down with my boxers until I'm standing completely naked in front of her.

I stroke my dick, and a bead of precum releases out of me. I graze my thumb at the tip and wipe up my cum. I stand in her space and bring my thumb up to her lips.

"Open," I demand. "Suck my cum off of me."

She obeys my command and opens her mouth slowly, then swirls her tongue around my thumb before closing it around me and sucking. She closes her eyes and looks like she just tasted the most amazing treat she's ever had.

Fuck, it's hot as hell. "How does it taste?"

She looks over me seductively. "I want more."

I grip her hair and pull her head back. "I'll give you all the cum you want."

Our lips come together in a punishing rhythm. I reach behind her and snap her bra off, then grab her breasts.

She moans into my mouth. "I thought you didn't want me. All these years. I thought I wasn't pretty enough for you."

I look at her in surprise. "You're the most beautiful woman I have ever met. But let's save this talk for another time. Right now, I just want to make you feel good."

I lean her back against the window and fall to my knees. My mouth is literally salivating for a taste of her. I pull her underwear to the side and spread her open with my thumbs. She is already glistening for me. But instead of giving her my tongue right away, I want to savor every second. I want to admire what's in front of me.

I run my thumb along her opening, getting it nice and slick, then run it over her clit. I do the same with my other thumb, alternating between the two as I continue to spread her open for me and stimulate her clit.

Her jaw is slack as she watches me. Her eyes tell me she's already in dire need of a release, but I'm not done playing.

"Does it feel good when I tease your clit like this?" I ask her as I continue.

Her eyes get heavy as she nods her head.

I slap her clit. "Answer me, Freckles."

"Yes," she breathes heavily. "It feels amazing."

While continuously rubbing her clit with one thumb, I use my fingers from my other hand and slowly push them inside of her. I go slow first, watching as they get coated more every time I pull them out. Then I leave them inside of her and work them quickly back and forth, flicking over her g-spot while my thumb is still working her clit.

"Holy shit!" she screams, and I can't help but smile up at her.

I replace my thumb with my mouth and moan the second I get a taste of her. She's perfect. While I suck on her clit, I begin to shake my fingers inside of her with more force, making sure to hit her g-spot repeatedly.

"Oh my god! I'm fucking coming!" she screams loudly.

Then I feel her release hit me. I smile up at her as I let it happen, and she screams in shock. After her body has calmed down, she looks horrified.

"What just happened?" she whispers.

"I just made you squirt, Freckles."

She seems baffled by this. I've done it before. It just takes a bit of research on the guy's part to know what to do.

"That felt..." she begins as her chest rises and falls quickly, "I don't know—weird, but amazing."

I stand up and reach behind her head. "Come here," I tell her as I bring her in for a searing kiss. I begin to stroke my dick as I break the kiss and turn her around.

"Place your hands on the window," I tell her. "Good girl. Now spread those legs wide for me."

She looks like a wet dream standing there with her round cheeks poking out of her lacy underwear, her face turned towards me with a freshly fucked looked on it.

I stroke my dick while her eyes take it in. I grin at her, knowing that beneath all of this, it's just Freckles and me. She smiles back at me.

Then I reach for the top of her underwear and pull them down her long, slender legs. Before I forget, I grab a condom out of my jeans and sheath myself. Then I grip her hips and slam into her from behind.

She moans loudly as soon as I bottom out, and I am right there with her as I groan my appreciation. It's like coming home. It feels like I'm exactly where I'm supposed to be, where I was meant to be.

Thank God I have the condom on. It gives me a little barrier between the two of us, which will hopefully help me last longer because just the thought of this woman can make me come. Let alone feeling the real thing.

"This pussy was made for me," I growl. "Do you feel it? Do you feel how perfect we are together?"

She turns around, and I think I see a bit of moisture in her eyes. "I feel it, Josh. I feel all of you."

I pull myself out, wincing at how good it feels to watch my dick come out fully coated then I slam back in. I keep the rhythm slower at first, just wanting to savor every second of our first time together.

The view from the window, the feel of her soft skin on my hands, her tight cunt squeezing my dick, but most importantly—the way she's looking at me right now.

"From now on, no one else touches you but me. Do you understand?" I demand. "You're mine."

I slap her ass. "Answer me, Freckles."

"Yes. I'm yours," she cries.

"That's right. You're mine," I growl as I begin to fuck her as hard as I can.

We both scream through our releases as I empty myself inside of her, now wishing there wasn't a condom between us.

I slowly pull myself out of her and throw the condom in the trash right beside me. Then I pull her up off the window and kiss her softly.

"Let's get cleaned up."

Chapter Thirteen

Layla

"How's it going?" Charlotte asks while I'm enjoying a cup of coffee on our terrace in Como.

We just got back from Venice, and I can't say that we got much sleep. It was amazing. Josh did things to me, made me feel things that I didn't know were possible. My entire body is sore but in the best way.

He's taking a shower now after spending three hours on the train this morning. We decided to relax a bit today and enjoy a day on the water by the pool. I hate to think about the fact that tomorrow is our last day here.

"Italy is magical," I reply, then remember I was supposed to be on this vacation with her. "I wish you were here."

She yawns. "Me too. We'll just have to plan another trip once I've had this baby."

I smile to myself, loving the idea of being an aunt to my best friend's baby.

"Why aren't you in bed?" I ask. "What time is it there?"

"Ugh, it's four. I woke up and got sick, then couldn't fall back asleep. I figured it was the perfect time to call you to see how it's going. Is Josh behaving himself?"

Absolutely not. Josh is not behaving himself one bit, and I couldn't be happier about it. A small smile breaks free, and I'm suddenly glad that we didn't video call. She'd know I was hiding something in an instant.

"Ugh, he's totally annoying," I lie, trying to sound believable. "I still can't believe you thought it would be a good idea for me to spend a week with him."

She sighs. "Hey, I did the best I could for it being last minute. Is he really that bad? Does Asher need to call him when he wakes up?"

"No, no..." I stutter. "Don't have Asher call him. He's fine, I'm probably just being dramatic. You know me when it comes to Josh."

"I still wish you would open up to me about why you hate him so much."

"We can save that for another time. I should get going. We are going to go lie by the pool today, make it a slow day. I hope you can fall back asleep. Love you."

After I hang up the phone, I lean my head back for a second. I hate lying to her, but I can't just blurt out what happened last night. This is my brother's best friend, and she just so happens to be living with said brother.

"Pardon me. Don't mean to interrupt you. I know I can be soo annoying," Josh says as he walks out in his swim trunks.

Fuck me, he looks good.

"Sorry, I panicked. It would be obvious if I did a total one-eighty and now happy with you here. It would be too obvious. You don't want me telling anybody about what happened last night. Right?"

He shrugs. "I guess not."

I'm not sure if I'm reading into things, but I think he's kind of hurt that I'm keeping it a secret. It's a bit surprising, considering only four days ago, we were both bitching about spending time together.

"I'm sorry. I didn't mean to upset you. I just thought that maybe we shouldn't...I mean, we don't even know what this..." I motion between the two of us, stumbling over my words.

"Yeah, got it. We don't know what this is. No need to explain." He lowers his sunglasses over his eyes. "Shall we go for a swim?"

I grab my bag and follow him down to the pool. The vibe still feels a little off as we sit down. I'm desperate to get it back to where we were this morning.

"I'm gonna go in," I tell him as I stand up and take off my cover-up.

I'm slowly descending down the stairs when I feel him behind me.

I turn around and smile. "You going to join me?"

I get in all the way and let my hands glide around the water.

"You don't see it, do you?" he says as he follows me in further.

"See what?" I ask.

"The attention you get in that damn swimsuit," he says with venom. "Every male around here, hell—probably even female, is looking at you in that thing. They're all wishing they can find a way to get you into bed."

I roll my eyes. "You're completely off base. No one is looking at me."

He grabs my hand and pulls my body against his. "You are just too sweet to recognize how sexy you are. Now, do me a favor and kiss me so everyone here knows you are mine."

I'm not sure why he asked because he just grabs my face and claims my lips. His mouth devours mine, making my body burn with fire. The water ripples around us as our kiss deepens. We move in perfect harmony with each other, a rhythm only we can hear. Every touch, every brush of skin against skin, sends a shiver of pleasure down my spine.

Whatever tension was there a minute ago is gone, replaced by a smoldering flame.

He pulls away and kisses my forehead. "There we go, Freckles. Now, I can go lie on the chair in peace, knowing that everyone here knows you are off limits."

He turns away and walks up the stairs out of the pool, and lies down on his towel. Except, now I'm all turned on.

I'm going to get him back tonight for that. He leaves me here all needy just so he can pump his chest and claim me in front of everyone. Okay, fine, it's sexy as hell that he's being that territorial over me.

Dammit, I'm so screwed! What are we even doing? We haven't even resolved our issues, and we've dove headfirst into this messy situation. Do I even trust him with my heart? I know I can trust him with my body. He has proven himself in that department.

Was it just bad timing all those years ago? Maybe he's different now, more mature. But what if he does it again? I won't be able to stand it.

I just need to keep reminding myself not to fall in love with him. This is probably just because we're alone in a romantic country. I'm sure when we get home, he'll go back to being cold and distant.

But I want to enjoy the last of the time I have left, and I know he can promise me a good time. I'm vowing to myself right here, right now, that I will not let myself get swept up in the romance of it all. I will recognize this for what it is: a fling in a foreign country.

With that, I dive under the water and swim a couple of laps. When I'm done, I join Josh on our lounge chairs.

"What's this?" I ask when I notice a fruity-looking drink on the table between us.

"I ordered you a peach Bellini," he replies.

"Ooh, that sounds so refreshing. Thank you," I tell him as I take a sip.

This must be fresh peach juice in here, it's incredible. I look over at the man lying next to me. His sculpted body and rigid lines, the view of the alps in front of us, and wonder how I got here. It feels like a dream.

I used to lie awake at night and think about a life with Josh. He was that one guy that always seemed unattainable, but my heart could never let go of him.

After dinner, we stroll along the water hand in hand. We talk for over an hour about everything. He makes me laugh along the way, in between deep conversations about our family and careers.

By the time we get back to our hotel room, I'm itching to get him out of his clothes. But he must've been feeling it too because he pushes me up against the door the moment we're in the room.

I can feel the urgency in his kiss. It seems he has also been on the verge of losing control. His hands rake my body as he presses me harder into the door.

"Fuck, Freckles. I can't get enough of you."

He reaches behind me and unzips my dress, then tugs it off until it glides down my legs to the floor. I couldn't wear a bra with this dress, so I'm standing in my black panties.

"Touch your breasts for me. I want to see you playing with yourself," he growls as his hand reaches for his belt.

I follow his command and let my breasts fill my hands. They are sensitive to the touch, but it's nothing compared to watching this man undress in front of me. His eyes are smoldering as they hold mine. Once he loses his belt, he unzips his pants and then takes a step backward towards the bed.

"Get over here," he demands. "Lie down on the bed and let me watch you."

My panties flood at his words. His domination in the bedroom really does something to me. I lie down on the bed and scoot back, leaning on my elbows as I wait.

"Tell me what you want me to do now," I whisper, then watch him as he loses his boxers. "Do you want me to touch myself here?"

I spread my legs and rub myself over my panties.

He groans as he takes his dick in his hand. I watch the veins in his hand and arm pop out as he grips himself hard. I begin rubbing circles over my panties, needing the friction.

"Lose the underwear," he insists.

I lie back and kick them off in seconds.

"Now spread those legs and let me see your perfect pink pussy."

With my legs spread open for him, I bring my hands between my legs and spread my lips open for him. I hear him cuss under his breath. I love knowing I can garner such a reaction from him. It only makes me more wet.

"Look at you, dripping wet for me," he says as he continues stroking himself. "Does someone wanna soak my face again like last night?"

I would've thought I'd be mortified by squirting, but he seems so into it, and it felt amazing. Before I can respond, he is on his stomach and burying his face between my legs.

His tongue moves quickly over my clit. I fist my own hair as the sensations in me build quickly.

I don't know if I'm going to last long.

Chapter Fourteen

Josh

With my mouth wrapped around her clit, I push two fingers inside of her and curl them up just how she likes it.

I could barely make it to our room to get my hands all over her. She looked so beautiful tonight and knowing that we don't have much time left here, I was desperate to enjoy every second.

She looks wild and free with her hands in her hair, panting and moaning. I grind my dick against the bed to try and relieve the ache. Watching her makes me harder than I've ever been.

"I heard about this thing," she starts mumbling as I lick and finger her, "where, like, if you put your finger…"

She stops and doesn't continue, so I lift my head up. "If you put your finger…" I drawl out, waiting for her to continue.

She shakes her head. "It's weird. People say it feels good to put your finger in…you know. Ugh, I can't even say the word. It's so not for me."

I chuckle, then take a slow lick from her ass to her clit. She sucks in a breath. "Are you sure it's not for you? Why bring it up?"

I start to lick her clit again, looking up at her, waiting for her response. Clearly, she's curious but is hesitant. I've heard similar things, too. I push a finger back inside her pussy and let it get nice and slick. Then I start to move it back while I keep my tongue on her clit.

She keeps talking. "I don't know why I brought it up. But no, it can't be for me, right? It's just so…"

I push my finger inside just an inch and watch her eyes fly open. She is on her elbows now, eyes on me while I slowly draw my tongue in circles around her clit then push my finger in another inch and wiggle it this time.

"It's just something porn stars do. You know?" she says through her panting.

She continues to talk while I suck on her clit and then push my finger in all the way.

"Fuck!" she screams. "I'm a lady, and ladies don't do this. They don't like this."

I try to hold in my smile. If she doesn't want it, that's on her. I slowly start to pull my finger out.

"If you fucking take that finger out, I'll kill you."

I smile through my licks but don't slow down until she is coming on my mouth. I let my tongue draw lazy circles around her clit until her breathing is back to normal.

"So, if only porn stars like stuff like that…" I start, but she cuts me off.

"Shut up," she pushes me onto my back while I laugh at her, trying to ignore what we just did. She straddles me and starts to grind all over my dick. The view is perfect. I grip my hands on her hips.

I realize I could just slip my dick inside of her right now, but I know we aren't there yet. She doesn't realize I fully intend to date her when we get home, but until then, sex without protection is off the table.

She slides down my legs and pushes them apart. "I believe it's your turn."

Shit. I thought we were gonna have sex, but I'll take this. She grabs my dick and wraps her delicate hand around me, dragging the tip of my dick over her lips, painting them with my precum.

"Fuck, you dirty little porn star," I growl, making her smile.

I don't remember ever laughing during sex, but with her, it's different. We're different. It's fun and sexy at the same time.

She wraps her lips around my dick and starts to glide her tongue along me as she bobs up and down my shaft. I fist my hands into her hair and help her along, trying not to be too forceful, but damn, it's hard when I just want to thrust my hips up and make her gag.

Like she's reading my thoughts, she pulls off my dick. "Fuck my mouth. Josh. Take me exactly how you want it."

It's like we're so entuned with each other we can read each other's thoughts. I'm surprised I didn't just shoot my load all over her just from those words.

She wraps her lips around my dick again and pushes down. I grab her hair and start to pull out slowly, then drive up until I hit the back of her throat, but she doesn't gag. She just fucking winks at me while taking all of me. I've officially been stunned into silence. Who the fuck is this woman, and why have I waited so long to be with her?

She has this mischievous look on her face, even when her mouth is full of my cock. I'm not sure what it's about until I feel her finger start to rim my asshole.

The sensation is foreign but not horrible. I should tell her to stop, but she looks so curious. But she doesn't stop there, she pushes the entire thing inside of me.

"Holy. Fuck," I growl as I grip her hair again and thrust harder.

Once the shock wears off, there's just pleasure. I don't know what in the world she's doing, but my entire body is aware. It all just spurs me on more. I can't control myself any longer.

I fuck her mouth while her finger penetrates me, all while I'm cursing and groaning. I don't even have time to warn her that I'm going to come. It hits me in an instant, and I'm in a whole other world as I spill into her mouth.

"Ah, fuck!" I scream. "Suck down my cum like a good girl. Yes," I hiss as I watch, slowing my pace down, "just like that."

She pops off me while I lie my head back, staring up at the ceiling. I can barely catch my breath from the full-body orgasm she just gave me. She joins me on the bed, and I wrap her into my chest.

"You are one tricky woman," I say as I tickle her side. "That was risky."

She smiles up at me. "When in Rome."

And then we both crack up.

Chapter Fifteen

Josh

As soon as the tires of the plane touch down on the Savannah asphalt, I get this unsettling feeling in my stomach.

We never talked about what happens when we get back home. I'm too afraid to even broach the subject. What if she goes back to hating my guts?

Maybe it was just Italy that provided this romantic ambiance that made her give in to temptation.

The jet lag is real as we find our luggage together, both in a daze. Asher and Charlotte agreed to pick us up at the airport and drop us off.

I'm not sure how to act around Asher. Guilt stabs at me as we walk outside, looking for their car. He asked me to take his sister to Italy and be on my best behavior. I don't think fucking her until her body gave out was what he had in mind.

"Oh, there they are," Layla points at the white SUV at the end of the terminal pickup line.

We roll our luggage down the sidewalk, my stomach aching a little more with each passing car. I'm picturing him sniffing it out instantly and then punching me in the face for betraying his trust. Until I can convince Layla that we are forever, Asher will just see this as me using his little sister for a little action.

I can't have that. I need more time to see where Layla's head is at.

"Hi!" Charlotte hops out of the passenger seat slowly. "I'm so happy you're back. I missed you!"

Her face looks a little pale and slick. I can tell she's still not feeling all that great but trying to put on a happy face.

Charlotte and Layla run into each other's arms while Asher joins me on the sidewalk. He claps me on the back. "You survived. I was expecting to see you limping or with a black eye. You know Layla when she gets angry."

I chuckle at the thought. He isn't wrong. The woman is a force to be reckoned with when you piss her off. I personally think it's kinda hot. "Oh, I know. I guess I lucked out. No black eyes or broken bones for me."

Asher looks over at the girls. "She looks different, super relaxed. I can see the tension in her has faded. Thanks for doing this for me, man. It means a lot. She really needed this."

"Not a problem. A free trip to Italy wasn't so bad. But we need to have a conversation about your spending habits. That hotel was way over the top."

His head falls back as he laughs. "I know. But if two of the most important women in my life were going there alone, I felt better that they stayed somewhere nice."

I get it. I would hate to think of Layla staying somewhere shady in a foreign country. It would keep me awake at night.

We throw our luggage in the trunk and hop in the backseat. Asher's daughter, Brie, is in her car seat in the middle. She is laughing and clapping when Layla and I hop in and take the empty seats beside her.

"Uncle Joshie, Auntie Layla," she giggles.

I don't think I've ever heard our names together like that. It sounds like we're a couple. I really like the sound of it.

Layla leans in and gives her a big kiss. "Hi, baby girl. I missed you so much."

Layla has always been incredible with her niece. Brie brings out the softer side of Layla, and I know she will be the most incredible mother.

"So," Charlotte turns around, "how was it? Tell me everything? Where did you go? What did you see? Keep in mind I was supposed to be on this trip and have major FOMO, so please don't make it sound too incredible."

Layla looks over at me, and we both try to hide our growing grins.

"It was alright," I lie. "Just your standard vacation. You didn't miss much."

Charlotte rolls her eyes. "I can handle a little more information than that."

We spend the next twenty minutes telling them about the trip, leaving out the details about how we spent our nights together. Asher doesn't seem to suspect anything. It makes me think he might be dumber than I thought.

At one point, Brie seems to be getting jealous that no one is paying attention to her. I don't like seeing my favorite girl so upset. She was only one when her mom passed away, so I was around a lot trying to help Asher adjust to being a single dad.

I scrunch my fingers together and have them slowly crawl their way to her before tickling under her chin. She starts to crack up, so I do it again. We play this game for a couple of minutes before she finds her snack up on the side of her car seat and gets lost in eating her goldfish.

I look out the window with a smile on my face. Brie always knows how to turn my mood around. I was nervous to be around Asher again with my new secret, but now I am completely forgetting about any awkwardness at all.

Asher pulls into my driveway a couple of minutes later. "Well, thanks for the ride, guys. I'll be seeing you tomorrow, Ash. Bright and early with a side of jet lag for ya."

Charlotte and Brie yell goodbye to me as I get my luggage out of the trunk. Layla looks back at me before I close the trunk, and I give her a wink.

She'll be seeing me again. She might not know it, but this isn't the end.

Chapter Sixteen

Layla

"Bitch, you are glowing. Italy certainly agreed with you!" Zane says from across my desk.

He's been catching me up on the week. We don't open for another couple of hours. Of course, the place ran smoothly without me. Zane had it all under control.

I'm actually more relieved than sad about it, which feels like progress. I think Italy showed me how much of the world is out there for me to explore. I don't need to hide away in my restaurant. I've worked my ass off. I should be able to enjoy the benefits of a successful career. Look what I would have missed out on if I refused to take the vacation.

"Italy was amazing! Seriously, the place is just indescribable. Every city, every town is unique. The people are so friendly and relaxed. It's impossible not to feel the same when you're around them."

"I'm so jealous you and Charlotte got to spend an entire week gawking at sexy Italian men without me."

"Oh," I sit up a bit in my seat, "I can't believe I never told you. Charlotte canceled last minute. She's pregnant, and her morning sickness just kind of hit her with a vengeance."

"What the fuck, Layla! You didn't tell me this. Who did you go to Italy with?"

Okay, I love Zane. I really do. But let's face it, this man is a complete gossip. I'm afraid that if I tell him the truth, it will only be a matter of time before my entire family knows what happened in Italy. All it will take is one of my brother's coming here to eat, and Zane will find a way to talk about it.

"Josh," I reply, crossing my fingers that my poker face works.

"Josh?" he drawls out, almost screaming. "You went to ITALY with JOSH?" he questions me, like he doesn't believe it.

I feign indifference, shrugging my shoulders like he's totally overreacting. "Yeah. He was so annoying."

"So, the trip was miserable? Shit, that sucks."

"No, no," I defend, somehow not wanting him to think that about the best week of my life. "It wasn't miserable. I mean, Josh behaved after a while. It's Italy, that's a hard vacation to ruin."

He gives me a strange look. I hold my breath, waiting for him to just come right out and tell me he knows what Josh and I did. How dirty our sex got.

"Hmm, I don't know. Anyone could ruin a vacation if you hate them that much. I've got some exes that could easily ruin a trip to Italy for me. But I'm glad you had a good time. I'm so damn proud of you for not reaching out to me. I gotta tell you, I didn't think you had a chance in hell of not calling or texting for an entire week."

I release the breath I was holding. "Yeah," I smile. "I honestly surprised myself. Maybe it was all the wine. It calmed my nerves and let me just enjoy myself. Maybe I should become an alcoholic." His eyes bug out, and I laugh. "I'm kidding, Zane."

"I think it's gonna take some time for me to get used to this new Layla."

I'm not sure if that's exactly how I would describe this. It's more like the old Layla finally breaking through. The Layla who would make dirty jokes and try new things. Who wasn't afraid to throw herself into any situation, not worrying about the repercussions.

I fulfilled a piece of my dream when I bought this restaurant but also lost a little piece of myself in the process. Truth be told, I lost a piece of myself before that, when Josh broke my heart and made me rethink trusting men entirely.

I can't believe I opened my heart back up to the very man who shattered it to pieces. That was not a very smart move.

Well, I can't think about that right now. I have a huge to-do list now that I'm back. First, starting with catching up on my emails. Zane leaves me alone to catch up on the administrative side of things while he takes care of making sure everything else runs smoothly.

Before I know it, it's already dinner time, and the restaurant is packed. That's one thing about owning the most popular restaurant on the peninsula: It's busy every night—a gift and a curse.

I'm walking around, checking to see that I'm happy with the quality of the food that is going out when I spot Josh walk into the restaurant. Like an idiot, my heart starts beating rapidly. I look behind him, expecting to see my brother or a group of his friends with him, but I can't spot anyone.

His eyes scan the restaurant while I stand frozen in place next to the bar. Once he spots me, a huge smile breaks out on his face.

He strides towards me casually, hands in his jean pockets, like he has all the time in the world. Why isn't he freaking out like I am?

"Hi," he smiles as he stops right in front of me.

"Hi," I breathe.

We both stand in silence for a moment, just looking at each other. I don't know what to say to him. I want to tell him how miserably I slept last night without him in my bed. How I replayed every detail of our nights together until I was so worked up that I had to slip my hand into my underwear to relieve myself.

He looks around the restaurant. "You guys look busy tonight."

"Yeah, it's that time of the year. There's really no slow night." I tuck my hands in my pockets, then feel stupid for mimicking his stance, so I pull them out and cross them over my arms.

His grin widens. "Are you nervous, Freckles?"

"Not at all," I lie. "Why would I be nervous?"

He shrugs his shoulders. "I don't know. That's why I'm asking. There's nothing to be nervous about."

"So, what are you doing here?" I ask, trying to get the heat off me.

"I just got off work and was passing by on the way home. I thought I'd stop in and say hello."

That's it? He stopped in to say hello. What am I supposed to do with that? I'm equally annoyed as I am turned on by the sight of him in his torn jeans and old shirt. I love him in his work clothes. He has a baseball hat on, and his muscles are poking out of his shirt sleeves. It's almost too much for my mind to take.

Suddenly, my body is burning up. It appears the reaction I had to him in Italy has extended to here in the states as well. That is going to be a problem. I was hoping I could forget what it felt like to have his hands all over me, or his dick inside of me, and his tongue. Shit, his tongue.

I realize I'm lost in my thoughts. I look back up at Josh, and his eyes are boring into mine.

"Where's your office?" he says in a deep, demanding voice.

"My office?" I question, wondering why he's bringing up my office out of nowhere. "Why?"

He steps closer to me. "Bring me to your office, Freckles. Right. Now."

That's odd. Is he suddenly taking an interest in how I run my restaurant? Maybe Italy inspired him, and he's curious. Here I am, practically drooling over him, and he wants to see my office. How embarrassing.

I turn around and lead him through the kitchen, around the corner, and down the back hallway until we step into my office. I turn the lights on and walk further in.

"Here it is," I tell him. "It's not really much to look at. Just a desk and some filing cabinets. Why did you want to see it? Have you never been in the back of a restaurant before?"

He closes the door. "I don't give a fuck about what it looks like."

Next thing I know, he lifts me up and slams me back against the wall. His mouth is on mine. I claw at his back and wrap my legs around his waist. The strange, uneasy feeling I've had since we've been back evaporated.

Everything feels right again.

His hand reaches up and wraps around my breast. I moan into his mouth, reveling in his attention. Then he moves us off the wall and places me on the ground next to my desk.

"Get on your knees, Freckles," he growls.

I should be pissed that he comes into my restaurant, tells me to take him to my office, then demands I get on my knees for him. But I'm too turned on right now, and the truth is, I've been wanting him in my mouth again. I think about it all the damn time.

So, I obey his command and slowly lower to my knees. I watch him unbuckle his belt then pull himself out for me. I lick my lips in anticipation, and a small grin peeks through his hard demeanor.

He grips his dick and then moves forward. He moves it in a circle around my lips, teasing himself. I'm too desperate for a taste, so I move my tongue along his tip.

He growls. "You're greedy for my dick, aren't you?"

I nod my head in agreement.

"Open your mouth, Freckles. I'll give you what you want."

I open my mouth wide, and he slowly pushes it inside of me, moaning instantly. I'm too aroused to go slow and build the pace. I wrap my lips around him and start to suck, moving up and down enthusiastically.

He closes his eyes like it's already too much for him, and he needs to gain some control. But I don't want him to have control; I want him to lose his mind.

I take my hand and place it at the base of his cock and move it up and down as I glide along his shaft. His hands are in my hair while his body tenses. I keep my pace until he pulls me off without any warning. I'm breathing hard as I gasp for more air, but I've never been more turned on.

"Hands on the desk, Freckles. Turn around."

Before I have time to do so, he's turning me himself and pushing me down on my shoulders. Then my pants and underwear are pulled down and at my ankles.

I hear the tear of a condom wrapper. With no warning, he pushes inside of me until he bottoms out. I do my best to stifle my scream. He starts fucking me roughly against my desk, his dick hitting the right spot over and over again.

"Ahh," I exhale as the feelings start to take over me.

Josh slaps my ass and grabs my ponytail. "I like your hair up like this. It helps me get some leverage so I can fuck you harder," he growls. "Like this."

I've never been fucked this hard. I didn't know it was possible. My orgasm comes barreling through. I grip the end of the desk with both hands as I do everything in my power not to make too much noise. I could only imagine what my restaurant guests would think if they were eating and heard a woman scream bloody murder through her orgasm.

Josh starts to slow as he empties himself inside of me, growling and cussing the entire time.

I don't even realize my office door has opened until I hear Zane.

"Oh shit," he gasps.

Josh and I both turn around quickly to find Zane's jaw on the floor. Then the door shuts, and there's silence for a minute.

"Shit," Josh whispers, his hands on the desk by my shoulders as he leans over me. "We just got busted. Was that Zane?"

"Yes," I whisper with mortification.

"Sorry, guys," I hear Zane's voice whisper through the door.

My head falls on the desk as I shake it back and forth. I can't believe he is talking to us right now, knowing what kind of position we are currently in. Josh's dick is still inside of me.

"I didn't mean to interrupt," he continues. "Keep doing what you're doing. Looks like Italy must've been a blast."

Embarrassment is an understatement for what I'm feeling when all of a sudden, Josh's forehead falls on my back, and I hear him laughing. His laughter starts to shake my body until I can't help but join him.

"That guy is crazy," Josh says through his laughs.

"He's a dead man," I tell Josh.

He pulls out of me and gets rid of the condom in my trash, first folding it into some tissues from my desk.

Very classy, Layla.

After we clean ourselves up, he pulls me into a hug. It instantly calms my nerves after just getting caught in such a compromising position. I wrap my arms around him and enjoy the warmth of his embrace.

I wonder what cologne he wears. Maybe I can find out and buy some and spray it on my pillow. It might trick my brain into thinking he's with me at night so I can sleep better.

"Well, that was unexpected," he whispers in my ear.

I pull away and look up at him. "You mean you didn't come here with the intention of having sex in my office?"

"No," he smiles. "I really did just stop in to say hi. But now that I know that sex is on the table, I might just stop in all the time. Maybe three times a day."

"Are you kidding me? We can't have sex in here again. The first time we did it, my manager got a full view of both of our asses. I don't even want to think about what else he saw."

He kisses my forehead. I missed him doing that, too. "Somehow, Zane doesn't seem like the type to scare easily. I think you'll be okay. But I should probably go so I don't get in the way any more than I already have."

His thumbs stroke my cheeks tenderly then he leans in for a soft, slow kiss. I'm barely able to remember my own name when he pulls away.

I want to ask him when I'll see him again. I want to ask what the hell we are doing. But instead, I let him walk away. My body feels satisfied, but my heart isn't so sure this is a good idea.

I take a deep breath and walk out of my office to find Zane. I apologize profusely and beg him not to tell anyone.

But before I even get out of the back hallway, I spot him in his office. He is sitting behind his desk, tapping his fingers. You would think he just met Chris Evans or something with the look he has on his face.

"Soo," he drawls out, "I see we did more than just sightseeing in Italy."

"I'm sooo sorry you saw that," I walk in and close his door. "I'm so mortified."

"Girl, don't be embarrassed. You should feel proud. In one week, you went from not being able to remember the last time you had sex to being fucked over your desk by a guy who clearly knows what he is doing. And his size is..."

"Okay, okay. I got it. You're not mad. And oh my god, you saw his thing?"

"Mad? Are you serious? No, I need details now. How did it start? How many times? How kinky did it get? That man has kink written all over him. And yes, I saw his thing, and you are one lucky girl."

I slowly take a seat in the chair across from him. "Details? We never talk about this stuff with each other."

He scoffs. "Only because you never had any details to share. I didn't want to depress you with the details of my epic sex life.

Now...spill. Before I go outside and tell everybody what I just saw."

"You wouldn't dare."

But I think he would, so I started talking. I tell him about our first kiss, our first night that he fingered me, and all the details about our sex. But I leave out the finger in the butts. That part feels too intimate of a detail.

He taps his chin when I look up at him. "What?" I ask.

"You're not telling me everything."

"What makes you say that?" I ask him, wondering how the hell he knows.

"Because the second you stopped talking, you looked anywhere but me and got all weird. What else did you two do? It must be dirty if you don't even want to tell me."

"It was...ummm...butt stuff."

Zane gasps. "Did you seriously have anal with him?"

"What? No! It was just a finger."

He leans back in his chair with a look of disappointment. "Aww, a finger is boring. But for you, it's a big deal. I never would've thought you'd be into that. I'm proud of you. You certainly knew your assignment to be adventurous and damn did take that seriously."

"Well, I wasn't the only one," I mutter to myself.

"You weren't the only one what? To take a finger?" He straightens his spine, mouth falling open. "Are you telling me the insanely sexy Josh took a finger, too?"

I nod my head slowly.

"Did he like it?" Zane whispers like there's all of a sudden a crowd of people in his office.

It makes me laugh. "He seemed to enjoy it. I mean, it was only for a second."

Zane begins to fan himself. "Holy. Shit. Layla. I'm dying. You just literally blew my mind. That is so damn hot when a guy doesn't shy away from trying kinky things."

"Josh is comfortable enough with himself to try something like that," I agree.

"So, what does this mean? Are you two dating?"

I swallow hard, trying to find a suitable answer. One that doesn't invite more questions that I don't know the answer to. "We're just seeing where things go."

Even though that satisfies Zane, my mind is congested with doubts and fears.

Chapter Seventeen

Josh

"I never really got a chance to thank you for what you did," Asher says as we sit on the back of my trunk eating our lunch.

The week has flown by as I try to catch up with the work I missed. Right now, I'm trying to manage this house renovation. It's a huge million-dollar house on the lake that needed to be gutted while simultaneously managing our first commercial project.

Asher and I are rarely in the same place at once, since we are always managing different projects, but he stopped by today to bring me some lunch.

"Thank me for what?" I ask as I shove a chip into my mouth.

"For going to Italy with my sister, you idiot."

"Oh, that. It's no problem. It turned out to be really fun. I would've never taken a trip like that otherwise. I'm glad I was forced into it."

Asher chuckles to himself. "Yeah, you're not the fancy vacation type."

I know it's not meant as an insult; he's just stating a fact, but it still hurts. I could be that person if that's what Layla wants. Why can't I be the type who takes trips to Europe? It was an amazing experience.

I'm starting to realize that maybe I was a total fucking idiot when I was younger and walked away from her. If I wasn't the man she wanted back then, I could've changed or at least been open to experiencing new things. Layla doesn't need a man with millions; she just needs a man who will love her. I can do that.

I am doing that. I've loved her from afar for years. It's about damn time she gets to see what it's like when I don't hide it away.

And honestly, if it makes her happy, then that's all that matters. If her parents are disappointed that she settled for someone like me, that's their problem.

"I could do fancy vacations once in a while."

He looks over at me with amusement flickering in his eyes. "I'll believe that when I see it. You'd prefer a week off right here at home just taking out the boat and enjoying some time with friends."

"Well, I like that too. But maybe Italy made me see things differently."

He shrugs his shoulders. "As long as you and Layla didn't kill each other and had a good time. Anyway, I just wanted to come by and thank you again. If you ever need a favor, I owe you one. I also wanted to invite you to our place tomorrow. We're throwing a birthday party for Brie. It's a bit last minute. Charlotte's just been trying to survive each day and keep some food down."

"Birthday for my favorite girl? I'll be there. What can I get her?"

"You don't need to get her anything. She'll just be happy that you're there."

I scoff. If he thinks I'm showing up to a four-year-old birthday party without a present, he's insane. I'm still gunning to be her favorite uncle, beating out her actual uncles Eric and Liam.

I'll be there. And knowing that Freckles will be there is just icing on the cake for me. I've been giving her space this week to get caught up at work, biding my time for when I see her again.

I walk into Asher and Charlotte's home, holding my present. Their house is huge. It's right on the lake and completely out of any of our price ranges. Charlotte's father passed away and left the house to her. It was vacant for a decade and left to rot. That's how Charlotte and Asher got reacquainted. She hired him to take on the renovations.

The kitchen is decorated with balloons, food and drinks laid out on the large island. Taylor Swift is blasting outside.

Yes, I don't have any daughters or a wife, but I can recognize a Taylor Swift song.

There are Taylor Swift balloons, plates, and cups—letting me know the theme of the party. It appears Brie is a four-year-old Swiftie.

I don't recognize the people chatting in the kitchen, so I wander to the sliding door that leads to a large deck overlooking the water.

The source of the music is evident when I see a large white bouncy house with pastel-colored balloons tied off at the corners.

"There he is," Liam shouts from the corner of the deck.

He's leaning against the railing with a beer in his hand, talking to Eric. I place my present on one of the tables and walk over to them.

"What's going on?" I ask as I approach and shake their hands.

"Just jamming to some Taylor Swift over here," Liam jokes, with Eric rolling his eyes. I forgot he's against fun right now.

I look over at the bouncy house again and spot Asher watching from the outside with some guy I don't know. Brie is in there with several other kids around her age.

"Who are these kids?" I ask.

"Brie's friends. I don't know, some kids from her pre-school, I guess," Eric answers.

She looks adorable laughing with the kids. How is she old enough to invite friends to her party?

I'm watching Brie laugh and giggle when I spot Layla standing out there on the grass next to the bouncy house with Charlotte. She's holding a glass of wine and laughing at something Charlotte just said. She's wearing a white summer dress, her hair down in loose waves. My heart begins to race as I watch, captivated by every little move she makes. Even watching her do something so insignificant, like tucking a strand of hair behind her ear, can get a reaction from me these days.

"There he is," Daniel, Layla's father, says as he approaches. "The man that saved my daughter's trip."

I reach out for a handshake. "Nice to see you again, Mr. Williams."

"I heard the trip was a success. Layla was raving about it just before you got here."

I grin. "It was a great trip."

"I heard you surprised her with a trip to Venice for a night," he says, sounding surprised.

"Yeah, well, she kept going on and on about how much she wanted to go," I lie as I panic.

I don't want him to find out like this and freak out at his grand-daughter's party. Thankfully, before we can continue, Layla's mother calls him from the kitchen.

"Excuse me," he says to the three of us. "Your mama is calling. Can't leave her waiting."

Liam and Eric are looking at me, brows quirked. "You surprised my sister with a trip to Venice?" Liam asks.

"Yeah," I reply, shrugging my shoulders like it's no big deal. "I mean, she had mentioned she wanted to go there, and I did a little research. It wasn't that hard to set up."

"Did something happen between you and Layla there?" Eric asks blatantly.

"What? Why would you think that? What would've happened?"

"That's not an answer, asshole," Liam quips.

Shit. I'm sweating now, and it has nothing to do with the Georgia heat. They can't make a scene like this. Layla will never give us a chance if this is how it goes down. I'm about to beg and plead for them to be discrete.

"Because if you two finally pulled your heads out of your asses and realized you were crazy about each other, I'd say it's about fucking time," Liam follows up.

Well, that's unexpected.

"Sooo, if something happened, you wouldn't be mad?"

"Why would we be mad?" Eric asks with confusion.

"Umm, because it's your little sister. And I'm not good enough for her."

Both guys start to crack up. "Please tell me that's not what's been holding you back all of these years."

I fold my arms across my chest, not sure I like this reaction either.

"It's part of it," I say in defense.

That just makes them laugh harder. "You're such an idiot. I can't believe you thought we would be mad," Eric says. Well, at least I got him to lighten the fuck up.

"Seriously, have you met any of the tools she's dated? Like that William douchebag. If we like you enough to keep you around, why would we be against you being with our sister?" Liam questions.

My jaw tenses at the mention of William's name. At least they agree he's a tool.

"Yeah, we're not some old-school protective brothers who will stop our sister from being happy. Plus, you're a good guy," Eric says.

How many years did I worry about what her family would think about me? I would lay around at night, picturing her brothers punching me if they found out, telling me I was trash and not good enough for their sister.

Did I project all my insecurities onto them and then use it as the reason why I couldn't be with the woman that I love?

I want to punch myself in the face for being so stupid.

"There she is," Liam says to somebody behind me. "I heard this man surprised you and took you to Venice."

I smell her perfume first. My body relaxes for the first time since I've gotten here. That's the effect she has on me now.

"Oh, yeah, he did. It was really sweet. Venice was amazing, too. It's so beautiful at night."

I don't want these two idiots to call us out right now and ruin it for Layla. I give them a look that I pray they understand. Eric nods slightly at me in understanding. "Come help me get some beers," Eric cuts in, gesturing to Liam.

Liam looks confused by the request. "That doesn't sound like a two-person job."

"Just fucking get over here, you idiot," he replies as he punches Liam's arm.

The two of them walk off, bickering at each other. With the two of them gone, I lean against the railing and watch Layla squirm like she's nervous to be left alone with me.

"I didn't know you were gonna be here," she says softly with her arms behind her back.

"I wouldn't miss being here for my favorite girl." Her lips part in surprise. "Brie," I clarify.

"Right. Of course," she replies.

"Aww, don't get jealous. She's my favorite girl. You're my favorite woman, Freckles."

She rolls her eyes like she doesn't care, but I know she does. I see that she wants to smile. I'll get her there. Right now, I'm guessing she is still questioning where we stand. I didn't call her this week, and it's probably messing with her. I just don't want to rush this and scare her.

But now that I'm with her, I don't think I can keep myself away.

"Uncle Joshie!" Brie screams as she runs up the deck stairs.

I bend down and lift her into my arms. While I'm showering her with kisses, I notice Charlotte pulls Layla into the kitchen for help. She may think she's escaped me, but I'll be back for her.

Chaos ensues as the birthday cake is brought out. We sing Happy Birthday, my eyes on Layla the entire time, and then everyone starts to disperse as they eat cake. It only takes about two minutes for the sugar high to kick in, and all the kids flock to the bouncy house again.

Layla disappears into the kitchen. I look around to see everyone deep in conversations on the deck, then put my beer down and walk inside. I find her putting out some more snacks. I know she sees me walk in, but she keeps her head down.

I walk up behind her, my body only an inch away from hers, then I grab her hand. I lead her down the hallway, into the bathroom and shut the door behind us.

Not giving her a second to talk, I grab her behind her neck and kiss her. It's a hungry kiss, letting her know just how much I've missed her.

Her hands fist the front of my t-shirt as she kisses me back with just as much desperation.

"God, I've missed you, Freckles," I say through our kisses.

I push her against the door and slide one of the straps of her dress down, exposing her breast. My hand wraps around it, massaging its fullness as my thumb glides over her nipple.

She moans into my mouth while I continue. Then I pull away and move my mouth to her nipple, sucking and biting lightly.

"I missed you too," she finally answers me.

I stand up and free both breasts, looking into her eyes while I take one in each hand. Her eyes are almost shut as she reacts to my touch. Then we hear voices coming from the kitchen, and her eyes are alert.

"Shit," she whispers as she pulls her straps back into place. "We can't be doing this here."

She's right. A child's birthday party is hardly the place to get her naked and fuck her.

"Come to my place after this," I insist, rubbing a finger across her smooth cheek.

I need to see her, need to hold her in my arms and remember what it felt like to feel content.

"Your place?" she whispers.

"Yeah, my place. You know where I live, right?"

"Of course, I know where you live."

"Good. Come back and spend the night with me." I don't give her a chance to overthink this and decline. I kiss her forehead and open the bathroom door.

"I'll go first," I whisper, then walk straight out to the deck.

Whoever was in the kitchen is gone now, so the coast is clear. Asher and his father are talking football, my kind of conversation, so I grab my beer and jump in.

My eyes follow Layla as she walks out a minute later. No one else can see the difference in her, but I see the extra spark of excitement in her eyes and the slightly swollen lips. Her eyes catch mine from across the deck, and I wink.

She bites her lower lip as she smiles and looks down. I chuckle to myself.

I try to mentally be present for the rest of the party, but it's hard. I keep finding Layla across the room, my eyes like magnets to her. Once everything starts to wind down, I start to say goodbye to everyone, saving Layla as my last goodbye.

I wrap my arms around her. "You better be at my place soon, Freckles. I'm feeling very impatient right now."

Once again, I don't leave time for her to respond. I walk away backward and wink again as her jaw falls.

Making her mine is going to be fun.

Chapter Eighteen

Layla

I shouldn't be following his orders like a puppy. I should be standing my ground and telling him he can't just tell me what to do.

So, why am I speeding across town to get to his place? Because apparently, my vagina is calling the shots, and she is telling me to get there fast.

I pull into the driveway of his two-bedroom home. It's a cute house with hundred-year-old trees towering over it, creating a nice feeling of seclusion. I've only been here to pick up Asher before; I've never actually seen the inside.

His front door opens just as I'm getting out of my car. He's changed into his sweatpants and a shirt. The sight brings me back to our hotel room.

He smiles as I walk tentatively up the front porch. "Hi, Freckles. Get over here," he says with open arms.

Who is this guy? Here I am freaking out over what this means, and he's acting like me sneaking over to his place is completely normal.

"Hey," I wave like an idiot as I approach then he wraps his big arms around me.

"I'm glad you came. Come on in. I bought some wine on the way home. I figured you would want a glass."

"Thanks." We walk inside, and he closes the door, leading me over to the family room.

His place is decorated nicer than I expected. I thought it would be a bachelor pad with mismatched furniture and nothing on the walls. I was wrong.

The brown leather couch is decorated with dark blue throw pillows. Pictures on the walls match the theme of brown and blue. It all seems to work really well together.

Two glasses of wine are on the tray on top of the dark blue ottoman. He motions for me to take a seat.

I don't know why, but my nerves just multiplied by a hundred. This is not quite what I expected for the evening. I thought maybe he'd pull me in and bring me straight to his bedroom.

He takes a seat and smiles up at me. "You going to sit down or just stand there like I'm gonna bite you?"

"Sorry, I just feel like I'm in some alternate reality right now."

His eyes grow with amusement. I sit down next to him and grab a glass.

"Please, tell me how this is an alternate reality," he says as he leans back on the couch.

His casual demeanor is starting to become a bit soothing. My muscles start to loosen slightly to match his comfortable mood.

"You know, a reality where you and I are not only fooling around but like…getting along."

He seems slightly offended by my words but does his best to adjust himself and recover. I feel bad, but it's true. This is not how we act towards one another, at least not here, back at home.

His head falls forward as he lets out a soft laugh.

"What's so funny?" I ask skeptically.

He smiles. "Not only did you just admit we're fooling around, but you were willing to admit it might just be more than that."

"I don't know if I'd go that far."

That makes him laugh more. "We'll see about that, Freckles. For right now, let's just enjoy the evening."

"And how do you suppose we do that?" my voice hitches a bit seductively.

He raises his eyebrows as his eyes look me up and down. "I have a couple of ideas. First, let's talk. How was your first week back at work? Did you and Zane move passed our awkward encounter?"

That makes me laugh this time. "Oh gosh. It did lead to a conversation I've never had with him before."

He seems curious. "What kind of conversation was this?"

I cringe at the thought. "He made me tell him everything we did in Italy." His face doesn't give way to his reaction. "Are you mad?"

"Mad? Why would I be mad?"

"I don't know. Some people don't want their personal details shared with others. But it's Zane, he would've locked me in his office until I spilled."

"I believe that," he says with a smile. "And I don't care if you tell him. You guys are close, you should be able to talk to your friends."

His response throws me a bit. He's so different when we aren't at each other's throats. He's so supportive and—nice.

"Thanks. He was so worked up when I told him how long it had been for me. He was beginning to worry about me."

He sits up straighter. "What do you mean? How long had it been before me?"

Crap. I just put my foot in my mouth. I feel like my cheeks are turning red.

"Like before I opened the restaurant or something. I don't know. I couldn't even remember the last time, honestly."

His eyes widen. Did I just scare him? I mean, I know it's out of the ordinary, but I was focused on work.

Suddenly, he stands up and looks down at me.

Is he going to kick me out? I can't believe I told him. Here I am, willingly telling the man I'm sleeping with that I'm basically a born-again virgin.

He puts his hand out. "Do you want me to leave?" I ask faintly.

"Leave? No, just come here."

I take his hand reluctantly, then follow him down a hallway. I'm not sure where the hell we are going until we are all of a sudden standing in what appears to be his bedroom.

His large hand takes my face and holds it gently. His arm encircles me, his hand landing on the small of my back. A mere touch from him sends warm shivers through my body.

He presses his lips against mine gently, making them burn with fire. His mouth moves slowly, taking his time with his exploration.

He pulls away, eyes looking drugged. "I'm sorry I didn't know that it had been that long, Freckles. I should've been gentler with you."

He seems torn up about this, and it actually makes my heart feel like it's cracking open.

"I love everything we did together. I have no regrets," I tell him honestly.

His thumbs rub up and down my cheeks as he closes his eyes. His forehead falls to mine.

"This time, I'll make love to you like I should have our first time together."

Make love? I swallow hard, trying to process what's happening. An undeniable magnetism is building between the two of us.

He moves the straps of my dress off my shoulder, this time pulling my dress down to my waist. I try to contain my erratic breaths as he takes in my breasts that are bared to him. He brings his hands up and glides the back of his fingers along my nipples, just barely touching them. My eyes close on their own accord.

"Open your eyes, Freckles," he whispers. "I like it when you watch me touch you."

I open them just as he leans in and takes a nipple into his mouth. He grips my breast to poke my nipple out further and sucks harder.

I let out a loud moan of appreciation. He pulls away and backs me up against his bed, then pulls my dress off completely, my panties going along with it.

"Lay down on the bed. Let me take care of you," he says hoarsely.

I lie down and watch him strip his clothes off before he joins me on the bed, right in between my legs.

His fingers gently traced a pathway along the skin on my inner thighs, and goosebumps broke out all over me. I squirmed around, shocked at my eager response to his touch.

His thumb dips into my entrance and starts rubbing wet circles over my clit.

"I've missed this pussy. I never got a taste of it in your office, and I've been starving for another one ever since Italy."

Then he replaces his thumb with his mouth and fireworks erupt in my body. The way he groans into my pussy like he's a starved man who finally got the meal of his dreams is just so hot.

I watch him devour me. I can't take my eyes off of him. I watch every single movement of his tongue, when he flicks to when he wraps his lips around my clit and sucks. The view is just as good as the feeling.

Then he slowly presses two fingers into me and it's my turn to groan. The feeling of my clit and g-spot being stimulated simultaneously is too much. I can no longer contain myself as I grip his hair.

"Fuck, that feels so good," I tell him.

"Mmmm...tastes good too." He looks up at me while his fingers start to pick up their pace, his tongue starting to match the tempo. "Are you gonna come for me, Freckles?"

"Shit. Yes!" I scream as my orgasm takes over me, a gust of desire shaking my body.

Josh climbs up my body, caging my head in between his elbows, and then kisses me. His lips are still wet with my own arousal, but it oddly doesn't bother me as his mouth moves slowly over mine.

"I need you, baby. I need to be inside of you," he whispers against my mouth.

"Yes," I agree, not sure why he isn't moving at all.

He pulls away, an almost hopeful glint in his eyes. "I want to be inside of you with nothing in between us."

It dawns on me what he is asking for.

"Are you on birth control?" he asks.

I nod my head.

"I'm clean. I get tested regularly. Based on how long it's been for you, I know you're clean. Do you trust me, Freckles?"

Do I trust him? The man who broke my heart a decade ago with no explanation. We still haven't even talked about it, and yet here he is asking me if I trust him. I think about everything he's done for me in the past week. How attentive he's been to my emotions and making sure I'm happy.

"I trust you," I whisper, surprising myself with how easily that answer comes to me.

A small smile lifts at the corner of his mouth. "That means everything to me."

He adjusts himself onto one elbow and then uses his free hand to grab himself. He glides his tip along my entrance, teasing me before he slides inside of me.

"Fuck," his forehead falls to my shoulder. "I didn't know it would feel this good."

"What are you talking about?" I whisper. "Have you never done this before?"

He lifts his head. "I've never wanted to experience this with anyone but you."

Tears well up in my eyes as he slowly starts to pull out and slide back in. I'm overwhelmed by his admission. I've never done this with anyone, either. I've never trusted anyone before.

He kisses me slowly as he finds a rhythm. It's slow, but that seems to give me the opportunity to really feel him inside of me. Every movement feels magnified at this pace. A hot tide of passion rages between us as he moves inside of me. His tongue dances with mine, his hand runs through my hair at the base of my scalp. It's like an overload of feelings that are being expressed between us right now.

I'm not sure I'm ready to really analyze what our bodies are saying to each other. I run my hands from the top of his shoulders, all along the length of his back, until they reach his ass. I squeeze his cheeks and pull him all the way into me.

We both groan. Then he breaks our kiss, balancing on both hands and starts to fuck me a bit harder. It's still a slow pace, but his thrusts are harder. My breasts bounce with the movement, and his eyes turn dark as he watches.

His chest and abs are on display. I drink in the sight, watching them flex each time he pushes inside of me.

We are both sweating, panting, a complete mess. It's too intimate and intense for words.

I feel my body tense, my orgasm starting to build. He must sense that I'm almost there because he starts to fuck me hard until we are both screaming our own release. His eyes close as he jerks and pumps his own release inside of me. Then he falls down on top of me, panting in my ear as we both try to catch our breath.

I sigh with pleasant exhaustion. Josh pulls himself up and looks down at where our bodies are still connected.

"I've never done this before, so I don't know if it's about to just fall out of you when I pull out."

The comment is so different from the mood that I actually crack up at how hilarious it is.

"What? What's so funny?" he asks. "Was that a stupid question?"

I can't control my hysterics as I try to answer him, shaking my head. "No, it's not stupid. I don't know either."

"Come on," he stands up quickly, then grabs my hand, dragging me out of his bed while I'm still laughing, "let's get in the shower."

As I walk, I feel some of his cum drip down my leg. Good thing he immediately turns his shower on. He steps in first to test the temperature before he motions for me to follow him in.

When I lift my leg to get in the shower, his eyes home in on something between my legs. I look down and realize he's looking at his cum.

"I guess we have our answer," I shrug and smile.

His broad shoulders are heaving as he breathes. I don't know what is making him react like this. I can't tell if he's angry or turned on.

Then, in one forward motion, he has me pinned against the shower wall. I gasp in surprise.

"What are you doing?" I whisper as I grab onto his shoulders.

"I need you to tell me you're mine, Freckles. My cum will be the only cum that ever leaks out of your tight pussy. Got it?"

He gathers his cum on my thigh with his finger and then pushes it back inside of me. His claiming me gives me a feeling of much more than sexual desire. Although my body is on fire, so is my heart.

"Got it," I gasp as his fingers writhe inside of me.

"Say it. I want you to say the words."

"I'm yours," I say as our eyes hold onto each other's.

"Good girl," he says with a kiss to my forehead.

His lips graze over mine as he brings me to yet another orgasm before we clean up together in his shower.

After we dry off, he hands me the same clothes I borrowed for pajamas in Italy, clean, of course. I'm wringing out my hair in a towel.

"Crap, my hair is gonna turn into a beehive by the morning if I don't brush it."

He looks over at me after he pulls his shirt down. "Well, sorry to burst your bubble, Freckles, but you aren't leaving here tonight. I haven't been able to sleep half as good as I was in Italy without you next to me."

"I haven't had great sleep either," I admit.

He walks into his bathroom and comes out with a comb. He sits on his bed and pats the spot right in front of him.

"What? You want me to sit there?"

He cracks a smile. "Yes, Freckles. I'm gonna comb your hair for you. Sit down. Relax."

I bite my lip as I crawl onto the bed and take a seat in front of him. He starts to run the comb through my hair tenderly, taking his time with each section. I close my eyes and enjoy the care and attention.

"When's the last time you've been home?" I find myself asking, not sure where the question came from.

"Shit, I don't know. Five years."

"Five years? That's a long time. Do you talk to your parents on the phone?"

I knew he wasn't super close with his parents, but five years is a long time.

"I'll occasionally talk to them on the phone. Maybe once or twice a year."

"They don't call more often or ask you to visit?"

"Nah, they aren't really interested in what I'm doing. They were pretty absent parents. They did just enough work to keep us out of poverty. I guess I'm not much better than them, huh? Not compared to what your family has accomplished."

I turn my head and see the pain in his eyes. He actually believes what he just said. I don't know his parents, but I know he is nothing like the people he's describing.

"Josh, you know there's no way you're like them," I say as I turn around so I'm facing him.

He chuckles. "How do you know, Freckles?"

"Because you trust people. You are like a second brother to Asher. Hell, even to Liam and Eric. You're a hard worker and have made a great living for yourself."

"It's not that impressive when it's your best friend who's employing you."

"Stop that," I push his chest slightly. "That's not why Asher has you as basically his co-owner. You know that man doesn't trust easily; his company is his baby, and he wouldn't put you in charge of so much if he didn't trust you completely. He does it because you are talented and trustworthy. You're kind and hardworking."

He looks up at me shyly. "You really think that?"

It breaks my heart that he doesn't know this about himself. "I know that. I may have hated you for ten years for breaking my heart, but that doesn't mean I didn't see how much his company thrived once he got you on board."

I realize I may have spoken too freely. I didn't mean to confess all of that.

"I broke your heart?" he whispers.

My head falls to the side. "Come on, Josh. You know you did. I was seventeen and completely in love with you. I thought we shared something special that night. I thought we were more than what we were. I didn't realize it was nothing to you. Not until I saw you with that other girl the next night."

My eyes water as I recall the events of the night. How excited I was to see him across the room. My stomach was in knots, my heart was beating erratically. I didn't think we would be going public with our relationship yet, but I figured he would at least smile when he saw me. Maybe walk up to me and tell me to meet him somewhere private.

I never expected him to look right through me then grab her hand and turn his head away.

"I didn't know you cared that much. I know what I did was wrong, and I've regretted it every second of every day, but I thought it just pissed you off more than hurt you. I'm so sorry I hurt you."

A tear escapes and rolls down my cheek. "Why'd you do it?" I whisper.

He sighs. "I've debated on how honest I wanted to be with you about what happened that night. But I don't want to start this with you with anything but complete honesty. I had already been scared about what people would think. You were only seventeen, I was twenty-three. I know it was only a kiss, and I would have waited for you to turn eighteen, but it still left me terrified that your family would hate me."

He pulls at the back of his neck as he continues. "I was just out of college, had student loan debt, a crappy job, and no sense of direction. You were used to a certain lifestyle that your father was able to provide for you. I didn't think your family would think I was good enough for you." He laughs, "I still think they won't find I'm good enough for you."

He looks up at me. "I was still willing to risk it all for you, but that night, William was at the party. I don't know how he knew about us. Maybe it was a coincidence, or he sensed it., but he pulled me aside. He told me if I ever pursued you, he would use his father's money, which he informed me there was an abundance of, and he would take me to jail for being with a minor. He threatened to have his father quit doing business with your family. Then he proceeded to tell me exactly what I had been worried about all along, that I would never be able to provide for you the way he could."

I'm stunned as I listen to his words. My body feels like it's in a state of shock, unable to move. He's kept this in for ten years, and I've hated him for all of that time. The story I told myself about him was that he was a player who stomped on my heart without a care in the world.

"Josh," my voice cracks as I begin to cry. "Why didn't you tell me?"

His hurt lay naked in his eyes. "I was embarrassed. I'm supposed to be strong and able to support you. Going to you, not only to tell you I can't financially support you like another man could, but to then tell you I'm all fucked in the head over it just felt like exposing how weak I am."

"Well, that sounds like some old-school bullshit if you ask me."

He gave me a sidelong glance of utter disbelief. "What does that mean?"

"It means that we aren't some nineteen-fifties couple where the man needs to make all the money and have no feelings, all while the woman sits at home depressed with nothing to do once her kids go to school. It means we are a team. We build the life we want together. We talk about our feelings. We support each other."

He leans in and presses his lips to mine. Parting my lips, I raise myself to meet his kiss. He runs his fingers through my hair as his lips move along mine. He pulls away and holds my head while he looks at me.

"I'm a fucking idiot. I'll never forgive myself for what I did to you. But can you forgive me, Freckles?"

I lean in and kiss him again. "I'll forgive you if you cook me breakfast tomorrow morning."

"That's all it takes?" He laughs. "Deal. I'll make the chef a fancy breakfast."

Chapter Nineteen

Josh

"Did you happen to see Layla get in her car and leave thirty seconds after Josh left the party last weekend?" Liam says slyly after he takes a sip of his beer.

I'm starting to wonder what the hell these two are up to right now. They asked me if I wanted to get dinner casually at Layla's restaurant tonight. Now, with the look they're giving each other, I'm thinking they have more conniving intentions.

"I did see that. I wonder where she was going since she went the opposite way of her house," Eric replies.

"What the hell is going on? What did I miss?" my buddy Kyle asks.

Kyle is dating Avery, Layla and Charlotte's friend, but Kyle has been a friend of mine since I came to this town after college.

"It appears that love was in the air in Italy," Liam replies playfully.

I shake my head. He's being a little over the top, but then again, it's Liam. I've learned over the years not to try and figure out what's going on in that head of his.

Kyle's jaw is hanging down like a puppy with a treat in front of him. "Shut the fuck up!" he shoves me from across the table. "You and Layla?"

"Can we all please keep in mind that this is new? You guys are the only ones who know, and most importantly, this is her restaurant, and she could pop up at any time. I don't want you to make her feel uncomfortable."

Kyle nods his head in agreement but also beams with joy. He leans forward, "You know that we've all basically been watching you two fight for years, knowing that you were really just suppressing feelings? Right? I mean, am I right, guys?" He looks to the other guys for confirmation.

"Of course. It was only a matter of time," Eric agrees.

Layla hasn't come by yet, even though I texted her to say we were here. She replied and said it's been crazy. Two waitresses called in sick, so she is trying to help the staff out.

I spot her for the first time tonight as she carries a tray of food to a table across the room. Her hair is pulled up in a tight bun and she's in all black with the company logo on the front of her shirt. She looks adorable, but I can see the stress through her fake smile.

"Where's Asher been? Haven't seen him in a while," Kyle asks.

"He's been busy with Brie and Charlotte. He can't come out with us all the time with a family at home," I defend, knowing I can't announce Charlotte's news yet.

Kyle shrugs his shoulders and moves on. Layla finally spots me and offers a small smile and waves. I can't take it anymore. I haven't seen her since Tuesday.

Is it only Friday? Yes. It's only been three days, but that feels like an eternity for me. I slide out of my chair.

"I'll be right back," I tell the guys.

Eric laughs. "Tell Layla to come say hi sometime tonight."

I roll my eyes. Why the fuck am I so transparent when it comes to Layla? It's like I have a sign on my forehead saying, 'Fool in love.'

Not bothering to defend myself or correct them, I find her when she's walking away from a table and grab her hand. I lead her into one of the private restrooms and close the door behind us. I step into her, caging her against the door, and lean in until our lips are connected.

Torturing her with long, slow kisses suddenly becomes torture of my own. When I pull away, her eyes are heavy.

"What was that for?" she asks.

"You seem stressed. I wanted to give you something else to think about until you come over to my place tonight."

"Your place?"

"Yes, my place. Come over after work."

"I might not be off work until after ten," she tells me.

"I don't work tomorrow, and I also am capable of staying up passed ten. Come on, I'll cook you breakfast again."

I'm rewarded with a smile. "I suppose I can just shower at your place tonight."

"Yes, you can absolutely get naked and lather your sexy body up at my place tonight," I say as I start running kisses down her neck. "It's actually encouraged."

"Okay, I'll come tonight," she sighs as I place an open-mouthed kiss on her shoulder.

"Yes, you will be coming tonight, Freckles. Now get away from me before I have you coming on my mouth right now for all your staff to hear this time."

She laughs as she opens the door and practically runs away from me. I smile the entire way back to the table. As soon as I sit down, the guys all look at me.

"You've got it bad, dude," Kyle says.

"I don't know what you're talking about," I tell him. "So, Eric, how's work going? You still gunning for the VP position?"

Liam rolls his eyes. "How you became another corporate scrooge out for only the money is beyond me. What happened to you?"

Eric stiffens in his seat. "You're like a broken record playing on repeat. I get it, you don't like what I've chosen for my career."

Eric has always been the buttoned-up one ever since I've known him. Sure, he can relax and chill with the guys, but he's never been interested in settling down or coasting through his career. He was always a determined guy.

"I'd like it if I thought it made you happy," Liam scoffs.

I let the two bicker over the same old shit while my eyes remain glued to Layla the rest of the evening. Just watching her work stirs up my body in ways I don't even understand. Like when she smiles and I see the crinkles at the corner of her eyes, it makes my heart race in my chest.

I head back home around nine, stopping at the door to wink at Layla before I leave.

It's nearly eleven thirty when she shows up at my house looking exhausted. I pull her into me for a hug, but it only lasts a second before she steps away.

"I must smell like grease and sweat. I can't believe you want to touch me. Let me shower first."

"Come on. I'll get you some towels. On my way home, I picked up some women's shampoo, conditioner, and whatever else I could think of that you would want."

Her eyes go wide as she looks at the counter in my bathroom that's covered with products.

"Did you buy the entire store?"

I chuckle. "I don't know what you like to use. Go ahead, pick whatever you want. I'll be in the bedroom waiting for you."

I give her some space to wind down and relax while I light candles in my bedroom and put lotion on my nightstand. She works her ass off and I'm sure her body is feeling it tonight. I want to spoil her and give her a massage.

She walks out of the steamy bathroom with a towel wrapped around her and wet hair dripping water droplets down her chest. My dick instantly gets hard. Down boy, this is about getting her to relax.

"What is all this?" she asks as she walks into the room.

"Come lie down," I pat the bed next to me. "This is spa night for Layla."

She doesn't argue as she sits next to me.

"Lie down on your stomach," I instruct her.

She looks at me skeptically. "You're serious? Is this gonna last like two minutes, and then you want sex?"

"Of course not," I laugh. "I'm pretty sure if I wanted sex, you'd be all for it."

I raise an eyebrow, waiting for her to try to deny it, but she knows I'm right.

"Good. Glad you agree," I tell her. "Now, lie down on your stomach. Are there any muscles that hurt more than others?"

"My feet and my back," she mumbles into the pillow.

"Got it, babe. Just close your eyes and relax."

I grab the lotion and pour some on my hands, making sure to mix it into my hands first to make it warm. Then sit on the side of her, and start with her shoulders. I can instantly feel the tension in her muscles.

I swear her stubbornness carries through even in a massage. I can feel her muscles fighting with me, not wanting to give up control. Finally, they give in, and she begins to relax.

I pull the towel down until it is just covering her ass and spend the next twenty minutes massaging the rest of her back, letting her moan her way through the entire thing like my dick isn't confused as hell. He wants to know why we are in bed with the woman of our dreams who is naked and moaning, and yet we are not allowed to get in on the action.

Then, I crawl to the end of the bed and grab a foot, working my thumbs into each section, before moving onto the other foot.

I start working her calves as I notice her heavy breathing. I think she's asleep. I smile to myself, thinking I've accomplished what I wanted, so I start crawling over to my space to go to sleep.

Layla lifts her head slightly. "You're done?"

"I thought you were asleep. Do you still want me to massage you?" I ask, still on my hands and knees.

"I want you to touch me."

"Touch you?"

"Please. My new boyfriend was somehow able to make it through an entire massage without trying to have sex. I think it's a little insulting."

I laugh as she makes a pouty face. Then I yank down my grey sweatpants and let my hard dick hang out. I grab it and give it a stroke. "It wasn't because I didn't want to, Freckles. I just wanted to make this about you."

"I appreciate that. Now, touch me," she demands, and I'm not about to make my girl ask me a third time.

I grab the towel and rip it away from her, exposing her ass. I lean in and kiss a cheek as my fingers gently run from her ankle up to the top of her thigh, then I push it out so I can see her pussy.

"Have you been this wet the entire time?" I growl as I look down at her glistening pussy.

"Yes," she whispers.

I spread her cheeks, then run some fingers from her clit to her opening, where I push them inside. From this angle, I need to push my fingers down to hit the spot that I know will make her come. I do it a couple of times, and she is already groaning and panting.

While my fingers continue, I kiss my way from her lower back up to her shoulder.

I whisper in her ear. "Is this what you wanted, Freckles?"

"Yes, please," she begs as she wiggles her ass, pushing my fingers further into her.

"Please, what?" I ask, wanting to know what else she wants.

"Please, fuck me."

She's needy for me and I love it. I pull my sweats off completely and roll over so my body is lying on top of hers, letting most of my weight rest on my elbow. Then I grab my dick and replace my fingers with it, fucking her while she's on her stomach.

It gives me the perfect access to whisper filthy things in her ear. I slide inside of her then lick the patch of skin behind her ear, and she gasps.

"Your ass looks incredible while I fuck this tight pussy," I tell her.

She looks up at me through hooded eyes, and my heart skips a beat. I'll never get over the fact that it's my Freckles who is letting me do these things to her. I lean down and kiss her lips as I pick up the pace.

I put both my hands on the bed so I can hold myself up and really get a look at my view. Her ass, her slender back, her pussy are all in my line of sight, then her beautiful face looking up at me. It's enough to make me feel like I'm about to start to lose it.

I fuck her hard and fast now, desperate and chasing my own release. She screams and tightens around my dick as she comes, letting me know it's for me to let go. As soon as I am done, I fall on top of her.

Both of us are breathing heavily as I pull myself out. I don't have to ask her to stay; thankfully, it's just understood now. A guy doesn't buy out the entire drugstore for just anybody.

Chapter Twenty

Layla

"Oh my god, you're the best," Charlotte says upon answering the door and seeing me holding up a bag of greasy cheeseburgers from our favorite fast-food joint.

She grabs the bags out of my hands and walks away from me. I laugh to myself as I walk inside and close the door. That's why she's my best friend. "Hello to you too!" I shout jokingly.

I walk into the kitchen to find Charlotte sitting at the table, scrummaging through the bags.

"What's up, sis?" my brother walks by with a hammer in his hands.

I don't even ask what he's working on now. He's always fixing or updating something around here. This house is huge and seems to have an endless list of things needing to be repaired.

"Where's Brie?" I ask as I sit down at the table.

"She's taking a nap," Charlotte answers over a huge bite of her cheeseburger.

I know we like this food, but she's on another level right now. She literally moans over her burger after she swallows her first bite.

"Everything alright over there?" I ask with amusement.

"Ugh, I'm finally feeling better and able to keep some food down. I'm just ravenous now. It's like my body has been deprived of food for weeks and wants to make up for its missed meals."

I chuckle as I open the wrapper of my own burger. "Well, you deserve it. I'm glad you're feeling better."

"Your brother must think I'm gross. I can't fit into any of my pants anymore, and I'm eating like I'm preparing for the finals of a food-eating competition."

"I'm pretty sure you could eat all the food in the world, and my brother would still be crazy over you," I tell her.

She rolls her eyes at me, knowing I'm full of shit but takes another bite of her burger.

"It feels like we haven't really had a chance to talk since you've been back from Italy. Are you settling back into work alright?" she asks through a mouth full of food.

I feel bad that I haven't told her what happened in Italy with Josh, but it didn't feel like a conversation to have in passing. I'm sure she'll have a million questions. There's also the weird dynamic of her being with my brother. She will have to keep it from him until Josh and I agree to tell him. I'm not sure how she will feel about that.

"Work is crazy, exactly what it was before I left."

"Ah, so the entire place didn't crash and burn because you took a vacation?" She raises an eyebrow at me.

"Yeah, yeah, yeah. You were right." I stick my tongue out at her. "But seriously, going away was exactly what I needed. It showed me that I was hiding in my work, not opening myself up to other things in my life."

"Really? That's so amazing. I love that you got so much out of the trip. To be honest, I was panicking the entire time."

"You were?"

She leans back in her chair, and I get a better glance at her growing belly. It's so adorable.

"Yes! I was totally taking a chance with Josh going. I thought there were two ways it could go. You two would end up killing each other, or..." she gives me a weird look.

"Or?" I drawl out.

"Or you two would finally see that you two have feelings for each other, and something would happen."

My hands freeze with my burger halfway to my mouth as my jaw falls open.

"I know!" she shouts. "I'm the worst. I kinda was hoping you would come back and have this like huge romantic story about how the two of you had sex the entire time and how amazing it was. I'm lucky he didn't ruin the entire trip for you with my stupid hopeless romantic delusions."

I can't contain my laughter. Her hopes for the trip is just so absurdly accurate.

She looks at me like I've officially lost it. "Well, I'm glad you're laughing about it. I thought you'd hate me."

I shake my head at the ridiculousness. I would never hate her. "No," I laugh, "it's not that. It's just that you may not be as far off as you originally hoped."

Her forehead scrunches. I can see her mind working overtime as she tries to put it all together. Then her hands slam down on the table. "Wait a minute. Are you telling me something DID happen between you two?"

I bite my lip, trying not to blush like a damn schoolgirl. "A lot more than just *something* happened in Italy."

"Yes!" she claps with excitement.

"Shhhh," I reply as I look around the house. "Look, I'd love to talk about this with you, but you have to promise me one thing."

Her shoulders sink. "You want me to keep it from your brother, don't you?"

"Look, I won't ask you to lie to him. If he suspects and asks, you can tell him. But I'm asking you not to offer the information. I think that's a fair deal, right?"

"Yes. That's fair. I promise I won't tell him unless he asks. Now, please, tell me everything. How did it happen? Who made the first move? Was it good? How big is he?"

"Well, it was this like, weird gradual thing that happened over the course of the week."

She leans forward. "Ooh, like how? Did it start with a kiss one night under the stars?"

My cheeks redden with embarrassment. "It kind of started with me accidentally walking in on him when he was—you know," I gesture with my hand.

She gasps in surprise. "Shut up!" she laughs. "You walked in on that? Did you run away mortified? Did you finish it for him?"

"Wrong and wrong."

She contemplates my response. "What the hell did you do then?"

"I told him to finish while I watched."

She inhales sharply. "You did not. I don't believe you." She throws down her fry on her foil burger wrapper.

"I swear, I don't know where the confidence came from. It was like the old me slowly started to return."

"Was it hot to watch?" she asks in a whisper.

I look around again to make sure Asher isn't nearby. "It was soo hot," I whisper back.

She eats a fry and does a weird dance. "I'm so excited. I wish I could drink alcohol. I feel like this conversation needs wine. Okay, so, then what happened?"

I tell her all about our kiss, the night he fingered me, and then our first night together. She grins the entire time while her eyes sparkle with joy. Every word that tumbles out of my mouth is met with contagious enthusiasm.

"This is all so romantic," she sighs blissfully.

I snicker as I drink my water. "I mean, aside from all the dirty hotel room shenanigans, I suppose it's pretty romantic."

"Oh, please," she waves her hand at me. "The dirtier it is, the more romantic, in my mind. Like when Asher uses his tongue and..."

"Ahhhh!" I scream and cut her off. "Look, I know I get to share my kinky little details with you, but I'm sorry, I draw the line with details of my brother's sex life."

She gives me a pouty face. "I know, but you're my best friend. Who am I supposed to talk to about my sex life?"

"Avery, a college friend, your therapist, anybody but me."

"Fine," she whines. "Moving on. So, what does this mean? Have you two done anything since you've been back? Oh, no, are you two gonna pretend like it was just Italy, then go back to hating each other here? I don't have the energy for that."

Charlotte has certainly gotten a bit more dramatic since she's been carrying life in her belly. She doesn't normally catastrophize like this.

"Calm down. At first, I was definitely weary about what it all meant. He broke my heart years ago, you know that."

She nods her head in understanding. She doesn't know all the details of what happened, I never told anyone. I was too mortified.

"But after talking to him about it, I don't know I guess I had it all wrong. Can you believe I spent ten years hating him when it didn't go down exactly how I thought it did?"

She rolls her eyes. "I only said that to you like a million times. I could tell from the moment I met Josh that he was a good guy. I figured whatever he did, there was more to the story. I told you to ask him about it, make him talk to you."

"Well, I still think he could've grown a pair and talked to me about it."

"Ok, I think we're getting off topic. One day, I'll make you tell me the whole story. So, you guys talked. Does that mean you're dating?"

I shrug my shoulders. "I guess. We haven't really gotten that far in our conversations. We get too distracted with—other things. But I've spent a couple of nights at his place, and the way he talks to me, it sounds like he has no intentions of being with anyone but me."

"So, you guys haven't talked about telling people about the two of you?"

I laugh. "I just told you, we don't get much talking in before other things happen. We'll get there. It's been two weeks since we've been back."

"Fine. But please have the conversation with him so I don't have to keep this secret for long."

"We'll see," I tell her, not wanting to promise anything. I need to see where Josh is in all of this first.

"Look who's here," Asher walks in, holding my adorable niece with her messy bedhead and tired-looking face.

As soon as she spots me, a bright smile spreads across her face. "Auntie Lay-lay."

I run over to her and grab her from my brother. "There's my girl. Did you have a good nap?"

She nods her head as she starts to play with my hair. There's something about when a kid just wakes up, they are willing to be held. They are super clingy and affectionate. I just love it.

Charlotte heads to the bathroom, leaving me and Asher alone.

He looks behind him to make sure Charlotte is gone. "Thank you for bringing her food and visiting her. I think pregnancy hormones are raging right now. If I ask her if she's hungry, she cries and tells me I think she's fat. If I don't, I'm not taking care of her and the baby."

I let out a snort. "Good luck. I don't think that's going to go away as the pregnancy progresses."

"I know. I'll get used to it. She's the one going through this entire process and carrying our baby. I can deal with some mood swings."

Although he is saying the words, I can see the concern on his face.

"Hey, she's not Lauren. Okay? Even if Charlotte deals with anything post-partum, it's not going to be like it was last time. She loves you like crazy. I promise," I tell him.

He nods his head. "I know, it's just sometimes my brain can try to tell me differently."

"I understand, but our brains can be liars. In fact, *most* of the time, they are."

"Thanks," he replies, looking down at his feet. I think he's trying to hold back his emotions.

I hate that what Lauren did to him will always be etched into his soul. It's not something that goes away, but he's come a long way. He has generally moved past it, but I imagine he will need to see for himself that Charlotte will love him after the baby comes.

I feel a little tap on my shoulder. "Yes, sweetheart?" I turn to Brie.

"Can we go outside and play?" she asks, looking much more awake now.

"Of course we can. How about sidewalk chalk?" I suggest.

That earns me a cheer of excitement. I walk outside with Brie and get both of us set up with the chalk. Being a part of this little family unit makes me think back to when I used to picture what life would be like if I married Josh.

I was seventeen and stupid, but I had it all figured out in my head. Who knew ten years later, those dreams would start to creep back in?

Chapter Twenty-One

Josh

"Did you pack an overnight bag?" I ask Layla as I lean against the frame of her front door.

She picks up a black bag from the ground by her shoes. "Overnight bag is packed."

She closes the door and locks it. As soon as we're settled into my truck, she grabs my cheek and pulls me in for a kiss.

I don't think I'll ever tire of her lips or the way my heart flutters every time they touch mine.

"Now, can you tell me where we're going?" she asks as she pulls away.

I put the truck in reverse and back out of her driveway.

"Nope. Sorry, Freckles. It's a surprise all the way to the very end."

I've been setting this up for a couple of days. My friend owns a huge beach house in Charleston that he rents out in the summer months. He is letting us stay there for the evening. But we are not driving the two hours to Charleston, we are taking another form of transportation.

When we pull up to the gate of the private airport, she looks at me strangely.

"What's going on? Are we flying somewhere?" she asks.

I find a parking spot in the front and cut the engine. "We are indeed."

I grab both of our bags and walk into the building. Carter is waiting for us at the opposite side of the building by the sliding glass doors.

"What's up, man?" I ask, placing our bags on the ground and shaking his hand. "Thanks for letting me do this."

"Not a problem. I think you've earned yourself a solo trip."

"You ready, Freckles?" I pick our bags back up, following Carter outside to the small aircraft that's being inspected at the moment.

"This guy is flying us somewhere?" she asks as the wind whips through her hair; looking like a movie star with her sunglasses.

We walk up the stairs and into the aircraft. I place our luggage in the closet and then sit down in the cockpit.

"Not exactly," I tell her. "Come sit down."

I motion for her to sit in the co-pilot seat, but she continues to stand in place.

"Josh, what the hell is going on?" she crosses her arms over her chest.

Her small white tank top pushes her breasts up and makes me want to take her right here in front of anyone who wants to watch.

"My buddy Carter is letting us borrow his plane. I'm flying us to Charleston, where we have a beautiful mansion on the water waiting for us."

"Be serious, who's flying us there?"

I chuckle. "I am serious. I've been flying planes for two years now. I took lessons, clocked my hours, and Carter has been teaching me. This is the first time he is letting me borrow his plane. This thing ain't cheap. But he trusts me and has been flying with me for a year, so he offered the other day when I was telling him that I wanted to do something special for you."

She still doesn't look very convinced.

"Josh, you've never talked about flying planes before."

"Well, Freckles, I'm not sure you and I sat down and had much small talk in the last couple of years."

She can't deny it, we've been dancing around these feelings for years, avoiding getting to know each other.

"How come Asher's never mentioned it?" she asks, still not completely convinced.

I shrug my shoulders. "I'm assuming Asher hasn't felt the need to bring it up to you. It's not like I've flown with him before. I generally have only flown with my instructors and Carter. It's not like I have a plane of my own to jet out with my friends all the time."

I pat my lap. "Come here. Sit down." I grab her hand and slowly pull her down to sit on my knee. "I'll explain all of this to you. I want you to feel comfortable."

I spent the next couple of minutes going over all the controls I will be using for the flight, showing her the communication I will have with air traffic control throughout the entire flight. She listened intently the entire time, her body slowly relaxing into mine.

"Most importantly," I tell her, "is that I would never allow anything to happen to you. If there is anyone in this world I would die before I let anything happen to, it would be you. Trust me when I tell you, I wouldn't do this if I didn't know it was safe for you."

"Okay," she turns around and looks at me. "I trust you."

I smile and squeeze her side. "Good. Now, you can go in the back and enjoy the trip. You can take a nap on the couch or watch a movie, or you can sit up here with me."

She bites her bottom lip as she looks behind me at the luxury jet and all its features. I really won't be offended if she chooses to sit in the back. I just want her to feel comfortable. But she smiles and leans down to kiss my lips.

"I think I'd like to be your co-pilot, Captain Crawford."

I suppress a groan. "Fuck, that sounds hot coming from you. We'll be exploring this name in the bedroom tonight."

She laughs as she hops off my lap and takes a seat next to me in the co-pilot chair. I give her her own set of headphones so she can listen to anything that comes through on the radio.

"This is so cool," she claps. "I can't believe I never knew this about you. You are full of surprises."

"Just something I've always wanted to do. Not that impressive."

She turns her head to the side in confusion. "You really don't understand how amazing you are. Stop downplaying how incredible this is. But just so you know," her face turns serious, "you would be equally amazing to me without any of this." She motions to the plane and everything around her.

My heart skips a beat. I think that's all I've ever wanted to hear from her. That I'm good enough just as I am, without any fancy accomplishments or skills. I smile at her, knowing words can't convey what that means to me.

I turn back to the controls in front of me and start the engine. It comes roaring to life, like the love I have had in my heart for this woman since our trip.

Once all systems are a go, I reverse the plane and start to taxi towards the runway. I make sure Layla is buckled up as I turn the plane, coming to a complete stop.

"This is it. You trust me, baby?" I ask, just wanting to hear the words.

She smiles. "I trust you."

"Here we go," I tell her as I get clearance for takeoff.

I push the throttle forward, and the plane begins to accelerate. As we gain speed, I steer the plane down the runway. Once we hit our rotation speed, I pull the controls back, and the plane lifts off the ground.

"Holy. Shit!" Layla screams next to me. "You're fucking flying a plane!"

I erupt into a deep laugh. Her excitement is contagious. A couple of minutes later, the plane is coasting in the air on the way to our destination. We should be there in thirty minutes. I'll be starting to descend in about twenty.

Layla keeps looking out the front windshield and side window with a big grin. Making her happy gives me more joy than I've ever experienced in my life. I could easily make this my mission for the rest of my life.

"Do you have any idea what you flying a plane is doing to me right now?" she says to me.

I bite my lip, just thinking about sliding my finger into her panties and feeling how slick and turned on she is.

I cover the microphone to my headset and whisper. "Having you sit next to me with that headset on is doing things to me, too, baby. You're, without a doubt, the sexiest co-pilot that has ever existed. If I weren't flying a plane right now, I'd have my finger so far up that cunt of yours, you'd be screaming my name."

Her skin flushes as her jaw hangs low. "Captain Crawford! Do you talk to all your co-pilots like that?"

I wink. "Only you, Freckles. You're the only co-pilot I want for the rest of my life."

Her eyes go wide. Shit. I think I just confessed I want to spend the rest of my life with her. Was that too soon? I know I should take my time, make sure we get this right, but it's so damn hard when it's the person I've pined over for a decade.

I turn back to the windshield, terrified to see what her reaction is once the shock wears off. Thankfully, air traffic control gives me the green light to begin descent. I just hope that I didn't ruin the whole trip by putting my damn foot in my mouth.

I take my time with the descent, sneaking a peek at Layla, who still seems enthralled by the entire process. As soon as the wheels hit the ground, I press my feet on top of the rudder pedals until the plane slows to almost a complete stop.

"What a freakin' rush!!" she claps next to me. "You did amazing!"

That's a good sign that the whole trip is not ruined. I breathe a sigh of relief. "I'm glad you enjoyed it."

As soon as the plane is parked, I cut the engine. The staff opens the door, and the stairs are ready for us to walk down within minutes. I go to grab our bags, but she unbuckles and jumps out of her seat.

She wraps her arms around my neck and throws herself at me, our lips clumsily crashing together. I pull her tight against me as her lips move along mine with fervor.

"Can they see us up here?" she asks breathlessly against my lips.

"Yes, it's not a commercial aircraft that's sixty feet tall. They can probably see us."

She pouts her lips at me, and I kiss her forehead gently. "Let's go. We can get to the house quickly, and I'll take care of you there, baby."

I grab her hand and our bags, then start to walk down the steps of the plane. I can't explain the feeling I get after flying. It's like my brain is completely calm and at ease. But with this beauty on my arm, it adds a whole new level.

I know every motherfucker in my vicinity is jealous of me, and they should be.

Just through the building, in the parking lot, is a black Ferrari Portofino waiting for us. I have several friends in the surrounding areas who have done very well for themselves, but I'm not very materialistic, so I've never reached out to them to borrow their things.

That's probably why they jumped at the opportunity to let me use their things because they know it's not the reason for our friendship.

"This is the car we're driving?" Layla stands in awe as I place our bags in the trunk.

Like promised, the key is on top of the back right tire. I grab her hand and lead her to the passenger side of the car, where I open the door for her. I hold out my hand for her to take a seat.

"It is," I reply, then walk over to my side and get behind the wheel.

"You didn't rent this thing, did you?"

"Ha! No, baby, I didn't. It's my buddy's car, the same one letting us stay at his place tonight."

"No one who owns a car like this owns a small little home in Charleston."

My lips twitch. "That's a very astute observation. I guess we will see if you are correct when we get there."

I grab her hand and place it on my thigh, holding onto her the entire time I drive along the roads. The neighborhood is secluded and nestled up against the water. I sent money to Tony and asked him to put together an array of items at the house for when we arrived.

It doesn't take Layla long to realize by the homes we're passing by that this house is gonna be huge.

"Okay, so you flew me by yourself in a private jet to Charleston, and now you're driving me in a Ferrari to spend the night in a mansion on the water?"

"It's not like I own any of these things and can provide them to you on a daily basis."

I don't know why I feel the need to downplay the evening, but I just want to make sure she knows this is not a typical weekend for me either. I can't do these things for her all the time. Just because I can physically fly a plane doesn't mean I have a plane to fly.

She sighs. "Giving you a compliment is like trying to give a kid a vegetable. It's nearly impossible."

Chapter Twenty-Two

Layla

How have I never realized the insecurities that run so deep in Josh? He's been such a fun-loving individual to everyone around him. It never occurred to me that he would be struggling internally so much.

There seems to be some conflict within him between doing what he loves, living a simple life, and being the man he thinks he needs to be.

Sure, having these experiences is amazing and fun. If we happen to get the opportunity to enjoy amenities like these, why not take it? But I don't need or even want these things in my life. I've lived a middle-class upbringing and got thrust into an upper-class life when my dad's business really took off.

I've seen the difference in the people who start to make more money than they know what to do with. I would choose any easy, middle-class life any day of the week.

The problem is getting Josh to understand that.

He pulls into the driveway of a massive white mansion with a huge southern wrap-around porch. The driveway runs up to the side of the house, where Josh uses the garage door opener in the car to park the car in the four-car garage.

"Alright, here we are," he cuts the engine and turns to me.

After he gets our bags, he takes my hand and leads me into the house. He walks me into the kitchen, which has large white cabinets and white marble countertops. The island is the size of my bathroom at home.

There are huge glass doors that slide back, creating no barrier between the back patio and the kitchen. There is a large pool with southern live oak trees all around. I can see the water in the distance, with a large dock.

The island is covered with food, and a wine bucket chilling some white wine with two glasses. There are candles lit all around the pool.

"Josh, what did you do?" I whisper as my eyes start to water.

He steps up behind me and wraps his arms around my waist, kissing a path along my neck. "I wanted to spoil you, to do something so you know how special you are to me."

I look up at him through my watery eyes. "This is incredible."

"You're incredible," he says, then leans down and kisses me softly.

I turn my body and wrap my arms around his neck, deepening it. I'm so overwhelmed with how he makes me feel. He's not shy with his actions or words, even after only two weeks together. No one has ever treated me like this. I don't even think I deserve all of this.

I want to repay him for this, but I don't even know what I can do. Then suddenly, I feel his dick harden against my stomach.

I think there's something I can do to show my appreciation. I break the kiss and get down on my knees.

His eyes follow me all the way down. "What are you doing, Freckles?"

I reach for his grey shorts and unbutton them while he watches, taking my time. Then I move onto his zipper, pulling it down slowly with a smirk.

"I'm saying thank you, Josh."

I pull down his shorts and boxers until they hit the floor. His long, thick dick bounces up into my face. I wrap my hand around the base and stroke it up and down.

He watches me intently as I lift higher on my knees then wrap my lips around his tip, giving it a tight suck.

"Fuck, baby," he whispers. "You don't have to say thank you like this."

I slide my mouth off him and look up through my lashes. "Are you telling me you don't want my thank you?"

He smiles down at me and shakes his head. "I'd never reject your thank you. I dream about your thank you all the time. I've wanted it since I met you, but I just wanted you to know I didn't do all of this for a thank you."

Ever the gentleman he is, making sure I'm not doing something because I feel obligated.

"Babe, I'm doing this because I love having your dick in my mouth. This is how I want to say thank you."

His eyes turn dark then a dirty smirk appears on his face. "Then continue, please."

I nod my head with a smile, then slide his dick back in my mouth all the way this time until it hits the back of my throat, and I gag.

"Fuuuck," he growls as his hands grip my hair. "You like taking all of me like that?"

I moan while I continue to move my mouth along him. His face, when he bottoms out in my throat, is hot as hell. His jaw falls slack while he watches, almost as if he is in awe.

"I'm gonna fill your dirty mouth with my cum. Do you want it, baby?"

"Mmmm hmmm," I hum while his dick still fills my mouth.

His dick is soaked with my saliva. It allows my hand to slide over his dick easily.

It doesn't take long before he's cussing and coming down my throat. I love watching him lose control.

I pop off him, and he lets go of my hair while he is still panting and catching his breath. I stand up and wipe my mouth off with the back of my hand.

He steps closer to me and kisses my forehead. "You really didn't have to do that. But fuck you are good at it."

"I like making you happy too, babe."

He laughs as he lifts me off the ground and places me on the countertop. "Keep calling me babe, I'm gonna lose my shit and fuck you right here."

"You like me calling you that?" I raise an eyebrow with a smile.

He steps closer and kisses me gently. "I love it. It makes me feel like I'm yours."

"Well, aren't you?" I ask hopefully.

"Fuck yeah, I am. I think I have been since the day I met you."

My heart jolts and pounds in my chest. Whatever this is between us, it feels like it's meant to be, like something bigger is working to bring us together. Maybe we have always been meant for each other.

"Now," he starts. "Let's get some food in you. You're gonna need your strength for what I have planned for you tonight."

He picks up a strawberry and places it near my mouth. I take a bite then he pops the remaining piece into his.

"Do you want me to give you a tour first? Then we can grab a plate of food and sit outside?"

"That sounds perfect."

I hop off the counter while Josh tries to navigate this ridiculous house himself. There are eight bedrooms, an indoor pool, an outdoor pool, a game room, a movie theater, and so much more that it's hard to even recall all of it.

At one point we end up in a closet, Josh thinking it was another bedroom. We find ourselves in a fit of laughter.

"What the fuck. I thought this was the room that had a good view of the water," he laughs as we back out.

"I'm beginning to think we're crashing in a stranger's place that was not loaned to us for the night. Did you steal that Ferrari?"

He wraps an arm around my neck and pulls me in. "Shit. You're onto me. And I stole the plane too. In fact, I just researched how to fly on the internet. I'm surprised we didn't die. All my ploy to impress you. Is it working?"

"Well, I didn't die on the plane. So, yeah, it seems to be working."

We eventually make it back downstairs to the food. He opens our champagne and pours me a glass. We both fill our plates with food and walk outside to the table that is off to the right of the large pool.

After we eat our food, we walk into the master bedroom, which is on the first floor and has its own little patio that leads to the pool. We put on our swimsuits and walk out the back.

The sun has started to set as the sky is painted with different hues of orange, pink, and red.

Josh runs and jumps in the pool instantly. I laugh and watch him as he swims over to the edge that I walk to. He stands and pushes his dark hair to the side. His rippling stomach is on display, chest hair soaked from the water, looking every bit like the man of my fantasies.

He rests his forearms on the edge of the pool and smiles up at me. "Get over here, Freckles. Take a seat."

"I can't get in the pool?"

"Not yet. First, I want you right here," he slaps the cement.

I sit down in front of him as he makes space for me between his arms. My red bathing suit is skimpy and shows off just as much as the one I wore in Italy, which pissed him off so much. But I figured this one is alright since he will be the only one seeing it. Plus, I like getting a rise out of him. It's fun and has proved to lead to my benefit in the end.

"Good girl. Put this foot up on the ledge."

He points to my left foot. I'm not sure what is going on, but I follow his instructions. Then, before I have time to process it, he hooks a finger in my bathing suit, pulls it to the side, and has his mouth on me.

"Ahhh," I shout at the shock of it all.

But my hand is already in his hair, pushing him harder against my clit. I lift my ass off the edge and grind into his mouth. He responds with a moan of his own like he loves my pussy being shoved further onto his face.

He grabs my ass with both of his hands and keeps me in place, then he shakes his head back and forth.

"Fuck, babe," I respond. "I'm not gonna last long."

How can I when he is like an animal eating his damn prey after a long hunt? He's ravenous, almost violent, as he works me with his tongue, sucks on my clit, then shoves his fingers inside of me.

I come on a scream, not sure if any neighbors can hear, but unable to control it. I bite my lip to try and stifle my cry of satisfaction. My body is still convulsing when he pulls me into the pool and kisses me. My trembling legs cling to him as they wrap around his body.

Then I rest my head on his shoulder and let out a sigh. I didn't know I could ever feel this content. I could actually fall asleep in his arms right here in the pool.

He walks us further in towards the deep end, all while holding me to him. There are no words that are needed. We float around like this for a while until my body recovers. I pull away from him and start to swim backward.

The water is the perfect temperature, cooling my body from the humidity of the late July summer air.

We swim for over an hour, Josh challenging me to a race from one side to the other, me winning each time. I was a lifeguard, and on the swim team, he didn't stand a chance. Then we stumble upon a freaking bowling alley in the basement where we play a full game, Josh killing me. I don't mind, though. It gave his ego the boost it needed after losing to me in the pool.

We clean off in the rain shower, grab the bottle of champagne, and lie in the large bed that looks out onto the water.

I lie my head on his bare chest as I begin to rub my fingers up and down him aimlessly as we talk.

"Did you actually hate me all of these years?" I ask out of nowhere.

His fingers start to play with my hair. "I've never hated you a day of my life."

I sigh, "Neither have I."

"Are you sure about that?" he asks.

"I promise. It was just my defense mechanism because I liked you so much. I didn't want to. If anything, I hated how much I didn't hate you at all."

We lay in silence as our admission hangs in the air. I don't know why I continue. "When I was seventeen, I used to lie awake at night thinking about what a future with you would look like."

"You did?" His fingers caress my arm. "What did a future with me look like?"

"It's silly. Just remember that I was seventeen."

He chuckles. "Tell me, Freckles. I won't make fun of you."

"We lived on the water. I know that sounds crazy with the prices of homes here on the water, but it wasn't some huge home. Just a normal four-bedroom home, big enough to grow a family. It had a huge wrap-around porch with enough yard space for me to have my own garden. We had a dog named Biscuit that you said I could get if I to wake up with him every morning because you aren't a morning person. He would be tan, the color of a biscuit."

I brace myself for him to laugh or, worse, get out of bed and never want anything to do with me. I did warn him I was only seventeen at the time.

"That sounds like a perfect life, Freckles."

It does still sound like the perfect life, even better today now that I know what it's like to be with him.

"It does," I whisper back as I look up at him.

"I think we should tell your brother about us," he blurts out.

"My brother? You mean Asher?"

"Yeah. Well, your other brothers kinda guessed it at Brie's birthday party."

My head lifts off his chest. "You mean they know about us? Did you admit to it?"

He nods his head. "I didn't want to lie. Are you mad?"

"No. I'm not mad. I'm just surprised. Were they mad?"

"Shockingly, no. They were kind of...excited."

"Excited?"

"Yeah," he runs a hand through his hair. "It was the weirdest thing. They acted like they knew we wanted each other for years. I don't know if they were messing with me or not."

Well, that's not what I was expecting to hear. Liam and Eric not only being observant enough to notice something between us, but then to be excited about it.

"Huh. That is weird. So, you want to tell Asher? Well, that's a relief. Charlotte knows and I made her promise not to say anything. But she doesn't want to lie to Asher."

"I guess if Charlotte knows too, it makes sense to tell Asher. He is my best friend, after all, and I'm not going anywhere. Not where you and I are concerned."

My heart flutters. He really doesn't understand how sexy it is that he is all in and so vocal about it.

"Then, let's tell him."

He pulls at his hair like he's a bit nervous. "I'm worried he's gonna hate me."

"What? Why would he hate you?"

"Because you're his sister, his younger sister, and I'm his best friend. There are rules."

He looks so cute being all worried, the crinkles in his forehead. I lean up and kiss his cheek. "I promise you Asher won't be mad. Surprised, sure. Mad, no. Okay?"

He nods his head. His gaze drops from my eyes to my neck to my breasts. His stare turns bold and assessing. I feel like the breathless girl of seventeen when a simple look from him would make me lose my breath. I swallow tightly as I hold his stare.

Then he twists me in his arms until I'm lying underneath him. He kisses me with a hunger that makes my body shiver with anticipation.

Chapter Twenty-Three

Layla

I hop into Josh's truck with a bottle of wine and a bag of groceries. I'm wearing my favorite navy-blue dress that cuts above my knees with some gold jewelry.

Josh is in a dark blue button-down. It kind of looks like we tried to match outfits. His gaze can't seem to hold mine or anything else in the car for longer than a second. He must be really nervous. I even have some butterflies in my stomach.

We are on our way to dinner at Asher and Charlotte's, but we are mainly going to tell my brother about us.

Last weekend, after we agreed to tell him, I told Josh that I would set up a dinner at their place. Charlotte agreed to do it under the guise that she wants to hear more stories from our time in Italy.

"You ready for this?" I ask him as he taps the steering wheel with his thumbs mindlessly.

"I just want to get it over with. The anticipation is what's killing me."

I reach over and rub the back of his neck, trying to relieve some of the tension he's feeling.

"Do you want to tell him right away or have dinner first?" I ask.

"I don't want to sit through an entire dinner without telling him, but what if we tell him right away, and it ruins the evening?"

"Well, to be honest, if he reacts that poorly, then I don't want to spend the rest of the evening with him."

I really don't think he'll be angry. I mean, sure, it might be kind of weird for a while, but let's not forget about the fact that he is with my best friend, and I didn't get angry about it. I'm sure he'll be able to see that.

We pull into the driveway, and he puts the truck into the park and then turns to me. "Before we go in, I just want you to know that no matter what anyone says about us, I want to be with you. Nothing will change how I feel about you. I'm done letting what other people think keep me away from you."

His hands cup my face. He leans in and gently presses his lips to mine. It's the kind of kiss that always leaves me feeling dazed as his lips move over mine so softly and slowly. When he pulls away, every part of me wants to dive back in and forget about going inside.

But I know we need to get this over with. We open our car doors, and Josh grabs the groceries for me as we walk to the front door. Before I knock, Charlotte opens the door with a bright smile.

"Hi guys!" she exclaims. "Come on in."

We walk through the door to find Asher hanging out on the back deck with a beer. Charlotte leads us out there to join him.

Asher stands. "Hey, man." He shakes hands with Josh.

I look around for Brie but see no sign of her. "Where's my niece?"

"She's spending the night at Mom and Dad's," Asher replies. "We figured if she were here, there'd be minimal adult conversation being had."

"Yeah," I laugh. "Brie is good at being the center of attention. What do you think she will do when the baby gets here?"

"We've been talking to her about the things that will change when the baby gets here," Charlotte says as she absentmindedly runs a hand over her growing belly. "I'm sure it will be an adjustment, but she'll be fine. She's a sweetheart."

"Are you guys going to find out the sex of the baby?" Josh asks, taking a beer from Asher as we all sit down.

Asher looks over at Charlotte. "Yes. We actually get to find out in three weeks."

"I can't believe you are already that far along. This pregnancy is going to fly by," I tell them.

"I know. It's already close to the halfway mark. It's unbelievable," Charlotte agrees.

Josh looks at me from his chair, his eyebrows raised in anticipation. I think we need to do this before he loses his mind. I don't think he can focus on anything else until we get this out in the open.

"Well, before I get started in the kitchen, Josh and I had something we wanted to tell you guys," I start, including Charlotte in this so Asher doesn't realize I've already told her.

"What's that?" Asher looks at me strangely.

"Well, when Josh and I were in Italy," I say, clearing my throat and looking over at Josh. "We actually kind of discovered that there might be something more than just friendship between us."

Asher's eyes shift between mine and Josh's. "You mean you would've called yourself friends before the trip?"

Josh smiles at me. "Fine," I laugh. "We realized underneath the anger between us were feelings," I pause. "Romantic feelings."

Asher's head falls forward as he lets out what seems like a bitter laugh while he shakes his head. Josh sits up straight while we all stare at Asher. I honestly can't tell if he's pissed or not. Charlotte shrugs her shoulders at me. Even she doesn't have a clue what the hell this reaction is.

Asher lifts his head and wipes his mouth with his hand. "You mean it took Italy to make you two idiots see that?"

"Well, I don't think there's any reason for name-calling here," Josh defends. "Wait...are you pissed?"

"No, you fool. I'm relieved that this whole charade of hating each other is finally over. It's been exhausting."

"For crying out loud, you too?" Josh falls back into his chair.

"What do you mean, me too?" Asher asks with amusement.

Josh looks frustrated now for an entirely new reason, and I find it kind of adorable. Charlotte smirks at me.

"Liam and Eric guessed it at Brie's party. They said the same damn thing to me. Does everyone feel this way about us? What about you, Charlotte?"

Charlotte shrugs. "I mean…I kind of guessed there was something between you two."

Asher winks at Charlotte. "We talked about it all the time," he adds.

"It's okay, babe," I tell Josh. "We were both fools for denying it to ourselves."

"Still," Josh mutters. "It's kind of humiliating that everyone knew but didn't say anything."

I place my hand on his knee and squeeze it. "At least we admitted it to ourselves eventually."

Asher looks at my hand and cringes. "I'm definitely happy for you two, but this touchy thing is going to take some time getting used to."

Charlotte rolls her eyes. "Oh, please," she touches his knee, "they do a lot more than that in the bedroom."

Asher stands up quickly. "Ok. Sex talk is off the table. I'm sorry, but I can't hear stuff like that."

A flash of humor crosses Josh's face, but I can also tell that he is relieved Asher isn't pissed.

"Fine!" Charlotte agrees as she pulls on my brother's hand. "Just sit back down, you big baby. Ugh, Layla does the same thing to me when I try to talk about us."

Asher's eyes bug out. "You try to tell my sister about our sex life? What is wrong with you?"

"She's my best friend. I want to tell my best friend these things."

"Well, find a new best friend, because you will not be discussing our sex life with my sister."

"Hey!" I interject. "She will not find a new best friend. But I do agree that from here on out, sex talk between anyone in this group is strictly off limits."

Asher puts out a fist for me to pump. He's such a dork, but I concede and hit my fist with his.

"Well, I'm gonna go get started on dinner," I announce as I stand up.

"Ooh, I'll come help," Charlotte replies as she follows me into the kitchen.

She's beaming as I start to get the ingredients out of the fridge.

"Oh my gosh, this is so exciting!" she exclaims as she leans against the island.

I start to chop the vegetables for the salad while she snacks on pretzels in front of me.

"I thought you were going to help," I joke as I continue to chop.

She waves her hand in the air. "I just wanted to come in here and gossip. I'd just be in the way if I tried to help. Anyway, does it feel good to have it all out and in the open?"

I turn around and drizzle some olive oil in a frying pan. "It does. Although, it's not like we kept it a secret for very long. Just a couple weeks."

"True. You two have moved along very quickly in this relation-ship."

I guess we have. I mean, it's not like we're talking marriage or anything. "I'm twenty-seven. He's thirty-two. We know who we are and what we want."

"True. I mean, I'm not saying it's a bad thing. Your brother and I were living together as a family before we were even together for a year. When you know, you know."

"We'll see where it goes. I don't want to move too fast, but I have a good feeling about this."

She claps her hands excitedly. "So do I. Promise me that you'll let me have the baby before the wedding so I'm not a fat maid of honor."

I laugh as I throw the shrimp in the oil. "Did I not just say we'll see where this goes?"

"Sure you did. But I know where this is going. I feel it in my gut."

"Maybe that's just the baby you're feeling," I say with a wink.

"Haha, you're freakin' hilarious. No, this is definitely my gut talking. I've got a good sense about these things."

I don't want to admit it to her yet, but I think she's right. I've got this feeling that this is it for me. I can't imagine anyone making me feel the way that Josh does. But it's too soon to be thinking like this. I try to take my mind off the idea while I cook, but it's kind of stuck in my brain the entire time.

A wedding here in Savannah would be perfect. Somewhere underneath the southern trees. Nothing big or fancy either. I know that wouldn't be Josh's style and I like the idea of something intimate.

Once my shrimp and linguine are finished, I pour them all into a large serving bowl, and Charlotte helps me bring the salad outside. I gesture for the guys to join us at the table, where Charlotte already has all of the plates and utensils set up.

Josh pulls out my chair for me. As I take a seat, he leans down and whispers in my ear. "Did I tell you how beautiful you look in that dress?"

He takes a seat next to me. "I don't believe you have," I whisper.

He leans in to kiss me on the cheek. "Well, you do. I can't wait to get it off you tonight."

A blush must form on my cheeks because I suddenly feel warm. I can't wait for him to take it off me either.

"Thanks for cooking for us, sis. You know how much I love whatever you make." Asher scoops some pasta onto Charlotte's plate first then his.

"It's no problem. You know I love to cook, especially since I don't get to do it at the restaurant."

"Speaking of your restaurant, Charlotte told me things went well there while you were away."

"Yeah, it went really well. Zane did a great job, and I was able to enjoy the trip without worrying about anything."

Charlotte giggles. "I'm sure Josh had a hand in the distractions."

I look over at Asher who rolls his eyes. I curl my lips, so he doesn't see me smile at his discomfort. I love him like crazy and appreciate that he just wants me to be happy, but if he thinks I've gone the last year without hearing things I haven't wanted to hear or seen things I never wanted to see, then he's delusional.

The amount of times he's groped my best friend in front of me or thought he was being quiet when he whispered something dirty in her ear is too many to count.

We spend the rest of the evening telling stories about Italy and reminiscing about old times. When it's getting late, Josh starts to shift around in his seat, working up the nerve to say something.

"Well," he eventually speaks up. "I appreciate you guys having us over. It's been a great night, but I think we should get going. It's getting late."

"Thanks so much for dinner and coming over. It was so nice to have a night with another couple," Charlotte says as we all get up off our chairs and walk back inside.

Asher pulls Josh aside and starts saying something to him that I can't quite make out. Josh is nodding along the entire time, then they shake hands.

Charlotte looks at me and shrugs her shoulders. Then the guys meet us at the front door, where we all give hugs and say goodnight.

Asher hugs me last. "I'm really happy for you, sis. But you tell me if he fucks up, and I'll kick his ass. I've always got your back."

"Thanks," I laugh. "I think."

Josh grabs my hand, and we walk to his truck, where he opens the door for me. I feel complete relief that this is all done and out in the open. My brothers all know, and nobody is angry.

I like that Josh just drives back to his house, knowing that I'm coming home with him. We're starting to get into this routine of staying at each other's places.

"That went well," he says as he grabs my hand.

"It did."

"He didn't even punch me."

I chuckle. "Were you expecting to get punched this evening?"

"It was a definite possibility in my mind. I've seen your brother pissed off before. You don't want to be the one on the receiving end of his fury."

"Ah, he's all bark and no bite. He wouldn't hurt a fly."

He throws his head back and laughs. "You haven't seen the other side of him."

"Oh, please, both of you guys are big softies. Hiding behind your scary emotions, but in reality, you're the nice ones."

He parks his truck in his driveway and then looks at me in a way that makes me need to rub my thighs together. "Did you just call me a softie?"

I bite my lip and lean further back against my side of the car. "I may have. What are you gonna do about it?"

"That's it," he says as he takes off his seatbelt, but I'm out of the car before he can get me. "You better run, Freckles."

I take off into the house, sprinting up the stairs while I can feel him hot on my heels. It's that terrifying feeling when you don't know when, or if, the person behind you will get you, like playing tag, but this time, I don't think I'll mind if I get caught.

I'm turning the corner into the hallway when I feel an arm wrap around me and lift me off the ground.

"You aren't going anywhere," he growls in my ear.

He takes large strides into the bedroom where he throws me down on the mattress. I turn around onto my back and look up at him. His eyes are smoldering as they focus on me. His lips are pressed into a hard line, yet there's a slight twitch to them, hinting at a playful side underneath.

Then he sheds himself of his shorts and grips his length. "I'm no softie, Freckles. There's not a damn part of me that is soft when it's around you," he says while running his hand up and down his hard dick.

My body shivers at the sight. I don't think I'll ever not react to watching him do this in front of me.

He lets himself go and grabs my dress, pulling the straps down and almost ripping it down my body, then throws it on the floor. He does the same to my underwear until I'm lying in only my bra.

But he doesn't seem to have the patience for that right now.

He steps forward, grabs under my legs, and pulls me to the end of the bed.

"Do you want to feel how not soft I am for you?"

He starts to tease me with his dick as he runs it along my soaked pussy. I suck in a breath at the sensations, especially when he reaches my clit.

"Talk to me, baby. Tell me that you want my hard dick inside of you."

"I want it," I beg breathlessly. "Please, give me your hard dick."

He smirks down at me. "Good girl."

Then he pushes inside of me until he bottoms out, and we both let out a satisfied moan. He cages me in with his arms and thrusts in and out with purpose until I'm clenching around him and screaming his name.

Chapter Twenty-Four

Josh

"So, you finally got it over with and told him," Liam yells over the music in the bar. "Did he get pissed?"

"No," I admit. "He was really cool about it."

I look over at Asher who is talking with Charlotte and Layla by the pool table. He really has been great about everything. This entire week at work, he didn't treat me any differently. He will never know how much it means to me that he trusts me with his sister.

"Told you," Eric nudges my arm. "Don't sell yourself short. You're a good guy."

"Uh, thanks. Anyway, did you catch the game yesterday?" I ask, desperate to change the subject.

I'm not sure why I'm so uncomfortable with any type of compliment. Probably because I never got any growing up. I don't know how to take it.

It means the world to me that these guys, my family, think highly of me. When you have parents who never noticed you a day of your life, it fucks with your head. All these years I've thought it was something I did, but maybe it was them.

The entire Williams family is beginning to make me see that I'm more than what my parents told me I was. Part of me wants to call them up and tell them off for how they've neglected me, but I'll probably just end up the one who gets hurt when they don't show any remorse.

Eric and Liam get called over to play pool. I take a sip of my beer and feel a small set of arms wrap around my neck. My smile is instant.

I turn around and see her looking up at me with dreamy eyes. I can't believe those are reserved for me.

"Hey, beautiful," I wrap an arm around her waist.

"Do you know how many times we would be out at this bar, and I would do everything in my power not to stare at you all night? It would piss me off because I wanted to want anyone but you."

"Each time you looked baby, it was after I forced myself to drag my eyes away from you. It would ruin my night if you spent the evening flirting with another guy. I would go home and be in the worst mood for days."

My lips take hers in a searing kiss. I get to take her home with me tonight and hopefully every night for the rest of our lives.

"Hey, get a room, you two. None of us want to actually see your love," Liam shouts across the room.

Layla covers her lips while she rolls her eyes.

"They'll get used to it," I tell her with a wink.

"So, you two…" a familiar voice interrupts, making my skin crawl in annoyance.

William is standing there in his stupid polo shirt with the collar popped up and far too much hair gel in his hair.

I tighten my grip around her waist. It's been a couple of years since I've seen him, but I still want to punch him in the face. He just looks like a douchebag; never mind the way he acts.

"Yes," I tell him with authority. "Us two."

"Hi, William," Layla says while tucking a piece of her hair behind her ear. A clear tell that she's nervous right now.

"How are you doin'?" he asks Layla, ignoring me.

"I'm doing good. Same old. Just restaurant and hanging out with friends. What about you?"

He stands taller and adjusts his belt. "Just got promoted to president at my dad's company. He's retiring soon."

"Wow. Congratulations," she replies. "Sounds like exactly what you were working towards."

"It is. You know, you're too pretty to be slaving away in that restaurant. You should be with someone who can take care of you."

He looks over at me the same way he always used to. Like I'm not good enough to be in their presence. I wonder if he ever even considered talking to her like a person and not some petulant child who's being stubborn by working in a "restaurant."

I squeeze her side when I feel her muscles tense. "I love working in my restaurant. That will never change, no matter who I'm involved with."

"I'm sure once you have kids, that will change."

Man, this asshole just keeps going. It's like the idiot can't take the hint. I'm literally standing here with my arm around her and he's basically asking her to marry him. The nerve. But this time, she isn't seventeen. He can't hold that over my head, nor can he make me feel like he can provide more for her, not more of what really matters.

I'm the one who will love and support her while he will just treat her like a trophy wife. She will be there to look pretty and cook for him.

"I think we can let Layla decide what she wants. She has a brain and even knows how to use it," I reply sharply.

Before William can respond, Layla steps in. "Well, it was so nice to see you, William. Congratulations again on the promotion."

She grabs my hand and pulls me away even though I wasn't done with the guy. I turn back around to see if he's watching and am met with a cold look filled with jealousy. I could be the nice guy and just walk away like Layla is trying to do, but I'm not.

This man made me think I wasn't good enough for her, and we lost ten years together because of him.

So, instead of walking away, I whip her around and slam my lips down on hers. I let my tongue mix with hers in a grueling kiss. I want him to see how hot we are for each other. I want him to witness what my lips can do to her.

When I pull away, she's breathless. Thoroughly kissed with swollen lips and a dazed look in her eyes.

I smile down at her. "Just so he knows who you belong to."

"I thought you made it pretty clear that I'm my own person to him," she raises an eyebrow.

I grab her ass and pull her against me. "Baby, you are your own person, but you are also *my* person, and he needs to know that. Got it?"

She nods her head and then leans in for a kiss. "I like you being all jealous and possessive of me."

I growl into her mouth. "I can show you possessive anytime. We can go home right now, and I'll give you possessive."

"I look forward to it," she says with a wink, then walks over to Charlotte.

I walk over to the guys and do my best to shake off our little interaction with her ex, but it wears on me the rest of the night. The stupid past is somehow repeating itself. Why did we have to run into him, of all people? And why is he still trying to go after her? Can't he find another woman to marry him for his money or is his personality that repellent?

Chapter Twenty-Five

Layla

"Okay, so she's already had some dinner, but since it's still kind of early, she will want a snack. She can have fruit and some milk," Charlotte says as we try to shuffle her out of the house.

"Got it. Fruit and milk," I agree. "Now, go out and have fun."

Josh is holding Brie while I get rid of Charlotte and my brother. Asher wants to take her out to dinner, so Josh and I agreed to babysit.

"Thanks so much for doing this," Asher says. "We owe you two. Bye, baby girl, have fun with Aunt Layla and Uncle Josh."

Wow. Josh has always been called Uncle Josh, but hearing our names together like that, like we're married. It makes my entire body break out into goosebumps. I want that, and I want it with him.

I close the door and turn around. Josh and Brie are smiling back at me, and I think my heart explodes into a million pieces.

"So, what does my favorite niece want to do?" I ask as I walk back into the kitchen with them.

"I want to play hide and seek."

"Ooh," Josh replies. "I must warn you that I'm awesome at hide and seek."

Brie giggles in his arms. "I bet you can't find me."

"I'm seeking first?" Josh asks.

She nods her head. "Uh huh. Come on, Auntie Lay-lay. Let's go hide."

Josh winks at me then covers his eyes and starts counting. "I'm only counting to thirty. You guys better hurry."

He begins counting while Brie and I run up the stairs.

She stands frozen in the hallway. "Where should I hide?"

Instead of pointing out that she just bragged to Josh about her hiding ability, I grab her hand and lead her to the laundry hamper at the end of the hallway. I open it, and it's miraculously empty.

"Would you be too afraid to hide in here?" I whisper.

She shakes her head, so I lift her up and place her down inside. Then I hear Josh on twenty downstairs, so I put the lid back on (making sure to crack it for air and start to scramble around for a spot.

I run into the guest bedroom and panic as I hear him shout that he's coming. Crap, I open the closet and try to wedge myself between some of the clothes.

This is such a weak spot. Although, I don't know why I care so much. We are doing this to entertain the four-year-old, not for me to actually show him up. But I just so happen to be super competitive.

The sound of doors opening and closing downstairs, as well as his empty threats of finding us, make me smile.

Then I hear him coming upstairs, and I hold my breath. He's being so dramatic. Every door he opens, he makes an 'aha' sound, like he just found someone.

That's when I hear the giggles coming from the hallway. I shake my head as I listen to Brie snicker inside the basket. I wait in anticipation for him to find her, but then I hear footsteps come into the guest bedroom.

At first, they sound like they are getting further, maybe from the other side of the room, but then I hear them get closer and closer. Light shines into the closet as he opens the door. I stand as straight as I can against the back of the wall, behind the clothes.

I hear a choked laugh, then the clothes part, and he is staring at me. "Found you, Freckles."

Stepping forward, I cross my arms across my chest. "It's only because I used all of my time to help Brie," I whisper so she doesn't hear me.

"Aw," he throws an arm around my shoulder. "Don't feel bad. I'm sure you'll do better next time. Now," he says louder as we walk into the hall. "Where can that little booger be?"

More giggles.

We both look at each other and silently laugh together at how damn cute she is.

"Is she in here?" he asks as he swings open a hallway closet door. "No, she's not in there."

More giggles.

"Is she in here?" he continues as he jumps into her bedroom. "Nooo, she's not in there."

More giggles.

"Wait a minute. Did I hear something?" he asks.

More giggles.

"I think I know where she is," he says as he walks back into the hallway.

More giggles.

He stands in front of the hamper while I lean against the wall and watch. He's always been good with her, but I don't think I've had this intimate of an experience with the two of them where I can really see just how great he is.

"How about in here?" He throws the lid off the hamper, and she screams with laughter then stands up.

"You found me, Uncle Josh!" she exclaims.

He lifts her out of the basket and onto his shoulder. She hangs off him and squeals with delight.

"I found you, you little rug rat."

"Aunt Lay-lay, he found me."

I come up behind them, laughing as she hangs upside down. "He did find you. I wonder how."

"I couldn't stop laughing," she giggles in delight.

We walk downstairs where we end up playing with her toys for a while. Then we settle down with some fruit and a TV show before bed. Josh gives her a kiss on the cheek before I take her upstairs.

She's an easy kid who just needs a nighttime story and a kiss before bed. When I walk back down, Josh has two glasses of wine waiting.

He hands me one.

"Thank you," I reply. "Would you like to sit out on the dock? I have the monitor so we can see if she gets out of bed."

"Sounds great."

We walk outside and down to the dock, where two adirondack chairs are positioned at the end. We take a seat together and look out at the beautiful sunset on the water.

He leans in until I smell his delicious cologne. "Cheers," he says. "To our first joint babysitting venture together."

I clink our glasses together and laugh. "We should start a business together. How much do you think they're paying us for tonight?"

"It better be at least twenty an hour. I'm no fool at what the going rate is these days."

I chuckle and take a sip of my wine. "Mmm, this wine is so good, but I miss my friend's wine."

"Oh, you got a wine person?" he asks slightly sarcastically.

"Shut up, it's not like that. I met her at this networking event years ago. She's in the wine business and obviously works with restaurants. But she lives in Cleveland, so I don't get to see her very often. She just knows all of the good wine."

"Well, why don't you just buy the bottles she recommends?"

"It's not that easy. She will recommend bottles that aren't sold in our local liquor store. Although, I should call her up and tell her I want her to send me another case of bottles."

"A case? That sounds like an alcoholic talking right there."

"Oh, stop it. That is very common in the wine world."

After we finish our glasses, he keeps looking at me funny. Could it be that he's drunk?

No, that's ridiculous. We only had one glass.

"Come here," he says as he pats his leg.

"What?"

"Come here. I want to snuggle with you and watch the sunset."

Swoon. I literally don't think I can handle the way he talks to me so openly. I shiver a bit as I sit on his lap and lie back.

He wraps his arms around me and kisses my cheek.

"Are you cold?" he whispers.

"It's you," I admit.

"Me? I make you cold?" he asks in confusion.

I turn my head up and look at him. "No, you make me shiver. Everything you do or say can make my body react like I'm seventeen again."

We both exchange this intimate embrace with our gaze as the world around us fades away. The moment transcends words. It's a silent conversation between the two of us, where our eyes reflect our soul's deepest thoughts and feelings.

My heart races as my body is ignited with a spark that only he knows how to light.

"Freckles," he whispers softly.

"Yes?"

"I love you."

My chest fills with a mix of emotions. The words hang in the air as I process the weight of his declaration. In this moment, everything has changed. I feel it deep down in my heart that this is the start of something amazing.

My heart is frantically beating as I catch my breath enough to say, "I love you, too."

He kisses my lips gently, then rests his head on my shoulder, wrapping his arms around me tightly. We watch the sunset in silence, but I know nothing will ever be the same.

Chapter Twenty-Six

Layla

"Are you kidding me?" Zane gasps in my office. "He told you he loves you? Girl, you must be dynamite in bed. It's only been like three weeks."

It's only been two days since he told me, but I still feel different. Knowing he feels that way has brought me an odd sense of calm.

"I'd like to think it was more than my bedroom skills that led him to say that," I tell him as I head towards the door. "Has the lunch rush started yet?"

We walk down the hallway towards the kitchen, where I see my team diligently working.

"We're about seventy-five percent full already. I think in the next half-hour, we will be maxed out."

It's still surreal that my restaurant is such a hot spot for lunch and dinner. I've worked my butt off to make sure the menu was trendy, and yet it still feels like you are getting something familiar.

"That's great. I'm just going to do a walk-through in the dining area to make sure everything is running smoothly out there."

I head over to the front of the restaurant to see how the hostesses are doing. Mindy and Becca are the two on the schedule today.

"Hi, girls," I say to them as I join them behind the stand. "How's everything going up here? Are we at a wait time yet?"

Mindy smiles at me. "Hi, Layla. We're getting close. I think we'll hit a fifteen-minute wait time soon."

"That's great. Do you need anything while you're up here? Something to drink? I can cover if one of you needs to go to the bathroom," I offer.

These girls are generally stuck up here during high-traffic times, so I try to make sure they are comfortable.

"No, I think we're good," Becca says. "Thanks for the offer."

I turn around to make sure the menus are stocked adequately. As I shuffle through them, trying to make them straight, I hear the girls whispering to each other.

"Oh my god, Becca. It's him. He's back. Ugh, he's so hot," Mindy whispers.

"Look at him in that black shirt," Becca responds. "You should ask him out."

I turn around to see who these two are talking about like that on the job. Clearly, it's a regular.

"Hey, sis," Asher stands there with a smile on his face.

He's in his white shirt with Josh next to him—my Josh, in a black shirt. My two hostesses were standing there crushing on *my* man. Becca even encouraged Mindy to ask him out.

I look at Mindy. Her long blonde hair, petite figure, and blue eyes. She's only twenty-three, but I doubt that would stop any man Josh's age from being with her.

What is Josh doing with someone like me when he can have his choice of any woman, like Mindy?

"Hi, Ash," I smile at him. "Josh."

"Hi, Freckles," he smiles at me.

"I'll seat them, ladies. What table?"

I see the look of disappointment on their faces as they look down at the sheet.

"Table 43," Mindy says sadly.

I grab two menus and walk the guys through the dining area, weaving around tables until we get to the table in the far corner. The girls didn't even ask them where they wanted to be seated. They must know the guys want to be inside to enjoy the air conditioning and, in the back, away from the crowd.

I wonder how many times they've been seated by Mindy and Becca. Does Josh notice them? What am I thinking? Of course, he does. He's a man after all.

We get to their table, and I place their menus down then turn around as I struggle to display a smile on my face. I don't want Josh to know I'm being irrationally jealous just because a beautiful woman thinks he's hot.

"Thanks, beautiful," Josh says as he leans in and kisses my cheek.

My cheeks redden at his public display of affection. I sneak a glance at Becca and Mindy at the front who are talking to guests. Dammit. I wish they saw that. I know that seems very high school, but I don't care.

"You're welcome," I smile up at him, noticing that he is resting his chin on his hand and smirking at me.

Asher sighs. "I can't wait until you two are passed this annoying beginning phase of the relationship. All the dreamy looks and constant touching." He makes a disgusted face.

Josh chuckles as he grabs his menu. "Layla had to put up with it with you and Charlotte."

"Yeah, well, I don't think we were as bad as you two."

Josh and I both start to crack up. That's the most ridiculous thing I've heard all day.

"You two still can't stop touching each other," Josh replies.

"Whatever. We didn't have the whole dreamy looks going on."

Josh winks at me. I tuck my hair behind my ear. "Well, I'll let you two look over the menu. Your server will be with you soon. Let me know if you need anything."

I walk away from the table and find myself pulled directly into a dilemma in the kitchen. From there, it's one thing after another. Zane is busy trying to order food from our purveyor, a task I have always done but have recently given to him in an effort to further let go of my control issues.

But since he's busy, that leaves me to manage today. I think it's about time I thought about hiring an assistant manager. I would like to have an option to work from home if I am dealing with office stuff.

I can't believe these thoughts are even crossing my mind. It's all thanks to the man sitting across the room from me. I look over at him, just to find him smiling over at me.

Every time I've stolen a glance in his direction, he's watching me. Any insecurities I had earlier about Mindy are gone. He hasn't looked in her direction even once. For some reason, he only seems to see me.

Chapter Twenty-Seven

Josh

I change my shirt for the tenth time, looking in the mirror at the button-down blue one I'm wearing. I actually ironed the damn thing, so I look clean and well presented. My hair is styled with some gel in it that I hardly ever use. I didn't go crazy with it, just enough to keep it looking neat without looking like I actually put any stupid gel in it to begin with.

I'm going to an end-of-the-summer barbeque at Layla's parents' house. It's already almost mid-August, and school is about to start back up for the kids. That is usually when everyone, even if they have no kids, throws their end-of-the-summer bash.

It's one last social event before the madness of the year begins and the weather gets colder.

I'm letting my stupid insecurities get the best of me because tonight Layla wants to tell her parents about the two of us. She is acting like it's the most casual thing in the world. Like we are going to walk into the party hand in hand, and they are going to nod a head and walk away.

I picture it going a bit differently than that. I picture her mom's face turning up at the idea of her daughter dating a man who works in manual labor while her father shakes his head in agreement with his wife.

Now, I'm not saying that her parents are bad people or have ever treated me differently. But I see the men her mom tries to set her up with, or the man, William, she is always talking about her getting back together with.

If that's the vision they have for their little girl, then I will be a major disappointment. And as much as I want to say screw them, who cares what they think, I'm also aware that she loves her parents, and I don't want to damage their relationship.

I promised I would pick her up at three, so I put on a splash of cologne and ran out to my truck.

When I park my car, I don't even have time to cut my engine before she's out the door with a big smile on her face.

Fuck, I love her.

This is the calmest I've felt all day. It's a feeling that happens in an instant when I'm with her.

She opens the door, dressed in a dark green dress, and hops into the truck. "Hi, babe," she says, then leans in for a kiss.

I need her kiss to distract me, so I put my hand behind her head and slam my tongue into her mouth. She seems caught off guard at first, but it doesn't take long for her to match my intensity. I want to live in this moment with her, just the two of us, for as long as I can.

She climbs into my lap, her dress scrunching at her hips, and puts all her weight down on my dick. I wasn't trying to take it this far, but I'm also not complaining.

"Are you okay?" she asks as we continue to devour each other's mouths.

"Just a little," I start when I can get a word in, "nervous."

She pulls away breathlessly. "You're nervous, babe?"

I bite my lip, slightly embarrassed, but nod my head. Then she proves to be the best girlfriend in the world.

She pulls the straps of her dress down until her breasts are exposed. "Do you need a little distraction?"

I grin. "It wouldn't hurt to try."

I grab one of her tits and wrap my lips around her nipple. She moans in response and wiggles her ass on my dick. I'm only thinking about how badly I want to sink my dick into her pussy and not at all about the party.

While I switch to her other nipple, she unbuckles my belt and unzips me until she frees my straining dick. Then she pulls her pink panties to the side and slides down my dick.

I lean my head back on the headrest and watch her as she takes control. Her hands hold tightly onto my broad shoulders for leverage. I grip her ass and help her move.

Her jaw falls as I watch her start to become frantic with need.

"You like riding my dick, Freckles?"

"Yes," she pants as she continues riding me.

When I feel her walls start to tighten around me, I decide I want the final thrusts.

"Lean back, baby," I demand.

She follows my directions instantly, leaning back towards my steering wheel. I don't even give a fuck if she honks my horn and draws attention to us. Let everybody watch me take her to orgasm, it's a beautiful thing to witness.

I grip her hip with one hand then start to rub circles around her swollen clit with the thumb of my other hand. I thrust upward as hard and fast as I can until we are both coming at the same time. Her tits bounce and shake as she screams out her orgasm.

I love how free she is with me. She never holds back. Once I've emptied myself out inside of her, she adjusts her straps and climbs back into her side of the seat.

"I think I'm gonna need to run inside and change my underwear before we go," she giggles as she opens the door and runs inside.

The thought of her sitting in my cum all night is tempting as fuck if we weren't going to her parents' house.

She comes running back outside and hops in my truck.

"Okay. I'm all clean now."

"I kinda like you dirty," I joke as I put the truck in reverse.

It's not even fifteen minutes later, and I'm pulling into their large driveway. Most people have parked in the street, but Layla insists we can park in the driveway.

We hop out, and I do my best to straighten my slightly wrinkled clothes. I still don't regret taking her in my truck. I could never regret a second of my time with her.

She takes my hand and leads me around the house and into the backyard, which has a large white tent. That's one thing about Stella and Dan's parties: They are always catered with a rented tent fit for a wedding reception.

I suppose if you have the money, it could be nice to never do any work to prep for a party, but I kind of like standing by the grill with a beer and the guys.

We spot her brothers sitting at a table under the tent along with Charlotte. Layla makes a beeline for them and immediately takes a seat next to Charlotte.

I'm so damn thankful her brothers know and are cool with it. That makes this so much easier. Maybe they'll have my back if her parents don't react well.

Liam looks me up and down. "What in the world are you wearing?" he asks as his head falls back with laughter.

"Seriously, dude," Asher joins in. "Why are you in a button-down, and why is it tucked in?"

"Fuck off, assholes. We're telling your parents about us tonight."

I look around the yard for the full-service bar and spot it just outside the tent behind me. Thank fuck.

"I need a beer before I deal with more of your shit," I tell them and turn around.

I'm standing behind a hoity-toity couple. The man is dressed similar to me, which makes my skin crawl, and the woman is in a fancy dress that looks like she should be at an actual wedding, not a backyard barbeque.

They order their drinks and stick a one-dollar bill in the tip jar. Classy. For all the money they are probably worth, I think they could afford more than a dollar tip, especially when they aren't even paying for their drinks.

The bartender doesn't seem phased as she plasters on a smile for me. "Good evening, sir. What can I get you?"

I nod my head. "Good evening. I'll take one of those beers and a glass of your red."

Once she gets me the drinks, I take a ten-dollar bill and place it in her jar.

I walk back to the table and hand Layla her wine while she's animatedly talking to Charlotte.

"Sorry, Charlotte. I'd get you a drink but…" I look around me. "Do Stella and Dan know?"

She pats me on the arm. "You're so sweet. Yes, they know. We announced to the rest of the family shortly after you got back from Italy."

"So, you guys are telling Mom and Dad tonight?" Eric asks across the table after I take the empty seat next to Layla.

"Yeah, why?" Layla asks as she takes a sip of her wine.

Eric shrugs. "Just wondering why your man is dressed like one of the preppy douches floating around here."

Layla sits up straight, eyebrows raised. "That's not very nice."

Eric has been acting more and more irritable lately. I don't know what the hell is going on at work or in his personal life, but he's about to snap. He's had a rough couple of years, but it's getting increasingly obvious that he is just getting worse, not better.

I squeeze Layla's thigh, signaling to her to let it go. It's not worth it right now.

"So, where are Mom and Dad?" she asks as she looks around the crowd.

"You know Mom," Liam replies. "She's walking around saying hello to every single guest while Dad tries his hardest to get away."

Asher chuckles. "Sounds about right."

"Where's Brie?" I ask, noticing her absence.

"We hired our neighbor's daughter to babysit her for the night. I didn't have the energy to chase her around, nor did I want to pass her off to anyone else," Charlotte replies.

"I would've watched her," I tell her, wishing she was here. She would be a great distraction. "And how old is this babysitter?"

Asher looks at me strangely. "She's in high school. Why? Are you insinuating we didn't do a thorough check of who is watching our daughter?"

I shrug my shoulders. "Just wondering if you chose someone who's trustworthy and old enough."

Charlotte laughs. "She's seventeen and a great girl."

Over the course of the next hour, we eat, drink, talk, and laugh with each other. I almost forget that we still have to say hi to her parents when they suddenly appear at our table.

"Layla, when did you get here?" her mother asks.

"I've been here awhile, Ma. You've been busy mingling."

"Oh, and Josh, how lovely to see you," Stella says happily.

I stand up and give her a kiss on the cheek. "Nice to see you too, Stella."

I shake Dan's hand and take my seat again. Asher raises an eyebrow at me with a little smirk, and if I could, I'd flick him off right now. They all think it's funny because I've never told anyone but Layla how I feel. She grabs my hand under the table.

This is it. She's about to tell them, I can tell.

"Why don't you two sit down and join us for a minute?" she suggests.

Stella looks around at the guests. "I think we can do that. We've made our way to all of the guests, and everyone seems to be mingling."

I sit up straighter, waiting for Layla to continue, when Stella and Dan's names are called from behind them.

Mother fucker. William and his parents are walking towards us.

"Oh, Martha and Frank. It is so good to see two. Won't you join us? We just sat down to chat with our children for a bit. Oh, William, you're here too. Won't you join us as well," Stella says as she beams at them.

My stomach churns as I watch William smugly take a seat next to his parents and then wink at me.

I haven't seen this fucker in years, and now this is twice in two weeks. Did I do something in another life to deserve this shitty luck?

"So," Martha says to Stella and Dan, "how are things going?"

"Oh, everything is lovely. Charlotte and Asher are expecting, so we are thrilled to have another grandbaby on the way."

"Congratulations. What wonderful news," Martha replies.

I watch the table exchange pleasantries while my entire body itches to get away. It shouldn't be this hard to tell her parents that we are a couple. Why is this happening? I'm not sure how long I zone out, but Layla appears with another beer and wine. She takes a seat next to me.

"Oh, and William just found out that he will be taking over at the company. Frank has finally agreed to retire."

"I'm sure you're so proud," Stella replies.

"I guess I'll be doing business with you from now on, William," Dan jokes.

"Watch out. I'm smarter than my old man," William says while they share a laugh.

I look around at the rest of the table. Liam rolls his eyes and looks away. At least I'm not the only one who sees through the bullshit of this conversation.

"Oh, Layla, when are you going to give my poor William another chance?" Martha looks over at Layla with a mischievous smile. "I don't know if you heard, but he is now the president of the company."

"That's right, my dear," Frank cuts in. "You won't have to work another day in your life."

Red, hot anger is now coursing through my veins. This is where William gets it. I almost feel sorry for the poor chump. He was bound to turn out this way with parents like this. Not that my parents are any better.

Mine are far worse. At least his are bragging about him and not treating him like a bug to be squashed.

Stella claps her hands together. "Oh, how sweet would that be. We'd love to see Layla settle down and with someone like William, who is so eager to take care of her."

I see Layla's shoulders deflate while Asher, Eric, and Liam are all cringing. They all know that must be a low blow for me.

I can't sit through anymore of this matchmaking. Standing, I straighten my shoulders, turn on my heel, and stride away. I don't know where the hell I'm going, but I find myself at the edge of the lawn looking out at the water.

I try to take deep breaths, reminding myself that I'm older now and that what others say or think about me doesn't matter. But even I can smell my own bullshit. I realize I've been gone for some time. I'm sure Layla will be looking for me, so I peek over at the tent to see if I can find her.

But instead of a worried girlfriend, she is still sitting at the table laughing at something William's mother is saying.

I'm stunned.

Is there a part of her that wants to be with William? Why is she sitting there with them and not coming to find me?

I feel like a needy piece of shit right now. All I want to do is storm over there and make a scene to let everyone at that table know that she is taken. But the more I stand and watch everyone laughing, the more I end up feeling like an outsider to their world.

Everything I felt comes flooding back. Then it happens: William finds me from across the yard and winks. It's like I've traveled back ten years to that very night when he made me feel the same way I'm feeling right now.

Nothing has changed.

My breathing is erratic, my body is trembling with anger, and I am in no condition to go back to that table. I can't be here for another second.

Instead of doing the honorable thing and saying goodbye, I prove to everyone that I'm the low-class man that they think I am, and I leave.

I storm around the house, hop into my truck, say a little prayer of thanks that no one is parked behind me, and leave.

Chapter Twenty-Eight

Layla

"Do you know where Josh went?" I ask Asher as I scan the backyard.

He shrugs his shoulders. "Not after he stormed off during your little matchmaking sesh."

Ugh, that was the absolute worst. I can't believe my parents had the audacity to sit there and continually put me in that position. It's so awkward and completely unnecessary.

"Yeah, that was brutal. Did you see his face? He looked wrecked," Liam joins in.

"I don't know why he stormed off. If he stayed, we could have put an end to it right there and just told everybody about us."

Why did he storm off? I know it's annoying, but I thought he wanted to tell my parents. William is an asshole. He always will be. I thought we were passed that.

I walk around the yard three more times, then go back into the house. Then I go outside to the driveway, and my breath catches in my throat. He's gone.

I can't believe he left. He left without telling me. What the hell?

Tears begin to burn my eyes as panic begins to take over. Did I screw up? What did I do wrong?

I didn't realize he was even taking the entire thing seriously. I think about his confession to me about not being good enough in the eyes of my parents. How he dressed completely unlike himself tonight to impress them, and how nervous he was.

All this just to have his worst fears thrown in his face before we can even tell my parents.

Shit. I fucked up. I should've stopped that conversation immediately and told everyone at that table proudly that Josh and I were together.

I'm just so shitty in those awkward situations. Surely, he will forgive me for not knowing what to do. Right?

I pull my phone from my pocket and call him again. With each ring, tears start to run further down my face. No answer.

Charlotte and Asher are walking out when they spot me.

"Layla," Charlotte says as she walks up to me. "Sweetie, are you crying? What's going on? Did you find him?"

"He left," I say through thick tears.

"Without telling you?" Asher asks, surprise evident on his face. "What the fuck?"

I wipe my tears away with the back of my hand. "I screwed up. There's a history there with him and William. I should've stepped in. I should've said something sooner."

"You can't blame yourself for this, Layla. You didn't do anything wrong. It was just unfortunate timing." Charlotte rubs my arm soothingly.

I shake my head back and forth. "You guys don't know all the details. It took a lot for him to be here tonight to tell Mom and Dad. I could've handled it better."

Asher scoffs. "Well, even if that's true, him just leaving you behind without a word is bullshit. Didn't he drive you?"

"Yeah," I whisper.

"I'm gonna kill him." Asher looks between me and Charlotte. "He's dead."

Charlotte rolls her eyes. "Okay, he messed up. But let's not pretend like you don't know the guy. He's not all of a sudden a bad guy. I'm sure he'll cool off and apologize. Don't pretend like you haven't screwed up before."

Asher huffs at Charlotte's response, but luckily doesn't have much to say back. He has screwed up before and can't deny it.

I mouth a silent thank you in her direction. I'm already in panic mode. I don't need to worry about Asher beating the shit out of my boyfriend.

"Come on." Charlotte throws her arm around me. "We'll drive you home."

The car ride is silent. My eyes are glued to the phone, waiting for him to call. His silence is deafening, and I hate to be that girl, but I decide to send a text.

Me: I'm sorry. I should've said something. I'm not good in those situations. Please call me back. Asher and Charlotte

are driving me home right now. Do you want to come over and talk?

By the time we get to my house, there is still no response.

"Do you want us to come in?" Charlotte asks after Asher parks the car.

"No, thanks. I'm just gonna get in my pajamas and relax. Thanks for the ride home."

As I climb out of the car, I hear Asher mumbling something about Josh being a dead man again. I don't have the energy to respond, so I close the door.

I lock my front door and head straight for my bedroom. There's nothing I want more than to get in cozy clothes, hop in my bed, and turn on a comforting show. In moments like these, I need the comfort of a show that I've seen a thousand times.

It's like having your best friends right there with you.

I put on New Girl, but Nick and Schmidt aren't making me even crack a smile. Nothing at this point is going to make me feel better.

My phone rings, muffled underneath my pillow. I grab it quickly and see Josh's name.

"Hey," I answer quickly, trying not to sound too desperate.

"Hi," he replies faintly.

"Josh, I'm so sorry. I know tonight was a complete disaster."

He laughs bitterly. "Yeah, you can say that again."

"Why did you leave me?" I falter in the stillness of the room.

I can just make out the sound of a sigh through the phone. "I'm sorry, Freckles. I shouldn't have done that. It was a huge mistake, and totally uncalled for."

"I had to get a ride with Asher and Charlotte."

"Do they hate me?"

"Asher's not pleased," I admit.

"I deserve it. That wasn't fair to you. I was just so angry."

"At me? Is that why you left?" I ask, my voice fragile.

There's a long pause on the line. It makes my stomach ache with dread as I wait for his response.

"I was mad at everyone. Mad at your parents for thinking someone like William would be a good match for their daughter. Mad at William for playing me like that again. Mad at you for not standing up for me."

I knew it. He is mad at me. I should've said something.

"I'm sorry, Josh. I'm not good in those situations. I don't know what to say to my parents, and I don't want to be rude to my dad's clients," I cry. "But you didn't have to leave me. I don't understand that reaction. It was childish."

He sighs. "It was completely out of line. You're right. The person I'm mad at most is myself. I reacted just as William wanted me to."

"What do you mean?"

"Nothing. He just winked at me a couple of times, knowing exactly what it was doing to me. He wanted to get under my skin, and I let him."

William really needs a kick to the groin. Someone needs to put him in his place.

"I'm sorry he did that to you. It was totally uncalled for."

I can't believe this is how the evening turned out. I was so excited this morning to tell my parents. I've finally found someone that I love. Someone that I can see myself spending the rest of my life with.

"Do you want to come over?" I ask, needing to feel his arms around me. I don't want to go to bed alone after our first fight.

There's this hollow feeling inside of me that only he can fill.

"I think I'm just gonna crash here. I'm exhausted. And about how I acted tonight, Freckles. You deserved better, and I fucked up."

"Oh, um, okay. I forgive you. It was a shitty situation all around."

"I'll call you later. Alright?"

That doesn't sound promising. Call me later, not see me later. Nothing about this feels right, but I'm too scared to press him on it.

"Ok," I whisper, trying to hold in my tears.

"Goodnight," he says.

"Goodnight."

I hang up the phone, and the last fragments of my composure are swept away. I slide down my pillow as my breath hitches in my throat. Tears well up in my eyes, blurring my vision. For a moment, I try to blink them away, but the effort is futile.

Then, like a dam breaking, sobs wrack my body as I bury my face in my pillow. The room around me fades as I lie alone while my thoughts spiral.

Chapter Twenty-Nine

I was looking forward to work today. After spending all of my Sunday moping around my house feeling sorry for myself, I knew I needed to get out of there and keep my mind occupied.

That's the thing about love, right? It'll make your highs high, but damn does it make your lows low.

I know I fucked up the other night. I let someone small and insignificant get in my head and play on my weakness.

I'm not sure if I'll always struggle with these insecurities. It's been a part of me since I was a child, and childhood trauma is real and lasting. But what I do know is that I don't want it to get in the way of the one person in my life that makes me feel whole.

Layla has made a mark on me from the moment she came into my life. Even when she was an innocent seventeen-year-old, I felt the pull immediately.

"Hey guys," I shout to my team as I come around the corner. "Why don't you go take your lunch now? I think we're at a good stopping point."

One of the guys places their tool down. "Not gonna say no to that, boss. Let's go, guys."

I walk around the lobby of the office that we're renovating. Asher started the company for residential construction, but my passion has always been in larger commercial work. He let me take this job on as a guinea pig to see how it goes.

We just gutted the entire lobby to the bare bones. This week, we will start installing the marble floors, which should be delivered this evening.

Now that I think about it, I want to make sure that delivery is on schedule. I don't want anything slowing us down. I pull out my phone and walk outside to dial the distributor's number when I see Asher walking towards the building.

He is approaching briskly, steps long and determined. As he draws near, I notice his clenched fists. His furrowed brows, narrowed eyes, and tightly pressed lips are unmistakable. With each step, there's a resonating tension that thickens as the gap between us diminishes.

Before I can brace myself, his hands land on my chest, roughly shoving me to the ground.

Instinct has me up on my feet quickly, hands in the air to try and defuse the situation.

"What the heck was that for?" I ask as I back away.

He takes another step closer. "You leave my sister stranded for a fucking pity party. I told you I give you my blessing to date her, but just don't hurt her. Here we are, one week in, and you made her cry."

My heart nearly stops in my chest. "She was crying?"

"Of course, she was crying. You stormed away, then left her humiliated and alone in the driveway with no idea where you were or if you were coming back. Give me one good reason why I shouldn't punch you square in the face right now."

I run my hand through my hair. Fuck, I can't believe she was crying.

"Shit," I mutter to myself, then turn to Asher. "I'm sorry, man. I know I fucked up. I called her that night and apologized. I've been racking my brain, trying to figure out how to make it up to her."

"What the hell is going on with you? You're normally the easy-going guy in the room. This isn't like you."

My shoulders rise with my breath, then fall as I exhale my frustrations. "It's—fuck—it's a long story."

Asher crosses his arms across his chest like he isn't going anywhere anytime soon. He looks around at the building. "I've got all the time in the world. Why don't we go inside out of this heat where you can tell me what the hell is going on."

I nod my head in agreement and lead the way inside. There aren't really any official places to sit, but I take a seat down on some boxes, motioning for him to sit on the other stack across from me.

My elbows rest on my knees as I clasp my hands together. I'm racking my brain, trying to figure out where the hell to start. My eyes focus on a particular paint stain on the ground.

"Did Layla ever tell you that we had a little thing when I first moved here?"

The silence grows as I wait for him to respond. I look up and see his eyes boring into mine.

"You mean my sister, who was in high school, and you, a recent college fucking graduate?"

I'm so sick of feeling ashamed of my feelings for her. It's a five fucking year age gap. I'm not a monster, and I am done apologizing for my feelings.

"Yes, your seventeen-year-old sister. She was seventeen, and I was twenty-two. If you want to do the math, that's five years. That's nothing. But if you must know, we only kissed at that time."

His shoulders seem to relax a bit at my admission.

"Anyway, there was just this instant chemistry that we shared from the moment I locked eyes on her. I tried to ignore it. I knew you'd kill me. I knew your father would dig the grave for you."

The corners of his mouth twitch ever so slightly, betraying his effort to maintain a composed facade.

I continue. "But one night at your parents' house, after everyone went to bed, we spent hours talking outside. One thing led to another, and we kissed. I want to tell you that I felt sorry about it, but that would be a lie. It was perfect. It only confirmed to me that there was something deep between us because that kiss changed my life. I knew right then, and there I would never find someone that held a candle to Layla."

"So, what the hell happened?" he asks, as he now mimics my posture, elbows on his knees like he is now riveted by my story.

"You had a little party at your parents' house the next night. Nothing big, your parents were out of town, so we were all hanging out on the dock and in the backyard. William was there. I think he knew there was something between Layla and me. I was always watching her, talking to her at your parents' house, even when he was around."

I pause for a moment. "I don't even think he knew what had happened between her and I the night before. It was probably just a coincidence. Either way, he approached me before Layla came out of the house. Told me if I touched Layla, he'd tell your dad. He threatened to make his father end the contract with your dad's company. And I know that your dad's business hit another level when they signed that contract."

That really gets Asher's attention. He knows what that account did to turn around his father's business. His eyebrows turn down. "That motherfucker."

"Yeah," I laugh bitterly. "In hindsight, he was clearly threatened by what Layla and I had, so he resorted to scaring the piss out of me. But honestly, that wasn't the thing that stuck with me the most. It was like he knew my weakest point, and it's my confidence in myself."

"Your confidence?" Asher questions doubtfully. "Dude, I've been to bars with you. Your confidence was never lacking."

I huff out a scathing laugh. "There's a difference between confidence to score a hot chick for a night and confidence that you're good enough to be the man she brings home to her father."

His head falls to the side. "What else did he say to you?"

"He told me your dad would never go for Layla settling for someone like me. A blue-collar worker who would never be able to provide the type of lifestyle she was used to."

"Fuck that. Layla doesn't care about those things."

I shrug my shoulders. "How was I supposed to know that at the time? She was only seventeen. She didn't know what she wanted for herself in the future. Back then, she had a lot of life to live. She had dreams to fulfill. And I'm so damn proud of the woman she has become. Where she is today only reminds me why I fell for her right from the start."

I look down again at the same paint spot. It gives me the confidence to continue. "She's ambitious but down to earth. She doesn't care about money or power. You know I didn't have the best upbringing, but I never truly opened up to anyone about it. Not until Layla. My parents basically treated me like a nuisance. Nothing I did or didn't do was enough for them to pay attention to me. I grew up in a trailer park. I came from nothing and was treated like nothing. So, to come into this world with people who have more money than they know what to do with, it made me feel like I didn't belong."

"That's bullshit. You've always belonged with us. You're like another brother to me. Shit, you're like another brother to my brothers."

"It doesn't mean I don't get lost in my own head sometimes. Sometimes, my thoughts take hold and tell me I'm just an outsider. That I'm never going to be able to offer her what William can. At twenty-two, I thought that would be the life she wanted. I know better now, but I'm still not anything special to bring home to your parents. I'm just a guy who works for their son in a blue-collar job."

"Is that really how you think of yourself?"

I shrug. "It's the truth."

"Fuck, no, it's not. And if it is, then that's all I am, too."

"You're the owner of a successful construction company," I point out.

"And that company would be nowhere without you. I let you run the company just as much as I do. You are the reason it's so successful. Every client fucking loves you. You're the reason it stayed afloat after Lauren died. I was such a miserable grump. I could've destroyed my reputation. I've tried for years to make you co-owner of this place, but you always deflect. Now, I see why. You don't see yourself as my equal, and that pisses me off."

He looks around the large lobby. "Look at this place. We got this job because of you. We took it because you have the balls and the knowledge to go after commercial work. I've always been terrified to expand to commercial. But you, you have that in you. If anything, you're the impressive one between the two of us."

I shift in my seat, almost uncomfortable with the compliment. "I don't think I'd say that, but I appreciate it. Thank you."

"This isn't over. We are going to continue this discussion about your role in the company later. But as for this situation, I'm sorry I never knew this happened. I'm sorry I didn't know how you felt."

"It's my fault," I admit. "I never said anything."

"Yeah, it would have been nice to know this shit was happening. I would have appreciated knowing you kissed my sister. I get it—I would've flipped out back then. Now, who am I to talk? I'm having a baby with her best friend who's the same age as her."

I chuckle at that. "I lucked out on that one. You can't tell me it's wrong if you're basically doing the same damn thing."

"You're fucking lucky it was only a kiss back then."

I roll my eyes. "Yeah, I get it."

"But what the fuck, man?" he switches gears back to anger. "That still doesn't mean you leave her stranded at an event you two went to together. That was some bullshit."

"I know. There is nothing I can say. It was inexcusable and will never happen again. I guess the only thing I would add is that I've spent a decade never interested in a serious relationship because your sister was always the only one for me, so I'm new to this boyfriend thing."

He looks at me skeptically. "Fine. You get one pass."

I smile. "Thanks. Now, I may need your help. I've been thinking all morning, and I'm done letting my life pass me by. I want to live my life, and I want to do it with Layla."

"Uhh, what exactly were you planning? Look, I love you, man, but if you propose, that's a surefire way to freak my parents out. You've been dating for like a month."

"I'm not talking about proposing."

I tell Asher what I have bouncing around my head. It's definitely bold, but there's just something about it that feels right. I want to do this for Layla. I want her to know I'm in this for good. I don't want her doubting anything like she is right now.

I can tell she is. I messed up, and I want to make it right.

Now that I have Asher on board, and he isn't adamantly against it, I have to get moving. Asher agrees to man my job site for the rest of the day while I go check out a spot I drove by the other day when all of this clicked into place.

Chapter Thirty

Layla

"Where are you right now?" Charlotte asks as I drive through the streets of my childhood neighborhood.

I took the day off from work. I'm just too emotional and on edge. Josh has been absent since Saturday evening when he disappeared.

He's calling and texting me but claims to be busy whenever I ask him if he wants to come over, and he hasn't invited me to his place. It's been four days. I know that sounds like nothing, but since we've been back from Italy, we haven't spent that much time apart.

"I'm on my way to my parents' house. I'm going to tell my mom about me and Josh. I just want this over with once and for all. I want her to stay out of my love life and stop trying to set me up with William. I've had enough of all of it."

"Do you want me to come with you?"

I turn into my parents' driveway and park my car. "I think I need to do this on my own."

"Did you tell Josh you were going to do this?" she asks.

I sigh. "No, but it's not like I've had much of an opportunity. He's been so distant since the party. I think if I just clear the air with my family, maybe we can get back to where we left off."

Tears well up in my eyes, but I blink them away. I'm done crying about this. I'm taking action now.

"I don't see why your parents like William so much. He's such a butt face."

I chuckle. "Butt face?"

Charlotte laughs along. "Sorry, I'm just used to trying to keep from using bad words around Brie. Not that I would ever encourage her to say butt face, but it's better than asshole."

"Well, William is a butt face. I don't get what my parents see in him either, but I'm going to find out."

"Good luck. Tell me how it goes right when you leave."

"Ugh, thanks. I'll call you later."

I hang up and take a deep, cleansing breath.

You've got this, Layla. It's about time you stood up for yourself. William interfered with my life ten years ago, he's lucky I didn't cause a scene on Saturday. He doesn't get to do this all over again.

I open my car door and take slow steps to the door. My shoes scuff against the pavement as my heart begins to race. My hand trembles as I raise it and knock on the large wooden door.

As I wait, my hands clench into tight balls as the tension grows. I'm not sure why I'm so nervous to say these things to my mom.

I've just always been afraid of disappointing them. I hate to admit it, but once my dad's company took off and they advanced into the high tax bracket, they changed a bit.

I love them fiercely but I was raised in a middle-class family for most of my life. They may have changed when they made more money, but I didn't. None of that matters to me.

The door swings open. Mom looks shocked to see me. "Layla. What are you doing here? Come on in. I don't know why you knocked."

I laugh. "I don't live her anymore, and I'm showing up unannounced. What if you were walking around naked?"

"Oh, dear. I don't walk around naked. I'm sixty years old. No one needs to see that, including myself."

I chuckle to myself as we walk into the kitchen.

"Can I get you anything to eat or drink?"

"I'm good. Thanks."

She points to the family room. "Why don't we sit in here. It's stifling outside."

"Good idea. It's getting to that time of year where it's miserable to be outside for even a second."

We take a seat next to each other on their large sectional couch. "I know. I can't even stand my morning walks anymore. There's no break from the humidity." I smile as my hands fidget in my lap. "Well, I reckon you came here to talk about something specific," she continues.

"I did actually have something in mind."

She straightens her back, but I can tell she's nervous. For good reason, it's not every day your adult daughter shows up out of the blue with no warning. Silence fills the air, as I try to figure out where I want to start.

"I actually wanted to talk to you about what happened the other night at the barbeque."

Her forehead creases as her eyes squint. "I don't understand."

My eyes dart around the room as if looking for an escape. I take a deep breath. "It's about William."

"Oh?" she replies as she shifts in her seat.

"Yes. I've never told you guys this before, but it makes me really uncomfortable when you talk about the two of us together. Especially, when it's in front of him and his parents."

Her head hangs a bit low, but I want to get this all out, so I continue.

"William and I happened in high school. That was so long ago, and I've moved on from it. If I wanted to be with him, I would."

"I'm sorry, dear. It's never been my intention to make you feel uncomfortable."

"I know. But to be honest, I don't even understand how you see me and William as compatible."

She looks up at the ceiling and lets out a small sigh. "In the beginning, you two just seemed to make such a cute couple. I thought he made you happy, and I suppose it was just a bit of fun to say those things. Then I saw you working so hard at the restaurant, I may have gotten a bit selfish in wanting you to settle down with someone and start a family."

"You do know William is kind of a dick, right?" I say bluntly.

"Oh, I know he comes from money. He has an air about him, but he always seemed kind enough to me. And he always seemed to adore you. That's all I've ever wanted for you."

"I know, and I should have just spoken up sooner. I just never wanted to disappoint you guys."

"Disappoint us? I never want you to think anything matters over your happiness. Is that what you've thought? That I'm trying to set you up with William for me?"

I nod my head as a tear slips down my cheek. Mom scoots closer and grabs my hand. I haven't had a moment like this with her in ages, it feels like something I didn't know I desperately needed.

"Honey, that breaks my heart. I'm sorry."

I shrug my shoulders. "It's okay."

She sighs. "No, it's not. Look, I know things changed a lot for us when you were in high school. Dad's business took off, and it was like a whirlwind ever since then. I let it affect our relationship, and I've hated myself for it for years."

She begins to cry, tears matching my own. "There was a lot going on. I understand you were thrown into a new world."

"It was a different world than what I was used to. All of a sudden, how I acted, how I dressed, it all seemed to directly affect your father's business relationships. It was a lot of pressure, but no excuse that I let it all affect us."

"Well," I squeeze her hand. "I'm glad we're talking about it now."

"Me too, honey."

"There's more about William you should know about, but to tell you, I first have to let you know something." I pause for a moment. "Josh and I are dating."

Her eyes widen in surprise. "You and Josh?"

"Yeah, it happened in Italy. But to be honest, there was something there ever since we met."

"Really?" she pauses. "Huh, I can see that. He has always been so sweet to you."

"So, you aren't mad about it?"

Her hand goes to her heart. "Why in the world would I be mad about it? He's a wonderful man."

That makes me smile. "He is. But Josh has some deep insecurities that stem from his upbringing. He always thought you and Dad wouldn't think he was good enough for me."

"That's not true. We've never talked about Josh like that. He's always been like a son to us."

"Well, when you guys try to set me up with William constantly in front of him, it doesn't help his insecurities. We were going to tell you and Dad about us at the barbeque."

I see the moment she realizes the situation. "Oh, I see. You guys were ready to tell us and here I am chattering away about how wonderful William is."

She looks disappointed with herself, but I realize it was all done innocently. "Yeah. But William has been getting in Josh's head for years."

I tell her all about what happened years ago, and how he got in Josh's head at the barbeque.

Mom gasps in horror. "I had no idea William was like that. Although, if I'm being honest, I'm not all that surprised. The apple doesn't fall from the tree. Your father can't stand doing business with his father. Those are just relationships he maintains strictly for business purposes."

"Well, going forward, can we just agree not to ever bring William up? I'm not sure where this thing with Josh is going." I decide to leave out that he's been acting weird since the barbeque. I don't even want to think about it because I'll just break out in tears again. "But he needs to know that you guys support this. It means a lot to me, Mom. He means a lot to me."

So much for trying to hold back my tears. They come in like a dam breaking. My chest vibrates with the rush of emotions bubbling to the surface. My face falls into my hands. I feel the warmth of her arms engulf me in a hug, and I cry harder.

I needed this. The ability to heal this with my mom, to feel her support and know that she's on my side.

"I hope you know you can tell me anything going forward," she says softly. "And I support you and Josh one hundred percent. I'm sorry I ever made you or him doubt that I would."

"Thanks. We'll see if we're even together by the end of the week," I mutter. So much for not telling her.

"Why would you not be together?"

After running through the events of Saturday night, how he left me, how he's been behaving since, she purses her lips for a moment.

I don't want to put Josh in a bad light, but if I'm going to heal this relationship with my mom, I think it starts with being able to confide in her.

"Well, if there's one thing I've learned about men in my sixty years, it's that they are not always the best at dealing with their feelings. Give him some time. What really matters is what he does with his feelings. Does he let this continue or does he learn and grow from it? Pay attention to that. We aren't always perfect, and we do deserve grace, but we must show that we are willing to accept fault and be better."

"Wow," I whisper. "That's very insightful. But," I begin as my lower lip trembles, "what if he doesn't learn from this?"

"Love is a gamble, sweetie. You have to look at the hand in front of you and decide whether you want to fold or keep going. But I don't think Josh will let you down. If he feels about you the way he has claimed, he'll come around."

I wish I felt better, but I suspect I'll be on edge until I can see Josh again. I'm not above showing up at his door and forcing him to talk to me. If I don't see him by this weekend, that may just be what I do.

As I drive away from my parents' house, I know I'm no closer to knowing where I stand with Josh, but I have mended my relationship with my mom. I pick up the phone to call Charlotte and fill her in.

Chapter Thirty-One

Josh

Okay, you can do this. Just be polite, but firm.

I must've repeated these words to myself a hundred times on the way to Layla's parents' house. After Asher gave me his blessing to move forward with my plan, I was pleasantly surprised at how easily it was coming together.

Now, all I need to do is get Layla's parents on board, particularly her dad.

I stand in front of their door, willing my hand to knock. I'm not sure how long I stand here, but if anyone is watching, I'm probably giving murder vibes, so I garner the courage to finally knock.

The door swings open and I'm greeted with a smiling Stella.

"Josh," she says kindly, "what a lovely surprise. Come on in."

I step past her into the house I've been in more times in the last decade than my own parents. "Thank you. I'm sorry for showing up unannounced."

"That's no problem at all. It seems to be happening a lot lately."

I don't know what she's talking about.

She smiles. "Layla showed up this morning unannounced. First time she's done that in years."

Crap. What could that have been about? Am I too late? Did they already tell her I'm not a good match, and I wasn't there to defend myself?

Stella walks me into the family room where Dan is reading a newspaper on the couch. He lowers it slightly to see who's here.

"Hi, Dan. Nice to see you."

"Josh. What a surprise," he says as he puts the paper down and stands, shaking my hand.

"Why don't you take a seat," Stella says as she gestures for me to sit down on the couch.

Even though every nerve in my body is on high alert and just wants to stand and pace around, I take a seat.

"What brings you by, son?" Dan asks casually.

Neither of them appears to be surprised that I'm here, which is a little strange. I look around the room, struggling to make eye contact with either one of them. I'm afraid to see the truth behind their stares. But I came here for Layla, to make it up to her. I want to put an end to this decade of shit that's been holding me back.

"Well, I wanted to talk to you two about your daughter."

Stella smirks knowingly, but she can't possibly know what I'm about to say. If she did, she wouldn't be smirking.

"What about Layla?" she responds.

My breath comes in shallow, quick bursts. The air around me feels thick with the weight of my unspoken words. My lips part slightly, my throat bobbing with the effort. I cast one last glance at both of them, their expectant gazes a silent encouragement to continue.

"Stella, Dan—I'm in love with your daughter."

There it is. The words are spoken. I can't take them back. My breath hitches in my throat as I wait for their reply.

Dan smiles at Stella who looks almost—happy. That can't be right. There's no way after all of this time, after ten years of agonizing over this, that they would just end up being happy about it.

Then Stella laughs. "We know."

My back stiffens. "I'm sorry?" I ask, wondering if I'm misunderstood.

"Well, it appears you and Layla had the same idea. She came by this morning to tell me about you two."

"She did?"

"I'm going to give you a piece of advice. Never leave a woman who's crazy about you in the dark," Stella says with a calm voice.

"I'm not sure I understand."

Dan chuckles. "It's good you're willing to admit that now, it'll come in handy. Don't feel bad though. It took me years to begin to understand."

Stella rolls her eyes at Dan. "I know about everything. What happened years ago, the barbeque, William. Firstly, I would like to apologize for our behavior on Saturday. It was never right for us to put that pressure on Layla, and had I known that you two were together…"

I rest my elbows on my knees as I try to comprehend all of this.

Stella continues. "I'm sure it's left you feeling confused and nervous about everything. I certainly hope you aren't second guessing whether you want to be with Layla. I can tell from our conversation this morning that she is crazy about you."

"I want to be with Layla more than anything in the world. I'm not second guessing anything."

She turns her head to the side. "Then why have you been distant from her?"

My head falls forward. I'm screwing this entire thing up. I can't believe that's what she's been feeling from me. Here I am trying to make everything right, and she's been worried that I don't want to be with her.

"I've been scratching my head trying to figure out how to make it all up to her. That night was a mess, and I know it meant a lot to her. I wanted to make it right."

"Well, you can start with treating my daughter a little better and never leave her behind like that," Dan says sternly. "I like you son. You're a good one. William has always bothered me. I've just gone along with it when his parents say shit like that. I never wanted to ruffle any feathers, but from now on, you have my word, I will never allow those remarks again. My daughter's happiness is more important than my business with them."

The relief that washes over me to hear him say that. The weight that's been sitting on my chest for a decade has suddenly been lifted.

Dan continues. "That's my promise to you. Now you have to promise me from here on out, Layla gets treated the way she deserves."

I nod my head. "Absolutely, sir. That will never happen again."

"Good. Now, tell me how you plan on making it up to her."

I go through my plans, hoping they don't think I'm jumping the gun on this. It's not a marriage proposal, but it might as well be.

To my shock, Stella seems to be fighting tears.

"Wow," she says as her voice betrays her emotions. "That's so romantic."

I smile shyly. "Thanks."

"But can I give you one piece of advice?" she offers.

"Of course."

"You need to do this now. She's devastated and really needs to know why you've been so distant."

"Now? I don't think I can pull that off. I don't have everything worked out."

Dan smiles. "We know people. What needs to be done?"

After an hour, I'm driving to a farmhouse to pick up something I need for the surprise. Dan and Stella have a good friend who was able to help. According to Dan, one of the things that would've taken weeks to obtain can wait. I'm just going to move forward without all my ducks lined up.

The last thing that I need is for Asher and Charlotte to get Layla to the location. I pick up the phone and dial Asher.

"Hello?" his deep voice sounds in my ear.

"Hey, man. Is Charlotte there with you?" I ask.

"Uh, yeah. She's right here."

I take the last left onto the street that I think is my destination. There's a large white farmhouse that looks tiny compared to the land that it sits on.

"Can you put me on speaker? I need to talk to both of you."

I hear him whispering to Charlotte before the background sounds of the house let me know he switched to speakerphone.

"Hey, Josh. What's going on?" Charlotte asks casually.

"I need you guys to help me out. I need Layla brought to an address in the next two hours."

"Ummm...why? Are you planning to murder her?" Charlotte questions.

"What?" I shout. "Geez, Charlotte. No, I'm not going to murder her."

Asher jumps in. "So, go on then. Why do you need us to drop my sister off at some mysterious location in two hours like some kind of Criminal Minds episode?"

"I don't have enough time to explain it all. I have to get something done before I meet her. Just please trust me."

"Is this something I should tell her to look cute for?" Charlotte asks.

"What the hell kind of questions are these? She always looks beautiful."

Charlotte chuckles. "Nice answer, but you're an idiot. I mean, if this is some kind of romantic thing, she will want to be sure she isn't in yoga pants and an old tank top with no makeup. Women care about these things, Josh. You have a lot to learn."

That's ridiculous. Layla looks beautiful in anything. But Charlotte is her best friend, and a woman, so I should probably listen to her.

"Fine. You can tell her to look cute, but it's not something that's necessary. We aren't going anywhere fancy. Look I have to go. I'll text you guys the address."

I hang up before they can distract me any longer with their questions. This feels kind of crazy that I'm putting this together so last minute, but also, it appears that I'm a moron and didn't even realize I was making Layla even more upset.

I was so focused on making this right, I never thought about how she would feel. But it makes sense. Sure, I've called and texted her every day, but I'm all of a sudden not making any initiative to see her.

Fuck, the more I think about it, the more I realize what I put her through. I really am an idiot.

Well, at least I'm an idiot in love who now has the support of her parents.

I really can't believe how well it went with Dan and Stella. It just goes to show you how much that negative voice in your head can manipulate you if you aren't careful. I let that damn voice tell me I wasn't good enough for ten fucking years.

No more. I'm done listening to those negative thoughts that creep in and tell me it won't work out. Right now, it's time to make up for all the times I listened to that voice.

Chapter Thirty-Two

Layla

"What are you doing?" I ask Charlotte as she walks straight into my house with no phone call or warning.

"Just coming to say hi to my best friend."

Asher walks in behind her with Brie in his arms. She smiles brightly. "Hi, Auntie Lay-lay."

"Hi, sweetie pie. It's so good to see you," I kiss her on the cheek than turn back to Charlotte.

"What's going on? This is an unexpected visit."

Charlotte shrugs. "We just thought we'd take you out for a drink."

She's acting strange, looking around the room, down at her toes. Basically, anywhere but at me. I glance at Asher who is avoiding eye contact too.

"Something's going on. Why are you two acting so weird? And why on earth are you bringing me out for a drink on a Thursday night with your four-year-old while one of you is carrying a baby and can't even have a drink?"

"That's it," Charlotte declares while she grabs my hand. "No more questions."

"Where are we going?" I ask as she heads towards the hallway.

"We are going to go change. You are going to put on a cute summer dress, and we are going out for a drink. If you ask one more question, I will not let you visit me in the hospital after I have the baby."

My jaw hits the floor. That's quite the threat coming out of her mouth. I can't believe she would resort to keeping me from her baby if I don't follow her ridiculous demands. But she arches her eyebrows at me, hand on her hip, as if challenging me to disobey.

My shoulders slump. "Fine," I agree.

I'm only agreeing now because I'm curious as to what's got her acting like this. It better be good if I have to get dressed up.

She pulls out my black sundress and some gold jewelry. I'm forced to change right in front of her, like I'll climb out the window if I go into the bathroom. Next thing I know, we are in my bathroom together while she fixes my hair and puts a little makeup on me.

Is she setting me up on a blind date? Oh my god! Does she know something about Josh that I don't? My heart starts to race as the temperature of the room feels like it instantly raised twenty degrees.

I don't even have the courage to ask her. I'd rather live in denial until we get wherever the hell we're going.

Asher and Brie have started the car and are waiting patiently for us when we hop into their SUV.

"So, do I at least get to know where we are going for drinks?" I ask in the backseat, sitting next to Brie who seems to be amused with her fake phone.

"I mean, we've made it this far. Why not add some further mystery to it?" Asher says with a grin on his face.

Right. Why not add a little mystery to it? That's exactly what my gut needs right now. It's already in knots over this whole situation with Josh.

We start to drive away from all the restaurants and bars that I know of. The longer he drives, the further away we get from all bars in the vicinity, when I notice he's looking down at his phone. Is he following directions? What the hell kind of bar is this?

Then we pull into some fancy neighborhood. It has beautiful homes that no doubt have incredible views of the water in their backyard.

"Okay, this is weird. There's clearly not a bar in this neighborhood. What is going on?" I demand.

"We're just about there. I promise everything will make sense soon," Charlotte says, but I swear I hear hesitation in her voice.

Then we pull up to the last house on the street. It's a lavish country style home with massive stairs that lead up to an even bigger wrap around porch. The white house looks pristine, like it's just been painted.

But we don't park in the driveway. Asher parks at the end of the street, where there's nothing but woods leading up to an old dock on the water.

"Ok." Charlotte turns around and looks at me. "We are under strict orders to send you off to that dock over there."

"Are you two having me whacked?" I ask.

I'd love to say I'm kidding, but what other explanation is there?

Charlotte and Asher smirk at each other. Have they been planning my demise for a while? Did I do something to upset them, and this is the revenge they've been secretly plotting?

"We thought the same thing," Charlotte giggles, as if that's going to make me feel any better about this whole situation. "But no, you are not about to be whacked. Quite the opposite, actually."

"What the hell is the opposite of being whacked?"

Asher tries to hold in his laugh, so it ends up coming out as a weird snort. "Just go out there, Layla. I'm your big brother. I wouldn't do anything to hurt you."

I look between both of them, and decide I'd rather end this charade. So, I agree to walk to the dock just to get this over with. What's the worst that can happen? They can't really be plotting my murder. What kind of psychopaths would make me get all fancy just to be killed? And would they really do it with my niece in the car?

Okay, I'm definitely being ridiculous. They wouldn't bring Brie along to kill her aunt in front of her.

I walk through an old stone path in the woods towards the dock. The large stones show their wear and tear as green moss and dirt cover most of them.

My hands grip my dress and lift it up a couple of inches. I'm trying to avoid the dirt along the path as well as not tripping and falling on my face.

I step onto the old wooden dock, the splintered wood evidence of its age. It's starting to get dark; the sun having set a little while ago.

The view is beautiful though. The homes are stunning, but it's the surrounding woods that I love the most. I don't understand why this property is sitting here vacantly.

Then I hear something crinkling in the woods behind me. I turn around, but there's nothing there. This is getting really creepy. I'm about to walk back to the car when a jingling by my feet distracts me.

It's a puppy.

I don't know where it came from, but he is wearing a blue collar and licking my feet.

I giggle as I squat down to pet him. His tail is going crazy with excitement as I scratch his head. I think he's a golden retriever.

"Hey there, buddy. Aren't you just the cutest?"

His tongue hangs out of the side of his mouth like a goofball, but he smiles up at me while I continue to scratch his head.

"Why did you run away from home? Let's look at your tags," I say gently as I pick him up.

I grab his collar and twist it around until I find a gold dog tag. My breath catches in my throat when I read his name.

Biscuit.

I look up to see if I can spot anyone, and that's when I see him. Josh is leaning against a tree looking devastatingly handsome in his jeans and black button down.

"He's cute, isn't he?" he says as he pushes off the tree and starts walking towards me.

When he reaches the dock, standing next to me, he scratches Biscuits head.

"His name is Biscuit," I tell him, like maybe he doesn't know this dog. Maybe it's all a weird coincidence.

His face breaks out in a wide grin. "Indeed. I thought Biscuit had a good ring to it. Don't you think?"

"You mean, this is your dog?"

He kisses the top of Biscuit's head. Tell me there's anything sexier than a strong, masculine man giving affectionate kisses to a puppy? Trust me, there's not.

"He's not my dog. He is *our* dog."

"Our dog?" I ask, stuck between disbelief and overwhelming joy.

A strange sensation starts in my chest, spreading like wildfire through my veins. Doubts and fears swarm my body, warning me not to get too excited.

He tucks a piece of my hair behind my ear. "Yes, Freckles. Our dog."

"I don't understand," I say on a breath.

"Well, there was a story you told me recently, and I guess it inspired me. There was once a seventeen-year-old girl who used to picture her happy ending with her prince charming. She wanted a house on the water in the town she grew up in, and a dog named Biscuit to keep them company."

Tears prick my eyes as I snuggle Biscuit. He continues. "But you see, her prince charming was an insecure idiot who had some lessons to learn in life. Even when he finally won the girl over ten years later, he fucked up again."

My lips curve into a faint smile as I let out a low chuckle. His eyes crinkle at the corners, sparkling with amusement. "He fucked up, huh? What did he do?"

"Oh, he fucked up big time. He let those insecurities rear their ugly head, and stormed off one night, leaving her stranded."

"Wow," I say, biting my lip. "What a dick."

"Oh, he didn't stop there. Then he decided he was done letting anything get in the way of his love for her. He got so into devising a plan to woo her, that he didn't realize he was ignoring her and making her feel that same way he made her feel a long time ago. So, he decided to accelerate the plan."

I raise my eyebrows. "The plan?"

"Yes, the plan to woo her. Keep up, Freckles," he says with a wink.

"Ah, yes. The plan. And what exactly does this plan entail?"

He extends his arms out and looks around. "Our happily ever after," he laughs lightly.

My heart skips a beat. The world suddenly seems brighter. The sound of his laugh carries a hint of mischief and joy, effortlessly infectious, making it impossible not to smile in response. "So, what does this happily-ever-after consist of?"

"I'm glad you asked." He looks around us. "This land. It's ours. I'm buying it off the owners over there. It's been vacant since this development went up. The original owner of the home wanted to build a large guest house, but never got around to it. With a little convincing, they agreed to sell it to me."

"You bought this land?" I whisper, shivers rippling through my body.

"I did. It will take some time, but I'm going to build our home right here. Our happily ever after is the dreams that my seventeen-year-old soulmate had. She was right all along. This is where we are meant to be." He wraps his hand around my waist and pulls me in along with Biscuit. "I may not be able to afford all the mansions on the water around here, but I can still figure out how to make all of your dreams come true. That is if you'll forgive me."

My heart feels like it might burst with the sheer intensity of its happiness. I feel a powerful, all-encompassing sense of joy that fills me with energy. I feel more alive than ever. Tears are streaming down my cheeks, but I don't even bother to wipe them.

"Of course, I forgive you. Josh," I say as I look around. "You didn't have to do all of this. A simple apology would have been enough."

He leans down and kisses me. A kiss that feels like we're sealing the deal on our love. "I didn't want you or anyone to ever doubt what we have ever again. But..." he starts as he looks around, "we technically don't own this property yet. The papers are being drafted by our lawyers right now. So, we should probably head back to my car."

"What? We're standing on someone else's property right now. Oh my god, Josh."

I start to take large strides back to the car with Biscuit curled into my chest. Josh is laughing behind me.

"I don't think they're going to get their gun out and shoot us, Freckles."

When I get to the top of the woods, I notice Asher and Charlotte are gone. Before I can turn around, Josh grabs my hand and leads me to his truck.

"Did Charlotte and Asher go home?" I ask after we close our doors.

Biscuit snuggles in my lap, and I scratch his head. I can't believe this is all happening right now. I don't even know how to process everything. And I have a million questions.

"Yep, I sent them back home. Man," he sighs while he drives us out of the neighborhood, "it's been a crazy day. I didn't know if Biscuit was going to take off and run when I put him down or walk up to you like he was supposed to do. I was considering telling Charlotte to rub some peanut butter on you to bait him in."

I erupt in a fit of laughter. "It's a good thing she didn't. If I caught Charlotte trying to lure me out into the woods while smothering me in peanut butter, I would have officially thought she was plotting to have me killed."

"You thought she was going to have you killed?" he laughs.

"Well, what was I supposed to think? She picks me up on a Thursday night for a drink, even though she's pregnant, with her four-year-old, tells me to look nice, then proceeds to tell me there's actually no drink but to walk out into the middle of the woods by myself."

Josh is now laughing so hard he has tears flooding his eyes. "You're right," he croaks. "That sounds exactly like a messed-up murder plot. I'm so sorry, Freckles. I told you I suck at this. I can't be romantic for shit."

My laughter dies, because that is so far from the truth. "Josh, this is the most amazing thing anyone has ever done for me. Like you said, you made my dreams come true. I couldn't be happier, even if I did briefly think Charlotte was going to kill me."

"Your dreams are my dreams now." He grabs my hand and squeezes it. "I really am sorry for how I behaved Saturday. It was awful, and I'm humiliated."

"Just don't do that again. We work things out together from now on."

"Deal, baby."

"I do have some questions," I ask as he seems to be driving a path to my house.

"Shoot."

"So, you're building a home on that land...for you and me to live in together?"

He smiles. "That was the plan."

"How long do you think it will take?"

He thinks for a second. "Well, we still need to deal with a loan and then I have to put a schedule together and hire the guys to start. It'll be about eighteen months."

"In the meantime, we live in our own homes? And who gets Biscuit until then?"

I realize I've lifted Biscuit to my face and am clutching him, daring Josh to tell me Biscuit isn't staying with me.

He winks at me. "Baby, I don't want to live a day apart from you. We can talk about the details later. One of us can put our houses up for sale. Until then, Biscuit can stay at your house."

I smile for what feels like the millionth time in the last half-hour.

All those years that I spent hating Josh, all that time wasted. If only we got it right the first time. Going back in time isn't possible, but second chances are. We didn't get it right the first time, but we spread our wings and grew. Luckily, life brought us back together. And sometimes, the second time is even better than the first.

I look over at the man next to me and smile to myself. We are definitely getting it right this time.

Epilogue

Josh

Four Months Later

"Biscuit, get over here now," I scream as he takes off on me again then proceeds to jump off the dock and into the lake.

This dog never listens to me. I told Layla I would bring him with me while she was at work, but she has no idea what that entails when we are at our property. Biscuit is obsessed with the water. I'd love to let him swim all he wants, but I'm in no mood to give him a bath when we get home.

I just worked for eight hours straight today on our home. The framing is up, and now the guys and I are putting up the siding. Wherever we can save money by doing the work ourselves, we are trying to do that.

"That dog doesn't listen to you for shit," Liam laughs as he uses his nail gun.

"You need to stop giving him everything he wants," Eric tells me as he holds up another large piece of siding to be nailed in.

"I don't give him everything he wants," I deny.

Asher laughs. "Dude, you are such a softy. That's why Brie gets whatever she wants from you."

"Whatever," I grumble to myself.

Even if I am a softy, I'm sure as hell not about to admit it to them.

Biscuit comes running back at us drenched in lake water. His tongue hangs out of his mouth as he pants while looking at us.

"Biscuit. Come here, lie down," I command. Thankfully, he listens this time. "See. He listens to me."

The guys just shake their heads and laugh.

Biscuit is six months old now. He is already forty pounds and still growing. Layla is absolutely obsessed with him, and I'm obsessed with making her happy.

We sold my house and have been living together in hers for four months now, and I've never been happier. I couldn't wait any longer, so I popped the question a couple weeks ago. I'm trying to get this house done in the next seven months, so we can move in before the wedding.

I wasn't even nervous to ask Dan for Layla's hand in marriage. Our relationship has only grown stronger since I've started dating Layla. We go over there a lot for dinner, now that Layla and Stella have been working on their relationship.

"Hey guys," Layla shouts as she walks down the dirt path that leads to our house.

She's dressed in her black clothes from the restaurant, hair up in a bun, and still so beautiful it makes my heart race.

"What are you doing here?" I ask as I give her a kiss and wrap my arm around her waist.

"I'm letting Zane take the lead for the night shift and over the weekend. I'd rather spend my time with you," she says as he smiles up at me.

I pull her closer into me. "I have some ideas of how we can fill the time."

"Dude, her three brothers are right fucking here," Liam shouts.

I lean down and kiss her with fervor, slipping my tongue into her mouth to mix with hers. If they don't like it, they can turn away. Now that we're engaged, my next mission is to get her pregnant. Although, she made me promise to wait until our home is ready. I'll keep trying to convince her otherwise.

When we pull away, I see the desire I stoked in her eyes.

"Guys, we're finishing this panel on the side and then calling it quits for the day," I tell them as my eyes remain glued to Layla's.

They all grown, knowing full well why I want to be done early today.

Layla looks up at the house. "It looks great guys. You got a lot of siding up today."

"Yeah, because your fiancé here threatened us if we weren't on board with helping," Eric grunts.

"Stop your bitching," Asher chimes in. "You need the manual labor to work off the depression your damn job has put you into."

"I'm not depressed," he defends weakly.

Even he knows that's a load of shit.

"I've been meaning to talk to you guys about something," Layla says, changing the subject. She never likes to see Eric put on the spot and get more upset than he is already trying to hide.

"What's up?" I ask.

"Well, I talked to Mia and think I may have finally convinced her to come stay here for a little while."

Mia is her friend from Cleveland who she knows through the business. They met at some conference or something years ago and have been really close ever since. Mia is going through some shit right now, and Layla has been trying to get her to come here and get away from everything.

We've told her repeatedly she can stay in our spare room. We almost got her to agree but then we got engaged. Now, she claims she doesn't want to be in the way of a newly engaged couple.

"Okay, that's cool," Liam says suspiciously, not sure why Layla is announcing it.

"Well, I couldn't get her to stay with me because she doesn't want to be in the way since we just got engaged."

Asher chuckles. "That's code for I don't feel like hearing you two fucking every night."

"Ugh, grow up," Layla replies. "Anyway, I think if she can stay with one of you guys, I might be able to get her here. I know Asher is out since he's got his hands full, but I was thinking one of you two," she looks over at Eric and Liam.

"Is she hot?" Liam asks like it's a perfectly legitimate question.

I roll my eyes. "Are you fucking serious? Is that what you're thinking about when your sister is asking for a serious favor for one of her friends?"

Layla turns to Eric. "Eric, you are the only one left. Clearly, I can't let Mia stay with Liam. You have a mansion and wouldn't even know she was there."

Eric throws his tool down and grumbles something. "You sure you want your friend staying with a depressed mean old man like myself?"

Layla sighs. "Trust me, it's better than what she's dealing with right now. I wouldn't ask if it wasn't really important."

"Good, it's settled. Mia will stay with Eric," I announce.

Eric's eyes open wide. "I never said yes."

"Yes, you did. Because you're richer than all of us put together and have like five bedrooms. Only a piece of shit would say no."

Layla smiles at me like I'm her hero. I wink back.

Once all the tools are put back into my truck, I hop in my truck and follow Layla back to our home. She got a head start, so I hit the gas as I try to make it back as soon as possible to get my hands all over her.

I pull into our driveway, and she's leaning against her car waiting with a mischievous look on her face. Biscuit must be inside because I don't see him anywhere out here.

She makes it to the side of my car before I even cut the engine then opens my door.

"What's going on?" I ask.

"You kissed me and got me all ready to go. I had to slip my hand down my pants while I waited in my car for you."

I groan as I think about how hot that is. "You didn't come yet, did you? That's my job, baby."

She bites her lip and smiles. "I saved it for you. You know how much better it is when you get me there."

"Damn straight." I reach for the keys but she stops me.

"Not yet." Her hand comes to my knee and glides all the way up to my already harden dick. "I want you right here."

I look around to see if anyone's around. "Right here?"

"It's been awhile since we've done it in the car."

Her hand runs along my dick making my head fall back. "Fuck, baby. That feels good."

She giggles. "I'm barely doing anything."

Then she unzips my shorts and pulls out my throbbing dick. She leans forward and wraps her mouth around it.

I don't know how I got so lucky. The type of physical reaction I have to her, it's unlike anything I've experienced. There's no other woman in the world that I could ever want over my freckles. She's end game for me.

It's far beyond our sexual chemistry. I think our emotional connection is what makes the sex so fucking incredible.

Every touch with her is like it's the first time, and every moment is better than the last.

Eric and Mia

Are you ready for Eric and Mia's story?

Ask and you shall receive. Mia's story is finally here!!! If you haven't read The Giannelli series about Mia's brothers, check it out! It will get you ready for Mia's story coming soon!

Also by Nicole Baker

THE BRADY SERIES

Enough

Impossible

Irresistible

Persuade

Protected

THE GIANNELLI SERIES-LOVE IN LITTLE ITALY

Where You Belong

Where We Met

Where We Fall

ISLE OF HOPE SERIES

The Last Time

Follow Me on Social Media

To have access to my bonus scenes– visit my website and subscribe to my newsletter. You will be directed to a special page on my website with ALL bonus scenes.

www.nicolebakerauthor.com

Follow me for exclusive news on releases, signings, and giveaways.

Facebook @nicolebakerauthor

Instagram @nicolebaker_author

TikTok @authornicolebaker